KRAZY KAT

ALFRED A. KNOPF NEW YORK 1988

KRAZY KAT

A Novel in Five Panels

JAY CANTOR

**THIS IS A BORZOI BOOK
PUBLISHED BY ALFRED A. KNOPF, INC.**

The author wishes to thank the Ingram Merrill Foundation for its
support during the writing of this book.

Library of Congress Cataloging-in-Publication Data

Cantor, Jay.
Krazy Kat.

I. Title.
PS3553.A5475K7   1988   813'.54   87-45233
ISBN 0-394-55025-0

Manufactured in the United States of America

FIRST EDITION

For M.G.M.
more stars in her train
than there are in heaven

'Tis a gift to be simple
'Tis a gift to be free
'Tis a gift to come down where we ought to be
And when we're in the place just right
We will be in the valley of love and delight.

Chorus:

When true simplicity is gained
To bow and to bend we will not be ashamed.
To turn, to turn will be our delight
'Til by turning, turning we come round right.

— *"Simple Gifts," Shaker hymn*

It's a gift to be Clever
It's a gift to be Smart
It's a gift to Ignore
The Promptings of your Heart
And when we've attained our truly proper Size
We'll be marching up to get our Nobel Prize!

Chorus:

When true Artistry is gained
To Plot and to Plan we will not be ashamed
To Crow and to Boast will be our proper Sound
Till by Scheming and Dreaming we come out ROUND!

— *"Clever Gifts," by Ignatz Mouse*

The Panels

The Gadget: In which Krazy and Ignatz watch the first atomic test, and Krazy becomes *very* depressed.

The Talking Cure: Ignatz's attempt to cure—and transform—the Kat is revealed in his letters to his new "colleague," the Pup.

The Talking Pictures: In which our cast, its leading lady ready to work once more, goes Hollywood.

The Possessed: We will get the rights to ourselves—by any means necessary!

Venus in Furs: In which, as always, fantasy makes reality.

Our Town

KRAZY KAT was the headliner of a comic strip—a long lyric delirium of love—that ran each day for thirty years in William Randolph Hearst's many newspapers. Against the desert backgrounds of Coconino County, a landscape that changed from moment to moment—mesas turning into trees into tumbleweeds—Krazy,  too, transformed, being somedays he-cat, sometimes she. What didn't change was the plot: Daily & Sunday Krazy sang  her aria of love and longing for IGNATZ MOUSE. And endlessly clever Ignatz, as if he spurned and despised the adoring Kat, spitefully delighted in hurling bricks at Krazy's bean. In her imagination—through Krazy alchemy—the brick-bruises bloomed as bouquets, proof to her of mousie's love. Lawman OFFISSA BULL PUP, the Kat's steadfast admirer, arrested the abusive Mouse and marched him to the clink.  From which Ignatz escaped next morning to give our Kat her daily brick.

Krazy's unexpected retirement has put the entire cast out of work: KWAKK WAKK, the gos-

 sipy duck who sang out Coconino's dirty linen, has no one to tattle on. JOE STORK, a lean decent creature who brought the babies and the mail from Outside, is a nearly dead letter man, for fickle fans no longer want to get in touch. DON KIYOTI, native-born long-eared snob, lacks an audience to lord  it over. BEAU KOO JACK, the black rabbit of thumping paws, finds fancy trade falling off at  his grocery store. KOLIN KELLEY, who fired the bricks that Ignatz threw, cleans and recleans his cold kiln, knowing that if Krazy never works again he is cursed king of useless rocks. And MRS. MICE, Ignatz's big-footed  spouse, with MILTON, MARSHALL, and IRVING, her Joe-delivered progeny, bicker pointlessly, Dad out of work and time on their hands.

Why did Krazy, they wonder, suddenly shy from the spotlight? And if only she would work again . . .

THE GADGET

morning. Krazy rolled up the rice-paper screens on the windows near her breakfast table and surveyed her world, her hemi-demi-semi-sandy paradise, her Coconino. This A.M. the harsh light transformed desert rocks into huge cacti, the cacti into tall church spires, split a mesa in the background into triplets, turned the triplets into maroon bells for the spires, and left only the Jail (empty now since their retirement) unchanged, eternally itself, the Pup said, like the Law. She no longer knew if the light was her friend or her enemy; not that the light played tricks, but that others, she now knew, could play tricks with the light, could make a light brighter than a thousand suns. Once she had used simply to like tricks, all tricks, unsuspiciously, indiscriminately (but the Mouse's especially, of course). No more. Standing by the window, stretching lazily, she stared at the raggedy edges of the sun, as if to force it to tell her the truth—*feel me at a distance and you live,* it said. Inside the sun she saw a smaller more compact ball of flame, falling inward into itself—*come too close to me and you die.* Her stomach turned. Was it others only that made mischief with the light? Since that day at Alamogordo, Krazy felt that she, too, might be rotten. But *she* hadn't done anything. (Had she?) Anyway, uncertain about herself, she had had to quit the strip, for her act, like a moral trapeze, required single-ness, and even one drop of guilt was gum-in-the-works. (But she *was* innocent!)

She waited for her insides to settle to the point where breakfast was imaginable, and, turning away from the light and its constant gifts of metamorphosis, she looked around her house. She loved her one large room, the five windows, the whitewashed walls. She liked her house's bareness, its "japonaise" quality: five translucent tan-colored screens, with widely spaced bamboo ribs; one square, thin-legged, low wooden table (almost mouse height) that reminded her of Japanese furniture, its sense that things were neither over-whelmingly solid nor foolishly fragile, but rather that their existence was a miracle; one Hopi rug, where she also slept, its delicate earth colors and sun pattern eccentrically per-fect—the daub *here* rather than *there* making all the differ-ence, though no one could have predicted it before the daub was made. Plus one set of Zuni eggshell-blue tea things, the small Indian cups broken and patched, and broken and patched again, the more precious the wider their tracery of lines, showing all the life they'd experienced together. She didn't have many things, but what she had was, as Tracy said about Hepburn's body, "cherce." In olden, pre-ettom days, her furniture had been overstuffed chairs you trustingly sank into, and lampshades with burlesque braided tassels. Then, one afternoon she had thought, This stuff is in bad taste; cooperatively, her disgusting things had disappeared, and these new spare items had moved in. (Only her plumbing had remained old-fashioned. Just as well, she would have hated for anyone, even an unknown force, to have gone into her private place, her toilet.) Less suddenly seemed like lots, and next to nothing was best of all. *Stay close to the ground. Don't show yourself.* Before the bomb, Krazy thought, I didn't spit things out, I didn't have *taste.* Still, she loved her new house because it was *hers* alone; and she hated it, because its emptiness could become too vast, too echoing—hers *alone*. Bareness or barrenness? Time for some tea? She heard the Lawman's kindly voice: *No*.

So she picked up a pile of newspapers and magazines and brought them to her breakfast table. Maybe, she thought, she would even have a gander at *Variety, Billboard,* and the *Hollywood Reporter*. She still (though she pretended indifference when the Mouse was around) pondered the comic pages, still studied the entertainment section, where their strip, moved from the funny pages, had, to Ignatz's and her mom's delight, run for its last ten years, placed alongside articles and reviews about the couples who she, too, liked to think were their colleagues—Fred Astaire and Ginger Rogers, Laurel and Hardy, Buck and Bubbles, Baby Snooks and her dad, George Burns and Gracie Allen (Oh, them especially!). It wasn't that, like Ignatz, she had gone high-hat—after all, his aspirations were much mightier. And it hadn't been *her* doing when suddenly, in 1933, their work had begun to appear on the entertainment page not just in one paper, but in every paper that Mr. Hearst owned. It hadn't been her doing, but she had immediately understood and accepted it: the move, she thought, had been a simple recognition on Someone's part (could it have been Mr. Hearst, himself?) that their art—hers and Ignatz's and the Pup's—was as legitimate as George and Gracie's. Surely in a fate so consistent one might fairly see a god's judgment at work? (Perhaps, she considered, in finding them her colleagues, in making a mental home for herself halfway between the panel and the stage, she was only accommodating herself to the world's choices, as she had always done—for she knew that the more popular strips had remained on the comic page itself. And some, she knew, had said that accommodation itself was her *true* art—the art, anyway, of her relationship with that difficult Mouse and his endless arsenal of well-aimed bricks.) But really she was no snob, she loved the comics as much as she loved vaudeville, or movies, loved nothing more than to lie on the floor, stretched out, and press her nose close to Snuffy Smith, Terry and the Pirates, and the beautiful pajamaed adventurer Little Nemo, whose exploits in Slumberland were more perilous, more vertiginous, more imaginative even than Terry the flyboy's go-rounds with that awful—yet seductive!—Dragon Lady. (Little Nemo! That was a long time ago. Does anybody, she wondered, still remember Little Nemo? Does anybody, she thought with a pang, still remember Krazy Kat?)

Seating herself as comfortably as she could (the table was closer to mouse than cat size and her knees had to be scrunched beneath), she turned to *Variety*. She brought her paw to her mouth to put a little saliva on the soft rubbery gray pad. To turn the entertainment bible's pages she needed some extra leverage; Krazy lacked Ignatz's almost human dexterity with his claws; besides she didn't like to let those menacing, almost . . . mechanimule things show. Distracted, she went on licking the fur around her paw, and up her arm, for a cat—even a krazy one—is a clean sort. Strands came loose, but didn't form hair balls; special stuff, it dissolved on her rough, pebbly tongue, leaving black spots, like freckles. She turned to *Variety*'s second page, wanting to see how her friends were doing at the box office and with booking agents, to keep in touch (but why did she want to keep in touch? It wasn't as if she'd been excluded. Stopping had been *her* choice—though choice was hardly the word, it had been so instinctual, almost intestinal; she *just couldn't* anymore). Still—when she was sure, as now, that Ignatz couldn't see her—she checked the grosses of the various acts in the various media. She would admit freely that she liked to read gossip, and grosses were, to her, really, just another kind of gossip—the numbers spoke of romances, poisonings, and Queen Audience's whimsical favors. Ignatz read reviews, read the critical essays about them, rummaged through novels looking for plots—towards the day (which, by the by, only *he* imagined) when Krazy would be ready to work again. But Ignatz, too, checked receipts. He said that they were a form of criticism, the judgment of the marketplace. The Pup was the only one who didn't care about the numbers. He read history, read big books of philosophy and moldy-oldy blue-bound works of theology. He said that all serious work was a vision of the Law—the enduring reality beyond the changing fashions (by which he meant the box office) that only the small cared about (by which he meant Ignatz).

And the numbers, nowadays, did just add to Krazy's confusion. Over the years Krazy had watched uncomprehendingly the slow shift from vaudeville to motion pictures, to radio, to television . . . and next? computers? video games? How would the next generation tell its stories? She knew she wouldn't be a part of those stories. But would she even understand them? She felt forlorn. Was it too early, she wondered weakly, for a little of that deliciously dangerous tiger tea? Pup warned—and she heard his kindly voice in her ear—that she was drinking too much tea, that it would build up in her blood and might cause hallucinations. His large face, his sorrowful eyes loomed in the air in front of her—proof, she thought, that affection, too, could cause hallucinations. But she supposed she could postpone her next drink a little longer. Till dark anyway.

It was Ignatz's influence, she decided, as she turned to the list of this week's top ten video games in *Billboard,* that had made her *so* conscious of the box office—but she knew that that was a lie as soon as she thought it; she tried to *say* that it was Ignatz's influence, and, of course, the words wouldn't form properly in the air in front of her. It wasn't in her nature to blame others; and she still, no matter how much else had changed, couldn't say what wasn't in her nature. Anyway, it wasn't as if the box office were her god, that whatever-sells-is-right attitude that she sometimes felt lurking behind Ignatz's spiteful judgments on other performers, the outward show on his part of what was really an inward biting sense of his—*their*—insufficiency. *Her* insufficiency, he would end up saying, after working himself up into an angry little snit; her blithe, unrealistic lack of concern for the marketplace, for what the audience wanted. Why wouldn't she vary the plot? he would scream. Why must she always forgive him? Then the black cloud settled round his shoulders: it's my fault, he'd say, that we're so flat and insipid. Followed by: the world is a dung heap. But even to make him happy, she couldn't vary the plot. Ignatz showed his love for her by beaning her with a brick. Offissa Pup drew his valentine for her by arresting Ignatz. And the readers adored her by reading about her. The plot was she herself! Her art had been what she was—how could she have been otherwise? done otherwise? But in his rage Ignatz forgot the essence of her heart—the very axis of their work. For only the Mouse, of all of them, gnawed at by some deep dissatisfaction, could dream that anyone could even imagine changing his nature. (Did Ignatz, spinning about in his discontent like a Comekissthedoor, almost have sides? Was *that* why she loved him?)

Ignatz had often ended up taking out his anxieties on her; he couldn't help himself. Why couldn't they do sex in the strip—as if it were her fault that neither of them knew what it was. Well, why couldn't they have insides, have souls, like *high artists* did?—naming two more impossible things before breakfast. She shrugged, motoring him to fury. For it galled him that they had never won the Pulitzer *or* scored the big killings, the enormous *Gone With the Wind* grosses, even in their cartoon days, their Hollywood years. She had chided him about his envy of others' big money and prestige. "Frankly, Krazy, I don't give a damn," he had said for a week. (He loved to do voices; though every voice ended up sounding like his.) It was a joke, supposedly. But it hadn't been a joke. He *did* give a damn. And, of course, because it was a lie, it had never found its way into the strip.

Yet it wasn't the shifts of the marketplace that most upset her—their slow fade from the public memory that was measured out in the widening disparity between their slowly diminishing (now quickly diminishing) royalty statements and the much larger figures next to other, newer names. Thut, thit, thot didn't bother her. (*Did* it?) No, most upsetting these last years were the comic pages themselves. *They* depressed her. Cartoon cats today were just as popular as in her time, perhaps more so—some of the cats, she noticed, even got top banana position, the upper right-hand corner of the daily page, the first strip in the Sunday supplement. But those cats were *cute!* In her art she had instinctively revolted at that sickening state. (If she worked again, though, she felt that every sinew of her imagination would have to fight off cuteness like the simpering disease of the spirit that it was. For now she would *want* to be cute! Why? Was it to say that little bitty innocenty kitty couldn't have done nothin' bad? Or was it the Fall Out! in the drinking water that made both audiences and actors want what wasn't good for them?) Think of it! To have so little dignity that you threw yourself like an infant on people's mercy, their protectiveness towards the bitty itsy thing—a tenderness that was only another face of their unconsidered overweening power. There was no deep involvement in such feeling. *That* kind of tenderness was one more cream puff of self-congratulation spooned up by already overfed burghers.

Burgher? she thought. Sophisticated word! Can I *say* that? (She no longer knew for certain what she could and couldn't say. No longer knew, from moment to moment, if the charm that *was* her still held, if she could not now suddenly send herself awry from her most basic nature.) Strok-

ing the tips of her whiskers with her paw, she tested: She
tried the word aloud.

"Burger!" She laughed to hear what had become of the
sound. She saw Wimpy chasing a fat German down the
street, trying to trap him in a fluffy bun. The boorshow as
food. Not where he eats, but where he is eaten!

Was she a radical, she wondered, anti-boowash? Or did
she really covet the big audiences the new cats got for themselves? Or was she just irritable because it was time for
breakfast? *Have I changed?* she wondered, have I *truly*
changed? *Am* I guilty? But of what? She was like a tongue
poking about, looking for a black spot in her *lovely* white
teeth that hadn't had a day of cavity in their lives. Well, *now*
I'm capable of worrying my motives, finding them as mixed
up as a ball of yarn! In the old days she would just have acted,
and known what was important to her from what had shown
up in the morning paper, read the true gist of her thoughts
from what had appeared in the next day's strip. She put her
jaw down to the table and rubbed it across *Billboard,* making the tablecloth slide askew and putting a black streak on
her white front fur. But no, she decided, the disdain she felt
wasn't *her* problem. It wasn't hunger, and it wasn't envy!
Cats today *were* servile. They acted like wise guys, certainly,
but that was the most slavish position of all, aping the pet
owners while pretending to yourself that you were mocking
them, and so—like all ironic court jesters—leaving everything just as it had been before. Those cats never created a
true realm of the imagination, a world elsewhere, as she and
the Mouse and Bull Pup and Kolin Kelley, the brickmaker,
and Mrs. Kwakk Wakk, the tattler, and Don Kiyoti and Joe
Stork and Beau Koo Jack Rabbit had done. They were Cute
Cats, not Krazy Kats, sentimental Hallmark cards of cats,
tasting of cardboard sentiments cooked up on assembly lines
by anonymous hands, each one indifferently adding a saccha-

rine word to a feeling that no one had ever had! Krazy lifted
a paw into the air, as if saluting herself.

And with all this sentimentality, she thought, came its
ghost, its ugly shadow—hardly its opposite!—obscenities like
a book (she looked at the best-seller lists, too, for, after all,
they had once been collected into a book) . . . a book . . . a
book . . . she could hardly bear to think of it . . . *a book of
things to do with a dead cat.* Sail it like a boat (a cat with
masts coming from its stomach). Or make it into a lamp (a
bulb stuck in its mouth, a shade over its head). Why a lamp?
There was nothing funny about that image, with its truly
disgusting overtones, nothing wittily contiguous about lamps
and cats. She shuddered to think of the repulsive history
behind that whimsy, the terrible unacknowledged hatred
that here found disguised expression, the Cat here substitut-
ing for the Jew. (Krazy wondered again why she could *think*
smarty words like "contiguous," but couldn't *say* them.
They belonged to Ignatz and Pup. When she spoke, the word
would come out—if it came out at all—as nexa eeek udda;
her own inimitable patois.) It was a sick, jaded audience that
wanted—as these moderns did—either to drown in sugar, or
to drink small amounts of strychnice . . . strike nine . . . poison
. . . mixed with amyl nitrate; it was a dead audience that
confused the galvanic kick of its limbs with dance steps.
Dead cats! At best it was a child saying poo-poo, mocking its
own emotions. More and more of the culture pages had
become, since the day of the Big Light, like a child saying
poo-poo. She felt giddy thinking the word. She wondered if
she could say it. "Poo-poo," she said aloud. It was fun. It
sounded just the way she had imagined it. Poo-poo. It was
fun, yes, but there were some kinds of pleasures one mustn't
allow oneself, even if one *could* have them.

What did Ignatz think of dead cats turned into lamps?
She thought she had heard him chuckling the day they'd first

talked about it, as they had walked up a mountain that became a tree on the horizon (so they would comically find themselves dangling from a branch at the end of all their climbing). Ignatz laughing: that would be too much. (But how many times had she thought *that*, only to find her heart mysteriously turned towards him again?) For one terrible instant she saw herself in his eyes, dead, a light bulb screwed into her mouth. She heard, as if it were outside her window, his high lispy laugh, and it was like an icicle in her heart.

The icicle became a snowflake, just as it always did with that Mouse's meanest gestures. She thought, *He loves me.* She tried to say it. She couldn't. The snowflake melted and left nothing in her heart but a puddle of confusion.

It really was too much.

For a moment she thought she actually did hear that *dear* laugh, that *terrible* laugh (the contrary feelings warred inside her and made all thought of breakfast anathema). She *had* heard it. It *was* his high, lispy laugh outside her window. He had come by, as he often did, for breakfast. She closed up *Variety* and pushed it under the tablecloth before—she hoped—he could see her reading it and reopen the old debate between them: when could they go back to work? (Though his little eyes were keen; they didn't miss much.)

"Where's breakfast?" Ignatz asked, swaggering into her adobe. "Where are my soft-boiled eggs?" He spoke in a mock-gruff sort of voice, not his own squeak.

Krazy felt flustered, for she was sure he was looking at the bulge of newspaper under the striped Navaho tablecloth.

"Your eggs," Ignatz said, in a falsetto voice, "will be ready in six minutes."

"Six minutes," Ignatz said wonderingly, his voice rasping again. He looked bemused, yet certain that something entertaining was about to befall him. "Why, Gracie, do two

soft-boiled eggs take six minutes?" He waited, staring at
Krazy, as if he could conjure words out of her with his stare.
She looked at the ground, tears forming in her eyes, unable
to speak. She knew now what he was doing: It was a Burns
and Allen routine, one from the moving pictures. "Yes,"
Ignatz as Krazy as Gracie said—recovering from the real
Kat's real silence, and carrying on as if playing a scene with
oneself were the most natural thing in the world (for Ignatz's
sense of timing had always been imppeckable). "Of course
it takes six minutes, George, silly. I'm boiling two three-
minute eggs."

Ignatz (as George) smiled at the krazy answer. (As Ignatz he wouldn't be smiling. It would have been brick time!
But he always stayed in character—though somehow all his
characters were Ignatz, the way Bogart was Sam Spade was
Philip Marlowe was Bogart.) "Gracie," he said, "I'll bet you
never finished the fifth grade." He looked over at the Kat
again, cheerful, expectant, waiting for her to say Gracie's
line.

Why didn't he stop? she thought, weeping now.
Couldn't he see what this did to her?

"George!" Ignatz said in Krazy/Gracie's falsetto, as if
shocked, but showing, too, that s/he didn't mind George's
insinuation one bit, that she couldn't be insulted, that it was
George's problem, not hers. "How can you say that! I spent
three of my happiest years in the fifth grade!"

Ignatz smiled; then, the routine over, he scowled, the
Mouse once more. He pulled up a seat at the table. Krazy
drew a paw across her eyes. She had always especially loved
doing the Burns and Allen numbers with Ignatz.

But she couldn't, hadn't for years, been able to play her
part in them, in anything. He *knew* that. He had done "The
Six-Minute Eggs" because he knew how much that would
hurt her; would remind her of her incapacity; and so she
wept. But even her tears weren't simple comfort anymore;

for to weep at his meanness reminded her of the joy she had once felt at the very same brick-brats; crying was another sign of her problem.

"What's for breakfast?" he said again, this time in his own high-pitched squeak.

She shook her head back and forth, back and forth, lost still in her confusion—not zaniness, not craziness, but a childish sullen bafflement that was like drowning in six inches of water.

"What's the matter?" he said. "Kat got your tongue? . . . Kat got a tongue?" His voice had a musing, stroking quality that she hadn't heard for a while. He was tasting alternative lines, shaping a new routine.

Shaping a new routine! Suddenly a sharper, more bitter pain stabbed at her heart. WHAT IF HE WAS PRACTICING BOTH PARTS BECAUSE HE PLANNED TO DO A SINGLE? She saw his new title, in some wild style of lettering that only half-recalled the old antic headline that had once been theirs. IGNATZ MOUSE! it would say, and then it would add, beneath the title, in *much* smaller letters, FORMERLY OF KRAZY KAT. No, she thought. Impossible. Unimaginable. But it wasn't. She could see it, her life turning into *A Star Is Born,* and her in the wrong part, the Norman Maine role, sliding into sullenness and loss as Ignatz ascended to the firmament. *A Star Is Born* without even the touching last moment; there would be no heart-rending acknowledgment of her importance for Ignatz, no graceful "This is Mr. Krazy Kat" for him. . . . But . . . but . . . but hadn't he sounded too ridiculous doing both parts, as if he were his own ventriloquist's dummy! Was that the sort of thing people *liked* nowadays? A mirror looking at a mirror, endlessly delighting in itself, as if there were no world outside, no world elsewhere? Would moderns want that? Did critics now prescribe it? It was the kind of question she usually asked Ignatz. She looked over to the Mouse, who grinned at her slyly, as if he knew her fear, had *meant* to provoke it. She couldn't ask him. She felt her loneliness, her own arctic isolation. Then, as always these last forty years, the narcotic of depression came over her, and the sticky black lassitude spread from her limbs upwards to her brain. *What did it matter anyhow? Let him go.* The six inches of water became a warm dark lake, gravity itself, endlessly inviting her downwards. All she wanted now was for the Mouse to leave so that she could sink into that inner shadow and sleep.

The Mouse, she knew, saw the light leaving her eyes. His sly smile turned angry, disappointed. He shook his head disgustedly. "Say good night, Gracie."

She said nothing, of course, so he put the final nail in, replying to himself in falsetto—Gracie making George's command silly by obeying the letter of it: "Good night, Gracie," s/he said. Then Gracie smiled warmly. Ignatz smiled meanly. And Krazy lay down to sleep.

■ ■ ■

Lay. Or fell, with her paws in the center of the blue sun design of her earth-colored carpet, her head on her paws, her backside in the air. And she dreamed. Or remembered? Since the strip stopped she had had a hard time finding the difference. She remembered dreams as if they were waking events; and vice versa, she thought, and versa versa too; also vice vice.

Memory had once been so simple. Each morning she had read the strip in the paper, and the cloudy melange of the previous day's events developed for her, clarified like a picture suddenly smiling up from its chemical bath. The strip had been her memory—not transcribed, but made clear; she found out there the truth of her day, all that she needed to remember, all that she did—at the moment she read it—remember. Maybe if there was a gap between the panels, well, perhaps she sometimes constructed a little continuity between. But the fixed points were sure, were certain. But now it had been forty years since depression had made her quit the strip; forty years that her memory had been a tossed salad, some uncertain producer cutting and recutting the story of her life.

One afternoon Ignatz had come by. That much she was certain of. The day always began that way, as sure as once upon a time. His lips had curled up in a close-mouthed mirthless smile. He said he had seen something, and Krazy had to see it too. It wasn't like anything else, this thing that he'd seen.

"How is that, dollink?" Krazy had asked, pleasantly, deliciously, confused.

"Just tell me what it is, and I'll figure out the profit, huh? Well, you couldn't do it, sir," Ignatz said. "Nobody could do it that hasn't had a world of experience with things of that sort and"—he paused impressively—"there aren't any things of that sort."

Ignatz, she knew, was working in a bit of the Fat Man's dialogue from *The Maltese Falcon.* Nineteen forty-five was tough-guy time for him—a response to the war perhaps, or his conclusion as to what fickle Dame Public wanted. In those days—before insomnia had clamped her leg in its trap—she hadn't had much use for that kind of story, hadn't been able to find a role for herself among the grifters, and the pretty deceitful women who double-crossed their playmates, the hard-boiled dicks.

She stared. Ignatz was patting the air in front of himself, turning his paw in half circles as if stroking the ether, a hypnotic gesture that nearly made her swoon it was so sweet.

"Where is it?" she asked, for that stroking motion had intrigued her.

He sneered. For "where?" was a silly question in Coconino. The mountain you walked towards became a building as soon as you stepped on/in it. Ignatz—like Bud

Abbott explaining wheres with whos—said, "The boys that built it call it the Gadget."

"Oh, a gadget!" Krazy smiled. Gadgets Krazy knew about from the comics. Each week in the Sunday color pages, Rube Goldberg—a nice-looking man with a big nose and a straight moustache of ten independent bristles—demonstrated one of his new gadgets, in a big diagram. That very week she had learned about a labor-saving device that helped your wife with her girdle. (What was a girdle precisely? Krazy wondered. What was it made from? Would Ignatz like it if she served him one?) The gadget had involved a bowling ball, an unupsettable bowling pin, weights, pulleys, ropes, a dog, a Chinese screen, and a shoe attached to the wall. Krazy liked having her mind pulled through one of Goldberg's gadgets. He was a real artist; he had a vision. She knew, because after contemplating his drawings she saw *her* own life *his* way. What were the umbrellas, the cactuses, the Pup, even the other Coconino characters, but a way to get Ignatz's lovely brick in contact with her yearning noggin, and so—like Mr. Goldberg with his devices—fulfill her heart's desire?

So she had set off happily across the hot desert to see the thing that wasn't like anything else, giving little skips in the evening air from the high spirits that bounced inside her like Mexican jumping beans. They walked briskly, watching the homeward heat rise from the sand in waves, and Krazy shouted phrases from her favorite songs, big-band numbers that were buoyant with hope and pleasure, even in wartime, lifting the nation above the news's chaotic swells. "Strut it out!" Krazy sang to no one in particular, her heart filled with unreasoning glee. Jazz was surely the brave strain of American life, that endless improvised existence, where all that held things together was the riff, a few chords, the daily plot (the dear Mouse's brick, her "He loves me!") and within that you had to ring fresh changes every day, making it new, yet still the same. "Oh mess around!" she shouted. The departing sun was big and orange and round. She leapt into the air and dove head first into the sand. Ignatz watched indifferently. "It's tight like that!" Krazy exclaimed as she pretend swam-rolled a few strokes across the desert floor—a warm sand bath was a good way to dust the fleas from her fur. "Mmmm, mmmm, it's tight like that!" She rose and let the silica drip from her head like water.

The Gadget, Ignatz said, was in New Mexico, which was a part of Arizona this evening. They had to be going.

"Play that junkyard music!" Krazy sang, holding her paws aloft. "Play it now!" She capered forward a few steps on her toes. Ignatz rewarded her with a lusciously mean smile.

Around the next rise the sand ended; they came to a flat plain, with low brown scrub on it, called Alamogordo. A tower stood in the distance.

When she saw the tower she was certain that it was the Gadget: a tall rectangle—almost a cone—made of crossed pieces of black steel; a platform three-quarters of the way to the top; a series of chain pulleys holding a football-shaped metal object. O joy! Immediately, she knew: *The Gadget was an amazing new device to deliver a brick to her head!* How would it work? she wondered sensuously, stretching herself upwards, curving her chest outwards towards the tower. What other elements of the world would the Gadget draw into its love plot? A flock of crows? The wind? A donkey that loves marshmallows? People on other continents? Had Ignatz, she wondered, imagined this all by himself? The dollink! She stared with wonder and delight at the tower, the embodiment of Ignatz's affection for her, and then looked back beneath long lashes at her mouse. He was as wonderful as the Gadget he had built for her, this natural extension in mixed materials of his steadfast love. He and the tower and the brick it would undoubtedly drop were all of a piece, an identity to her loving eyes: poised, delicate, yet strong and homey, too. Ignatz, she saw, peered away from her, to his right, his little head turned to one side, his mouth a crooked line. His upper lip was raised, and his sharp front teeth bit half his lower lip inward. Just the way he looked before brick launching! His right arm swung backwards and held itself poised, as if about to send forth a spectral missile! Hot joy flooded the Kat's heart. This device was the most complicated delivery system he had ever devised for her!

Was it, she wondered, a little, you know, too much? Perhaps love shouldn't require appliances? (Ignatz had had some odd ideas lately, ones from novels she didn't even want to hear about.) Was this tower like playing dress-up? (The only ornamentation she ever had was a parasol.) Or wearing leather, or dildos? (She had meant to ask Ignatz what kind of bird dildos were.) But how could there be any harm in such a beautiful-looking Gadget!

Krazy looked to her right, following Ignatz's intent stare, and she saw four cacti that bent the sun's rays oddly, creating a glow around themselves. The cactuses soon had heads; the heads developed the shoulders, arms, and legs of men; and the men, too, looked up at the tower expectantly.

As the sun started to set and the beams no longer blinded her, she saw the men more clearly, and once she saw them she couldn't look away. Oh, would that she hadn't seen! There was something luminous about their shape, even without the sun behind them, a glow that still remained. Her eyes wanted to gaze all along their surfaces. She wanted to scurry up and run about them, but she knew—for wherever she is is Coconino County; assimilated to its air, she never will be out of it—that if she took a step towards them it would as likely land her on a mesa miles away. And why "scurry"? she wondered. She was no one's pet! She walked on two legs, just as they did! (Is this what it means, she had thought for

the first time, "not to feel oneself"?) And why did she want
to go up and walk around them at all? Because, she realized,
these were real men, not pictures, not movies, but actual
men, the first she had ever seen! And she wanted to walk
around them because there was more to them than met the
eye!

This part the Pup hadn't had to explain to her. She had
known it immediately, with the force of sight. *There were
more sides to them, sides that were hidden by the sides she
saw.* They had *backs,* and not just in a way, like her and
Ignatz. Their sides weren't flickery, here and gone, like the
ones in Coconino, or the people she saw in movies, where
you felt that if you could just walk into the screen, but of
course you couldn't, so you just settled back down into your
seat. Anyway, watching Ignatz or watching the screen, it was
all kind of there. It was implied. But with these men—one
of them in a business suit, two of them in jeans, one, the most
beautiful, in khaki pants and a blue work shirt, open at the
collar—the backs weren't flickery implications. These sides
were permanent. That was the glow to them; their roundness gave them their aura, as if each were a planet unto
himself whose gravity could bend rays of light. How beautiful it all was, and how deeply mysterious! They could be
hiding something behind them—a nice surprise for her!
Their backs might be different from their fronts, and even
more lovely. They could even put something inside themselves; and unlike her and Ignatz, who could never keep a
secret for long, they could do it forever. Why, there could
even be another person within, different from the one you
saw!
     Without any thought, her hand moved in the air, curv-
ing in its motion, shaping something, just as Ignatz's had
when he had first told her of the Gadget. She wanted to draw

her hand all over them, feel their surfaces. Ignatz, she saw, was doing it, too. One wanted to pet them! Helplessly, the growly sound—that awful humiliating purring—began in her throat. She hoped to God they couldn't hear it.

"O, wonder!" Krazy exclaimed. "How beautiful men are!" In her joyful surprise she forgot that her words might make Ignatz jealous. "And what a brand-new desert that's got good-looking stuff like this on it!" The world itself seemed brave and beautiful to her; for a lovely thing always just burnished the whole place up.

"New to you, Kitty-Kat," Ignatz said.

The poop, she thought. So what that he had seen them first; why harp on that before such sights as these?

And *this* part she was sure the Pup must have explained to her later because she still didn't understand what it meant. The New Clear scientists—for those, she had learned, were the onlookers—were rounder than she, just as she had thought; they had more dimensions. And the ideas that allowed them to make the bomb, the Pup said, depended on their knowing about lots of dimensions—including time.

"Ah," Krazy said, ever agreeable. For she knew that kindly Pup, his face like a good big potato, meant these explanations not—like some Mice she could mention!—as a way of showing off, but as a bouquet, an act in his impossible, never-to-be-resolved courtship of her. Which was almost a game really; for Pup *knew* that her heart belonged to Ignatz. (If, she thought sadly, it belongs to anyone anymore. If it even exists.) Pup, she thought, was like the father she had never had. (Pup, Ignatz said, was like the father he *did* have.)

The more dimensions you know, the Pup had continued, the closer your comprehension is to God's own—for the Pup's faith was strong, and God was something he brought into almost any conversation—Who knows and occupies all dimensions. So the more dimensions you apprehend the greater your capacity for evil.

But they were so beautiful! Krazy had exclaimed, understanding only the word evil. Especially the thin one with the plangent pleading eyes!

"The one with the kindly sad eyes was Oppenheimer," the Pup said, smiling. "They called him Oppie. He was the man in charge." Oppie knew many more dimensions than flat Krazy did. He probably seemed as round as a god to her. As the Comekissthedoors had seemed to the Inkers.

"Comekissthedoors?" Krazy began. "Oh, yes. The ones who. Those ones. Sure!" She rubbed her eyes as if her confusion had been physical. "Yes! Yes!" she concluded. She looked out of Pup's lace-curtained window where a brown piece of tumbleweed blew past on its way to becoming a mountain.

The Inkers, the Pup said, were like her and Ignatz and himself, comparatively flat, they just wanted to do the same things over and over. The Comekissthedoors were round, because they were sick of their own lives, hungry for change. So they had history—an extra dimension—and a greater capacity for mischief. The Inkers looked at them adoringly. As you looked at Oppenheimer.

Krazy blushed. She, she thought, clearly was an Inker; no insides, no hiding place. The Pup had known what she had felt at Alamogordo, looking at the lovely man with his long nose and his sad eyes. And that day she had even hoped—Oh God, she prayed now that Ignatz would never find out—that *Oppie* had built the tower, that the brick that was about to come was *his* brick, launched by *his* hands with their graceful, long patrician fingers.

Dusk had fallen that day, not suddenly, but as if it meant it, was giving the world a long good-bye. The four figures became shadowy, looked again more like her and Ignatz. The men stared at Ignatz's tower, as if they, too, awaited something from it. The fat man with a clipboard and an Italian accent—he was the one in a gray business suit—asked each of them how many meggietunes the Gadget would make. "Anna sida bet Oppie," the portly man said, "onna whether ahr leetle gadgeet wella egnite the earth's etmosphere?"

In the sky the stars, oblivious, set up shop.

"Difficult to collect my winnings," Oppie said dryly, and the others laughed. Krazy felt the authority he had over the other men; they, too, wanted him to look their way. One of the men passed a bottle around, and the men slapped lotion on their faces, preparing for the next day's sun bath.

Then everyone just stood and watched. The men watched the tower; she and Ignatz watched the tower and the men; and the night air grew cool as the desert reluctantly surrendered the last of its heat. One of the men counted backwards, softly, as if whispering sweet nothings to himself.

She didn't know how many pleasant hours they had stood watching. With a long sigh the night, too, came to an end. The stars that weren't going to fall that evening went on their way back to wherever they were kept. She would have been happy if the night had been—just this once— allowed to go on forever; or if, like tomorrow's brick, she were certain it would come again and again. She wanted her surprise, sure, but she also just wanted to gaze—at the tower, at the men, and at Oppie especially.

The slow backwards counting reached ten, and the men's bodies stiffened. Then, as the recitation continued, they bent over, as if shielding themselves against a blow.

She had been looking at Oppenheimer when the big light came up in front of him. She thought—the sun is rising in the west today. Then it was like she had Superman's X-ray eyes, and she saw the bones beneath Oppie's skin! She screamed.

Or was that sound the roar from the bomb? The earth shuddered like a piece of shook foil, and a tremor ran through her body; both, together, undone. The air shimmered in front of her like an out-of-order television screen. A piece of the ash from the fireball floated down from heaven and landed on her fur. The ash stung; she put out her tongue to stroke and soothe her fur, but stopped, her mind filled suddenly with a vision of the ermine: Arctic hunters sprinkle salt on the snow. The ermine licks it, and her tongue freezes to the ice. This white heat was ice cold. Opposites touch, she thought, just as the Pup had said. (Had said? Would say?—for the pain was the beginning of the end of her memory.) And this vision was a warning: she must not lick the ash. She must not turn her head. *She must not move!* This icy spot on her skin was hotter now than anything she had ever felt, yet she didn't hop about to escape the pain, the way she had the time that Ignatz had lit a piece of newspaper stuck between her toes. She stayed still, feeling it, as still as if transfixed by something seen, a scene behind a door that she shouldn't have opened. (Whose door? What shouldn't she have seen?) The agony that had begun on her fur drew her inward; she couldn't turn her mind away from it. She followed the pain as it took her deeper inside herself—*it was giving her an inside! An inside,* she thought, *is a terrible thing to have!* It took her to a core, a heart within her physical heart. This pain wasn't content with burning her fur and her flesh and her blood, it wanted to eat up her soul! And until that moment she hadn't even known she had a soul! So a soul was something you found only as you lost it!

Most of all she stood still in order to keep her body together. This heat made whatever it was that made her want to jump around, to split her sides and their sides. Molecules, the Pup had told her later. And then years after that he had said quarks. Higgs Bosuns. Leptons and Baryons. But she had already known then that each little itty ettom had a littler thing inside it that wanted to get out—to shatter its walls, even itself, with a mad leaping—for the parts were in a rush to stream outwards together in an arc that would join the ball of flame on the horizon, the god they had always unknowingly worshiped. The bomb was teaching her *that she was not single*—for she had wrongly thought that she was only one substance—her body, her soul, herself, all the same. But now she learned that she was made up of separate particles, opposites only momentarily attracted—ettoms, quarks, bosuns—oh, whatever! This chilly heat was an agitator, going from piece to piece of her, inciting rebellion, saying that all should be, must be, would be transformed, changed utterly, in the twinkling of an eye. But she couldn't change! Mustn't change! She was what she was, over and over, and that over and over was what she was! She delighted in one day being like the last. She just wanted to repeat herself. To be multiple would be to die! To change would be to die! She wrapped her paws about herself, like a mother holding a child back from disaster, and she squeezed as hard as she could. She had to stay very very very still. Now. Here. Always.

As Oppie looked at the explosion, she had heard him say, "I am become Death, destroyer of worlds." He had a black face and his lips were stained with blood. He wore a necklace of human skulls.

Ignatz had heard him, too. The Mouse said, "The cheaper the hood, the gaudier the patter." He looked angrily over at Krazy.

Was Oppie boasting? Was Ignatz jealous? Krazy looked at the burn on her fur, then up at the sky. She didn't have time right now for jealousy; she had to hold herself tight to keep her molecules together. "THE TOONERVILLE TROLLEY," she shouted, "MEETS ALL TRAINS."

Ignatz smiled at her with a look that meant: Bricks.

Krazy thought of the bonk on the bean. She felt an imaginary bang, and a cold brick raising a hot bump. For the first time she thought, *it will sting.* And she couldn't help herself: *she flinched.*

The ash had turned her hair white, in a patch the size of a quarter, on her shoulder, just near the back. She could see it from the corner of her eye.

The spot had stayed white, and had never grown back black again.

■ ■ ■

When she awoke the next morning from her memory newsreel, Ignatz stood in her doorway. She looked down, ashamed that she had been remembering—dreaming?—the moment when his bricks had begun to hurt her. "It's Mr. Mailman," Ignatz said, his small face festooned with an uncharacteristically inviting smile. He entered and dropped a bunch of letters on the breakfast table. Krazy pressed her paws to her temples, in imitation of a psychic. "Seven," she whispered. The number clanged like a prison door closing. For forty years she had mentally graphed the mild ebb and flow of her fan mail. Throughout the fifties—only ten years after she had stopped work—she had been utterly forgotten by her supposedly devoted public. Perhaps, she had thought at first, King Features wasn't forwarding her mail. (After all, Mr. Hearst hadn't even replied to her telegram of resignation!) Or perhaps the post office had lost her letters. Fire destroyed them. Lions eaten them. Or maybe nobody wrote. Anyway, who cared? The emptiness, frankly, matched her mood. Then, on a day that was like all the others, Ignatz had angrily hurled a batch of envelopes at her doorstep. And the letters came every morning thereafter. Sometimes eight, sometimes six, even one year, on her birthday, ten (most of them homemade cards, half of the sick-comic variety, half very sweet). But the average, day after day, week after week, was seven. Same, same, same. Before the bomb she had felt as if she had chosen her life, had instinctively willed always the same again. Flat Krazy had been content, unrestless. She had wanted each day gleefully to repeat the last, and everyone stayed wonderfully, beautifully young. Now each day was the same as the last in a gray muddle. The world just *happened* to her over and over (but God forbid she might change, might age).

True, the first fan mail had cheered her; but then, in its dim regularity, it, too, had come to depress her—for she remembered the bulging sacks she had once received, the bags that Joe Stork (all-purpose messenger) had dropped daily. Her children, she had once thought happily. Her children, she had later thought ruefully—an aging career girl who never really aged. (Mrs. Ignatz at least had little ones, had, in that way, Ignatz.) She hardly read the mail anymore, with its sweet pointless sentiments. Like yesterday's, "You're the purple light of a summer's night in Spain." Or: "Funny lady, you're the National Gallery!" Or, "Dear Fur Ball, You're Garbo's sal'ry." Or, "Krazy: you're cellophane!"— nonsense like that came every day (plus the occasional "P.S. Loved the Lawman," or a tiny "Please, more of the Mouse!"). They might as well have been the very same letters coming again and again. Same. Same. Same. Seven. Seven. Seven. (She did sometimes glance at the signatures, though. Her fans had such funny names! Yesterday had brought notes from Big Nate Grouse, and Beul Leap-upp, I. Gnat Moose, and O.F. Sassy Phup.)

Ignatz held one envelope back. "You have a famous admirer," he said. His face was wicked, teasing. He dropped the letter in front of her on the carpet and sat down at her table.

Indifferently she pushed the envelope away with her nose.

But she was curious, too, and pulled it closer with her paw.

Anyway, what did she care about admirers, famous or not? She pushed it away again with her nose.

What famous admirer? she wondered, pulling it closer with one paw, but keeping the return address out of sight, to show Ignatz her disdain of worldly glory.

"You look," acrid Ignatz said, staring down at her, "like a cat playing with a wounded animal."

Ghostly strings of blood filled Krazy's mouth and formed a spectral hair ball in her throat. She gagged. She *wasn't* an animal! I mean, she thought, I *am* an animal, but I'm *not*. I mean. And he knows it! Why did he say things like that? She saw her straight black tail from the corner of her eye and cringed, for there was something about that skinny useless thing that embarrassed her, as if it spoke of forests, of dankness and hunting, of a self that someone who was like her— but *not her!*—had been long long ago. She curled the pointless appendage behind her, out of sight.

Yet cunningly read the return address with her head still turned away. (This envelope, Krazy thought, *did* feel alive. But *it* was playing with her.)

The address was: *Princeton Institute for Advanced Studies. Office of the Director.*

"Prance tune?" she said, wonderingly.

"Oppenheimer," Ignatz replied magisterially, from above. "Oppie. The gunsel at the bomb site."

"How did you know who it was from?" Krazy said, with, to her own ears, surprising sharpness. But after all, it was *her* letter! The little buttinski know-it-all who-asked-you Smarty Pants!

"I . . . I . . . saw it in a book."

Glib Mouse attacked by stutters, Krazy thought suspiciously. Was he hinting that he had solicited this letter? "Did you write him?" she snapped. She disliked Ignatz's snobbish claims to friendship with scads of famous people. Perhaps long ago his name-dropping had been endearing—names were bricks, then, and bricks were bouquets. But since the bomb it troubled her—it showed an insecurity on his part and a desire to make her into his pet. Besides, wasn't their life sufficient? Wasn't her company enough? (And she felt this the more their life seemed insufficient even to her, the more she wanted to be alone, making her company—even if it would have been enough for the Mouse—impossible.)

Most of all, she had to admit, she didn't want Ignatz to be responsible for *this* miracle. She wanted it to be between her and Oppie, far from the Mouse's prying eyes. Why shouldn't she have just one thing, not a secret exactly—for she knew that without real insides, without more roundness, she couldn't have secrets—but something that was, well, not Ignatz's, not her mother's, but just *hers?*

Anyway, she had already ripped the envelope flap open with her sharp teeth (perfect for such civilized tasks!) and spread the pages out on the rug.

Dear Krazy Kat:

My friend Mr. Ignatz Mouse has probably already told you of my great admiration for your work, and the importance that I place upon you, the greatest of the comic-strip artists.

For each age's art, I think, offers its people a fresh imagination of the self, with the new ways of seeing and feeling that are needed to master the difficulties of that time. It was the modern era that produced both the comic strip and the atomic bomb, so I think it's you comic-strip artists who have the knowledge that we desperately need to deal wisely with this new danger.

She imagined Oppie seated at his breakfast table, turning eagerly to look at her first in the morning newspaper—to learn her new ways of feeling. Oppie had dark rings under his lovely eyes—for she was sure that, like herself, he suffered from insomnia and distracted himself from distraction with detective stories. Probably he had lain awake all night, waiting for the moment of joy and release that she would offer him in the morning. But the image frayed as she remembered that those panels were now filled by other cats. (. . . Perhaps, she thought, someday she *might* go back to work—if it was so important to someone like Mr. Oppenheimer! Not quite yet, of course. But perhaps that might be possible someday.)

In the atomic age, Mankind [Mr. Oppenheimer continued] can no longer support the contradiction between its animal nature and its angelic part. Unable to bear that split we are about to resolve it in a demonic unity—a fireball.

Krazy, you, alone, have resolved that very division into an image of life. The cat has always represented the animal in man, the sexual, the woman. But you—a Krazy Kat, a *cat* that talks!— you accept the pain of our divided condition (redoubled!) and you transform it into graceful love.

Krazy Kat knows who she is: she's no one's slave—and no one's master. The gracefulness of Fred and Ginger are all contained in your person.

You are Self and Other dancing together. Dignity without pomposity. Pride without revenge. Civilization without the discontents.
That's entertainment!

Oppie's praise fizzed in her head. She had known, of course, that she danced reconciliation for them. Her mother had taught her *that* long ago, and they had made it the "time-step" of Krazy's career. Still, it was nice to be understood and appreciated. But why must there always be this harping on *animals!* she thought irritably. She wasn't *really* any more an animal than he was! (Was she? She curled her stupid ugly vestigial remnant, and tucked it out of sight under her bottom. What, she pondered sadly, would Oppie think of her tail?)

> Dear Kat, I hope that in this dark time I may soon look forward to the pleasure of seeing your work again, of seeing, if I may say so, *you*, for I always felt that your work was a direct communication of the special Krazy essence, as if there were no real separation between you and your comic strip, as if its images were no more—or less—than the imprint of your very being.
>
> With fond regard,
> *J. Robert Oppenheimer*
> (but please call me Oppie—all my friends do)

"Oh sure," Ignatz said. "He's right. Comic strips *are* important."

Krazy jumped off her tail. She hadn't realized that the prying Mouse had been reading over her shoulder. She looked around. He wasn't. He still sat at the table across the room.

"But our old strips," Ignatz said, shaking his head, "were shallow water."

"It's a gift to be simple," Krazy said. Not, she thought proudly, that she had ever lacked for *that* gift. Ignatz, Krazy knew, let his dear head get turned around by each new critical manifesto. He had even started a correspondence college doctorate, looking for ways to please the critics, to prove he was *their* kind of professional. Then he'd suddenly abandoned the degree, unable to write his dissertation. He said he just didn't want to; if he couldn't have a diploma from the kind of school critics respected, the non–letter writing kind—and he couldn't, of course, for their work had made them fit only for the air of Coconino—then he didn't want any degree at all. If it weren't for *her* feelingful heart, Krazy thought, that compass needle, Ignatz would turn and turn about. He'd dip his feet in ink and walk about the world in a zigzag that covered the page in meaningless scribbles. Besides the heart, Krazy thought, there is no map. If only she could get her heart pointing true north again!

"Let's face it," the Mouse said, leveling with her, "we were off the cob. If we're going to work again, it's gotta be less repetitive, and more roundabout. There are no simple routes anymore, dear Kat. We can't just say Yes to everything, over and over. We have to be rounder."

The Kat nodded, the Kat smiled, though she knew that she couldn't change, she was who she was, the simple yes to everything over and over. Same! Same! Same! In a different mood she might have felt betrayed. But today she didn't care. The sun shone on her letter and was reflected on her fur. She was adrift in her own warm reverie, far from Ignatz's critical gadgets. "I'm going to write him," she said.

"Write who?" the Mouse said, exasperated. "Oh, him. Sure. Good idea." And he even took out his penknife and sharpened up a pencil for her.

* * *

He had made the bomb, and the bomb, she thought, had made the world she couldn't work in anymore. Who better to speak her sorrow to than he? For she was sure that he, too, looked out at a world that he had never intended, and he was bound to grieve over it even more closely than she did. So she set to work, telling him of her confusion, the reasons that she couldn't—up till now, anyway, for who knew anymore what surprises the future might hold!—find her way back to the art *he* wanted from her. The bomb, she thought, was like . . . was like . . . well, the black bird, the Maltese Falcon. They didn't own *it. It* owned them. It ruled everyone's life—everyone's but Mr. Spade's. *He* was no one's pet. He knew who he was, and there were things that who-he-was just wouldn't do. (Immodest and unnecessary, Krazy thought, to mention who *else* was like that!) He wouldn't play the sap for Brigid O'Shaughnessy, that lovely betrayer. Spade wouldn't have cared about any critic's opinion, but would have just gone on as he always had. Same. Same. Same. And *he* certainly wouldn't sell out a partner—even if he didn't like him much.

Krazy looked wonderingly at Ignatz, who smiled down at her. But who knew, anymore, what a smile meant? Hadn't some of the fizzyisits . . . the sighin . . . the smart guys smiled at their success at Alamogordo?

Spade had a code to live by, but after the war those rules hadn't seemed like enough for a bump-em-car world careening out of anyone's control. Peace hadn't meant a united nations, but cynicism and suspicion. Heck, maybe *the detective* was *the murderer!* And maybe because of Oppie's bomb, even the machines didn't seem so friendly anymore. But the gadgets *worked* great. Stuff poured out. And even cynicism was canceled for the easy drift of extra cream, that "why resist" in which all distinctions were blurred—that night, she thought ruefully, in which all cats are gray. 'Cause lies made the world go round, till no one knew the difference and, so what? it's real Arnel. Nobody claimed anymore that he knew who he was, or that there was something he just wouldn't do. We all played the sap for each other.

The bomb and the shopping spree seem part of the same thing, and *it* owns us. We hug ourselves so we won't change and lose what we have—our fave TV show interrupted by: *Bulletin: World Over! Everybody Dies!* And art had become dead cats as lamps! Anything goes! "I know, Mr. Oppenheimer, that *you* must hate things like that as much as I do. You seemed to me the one time that I saw you, and in your nice letter to me, the kindliest of people. Well, frankly, I was wondering how someone like you could have been the one to start a terrible business like this? I mean . . ."

She paused. It might hurt him, but she had to say what was in her heart. "I mean, *how could you have done it?*

> With my sincere admiration,
> *Krazy Kat*"

Writing, she felt as if she spoke directly to the man with the feelingful understanding eyes, the one she had met, well not met exactly, but *nearly* met, at Alamogordo. And as she licked the flap of the envelope, she felt, as she hadn't since 1945, that she wasn't entirely alone in the world.

"I'll take care of that," the suddenly kindly Mouse said. His squeak startled her, for she had forgotten all about him— perhaps for the first time in her life! "I'll address it," he said rapidly. "I'll give it to Joe Stork. I'll see that he delivers it right away. I'll take care of it. Give it to me!" He grabbed her letter from her paws and ran to the door.

"Mmm," she hummed, as he left. The world was flooded with a new and friendlier light. "Mmmm, it's tight like that! Strut it out horns!" She wouldn't want, wouldn't *need* any tiger tea to face the dark tonight. "Come on, now, strut it out!"

* * *

"I'm back," Ignatz said breathlessly, an envelope in hand. It was evening of the same day. "How's that for service?"

"Good," Krazy said. The time between Oppie's letters had been forever, yet the intervening time disappeared the moment she saw what was in the Mouse's ink-stained paws. (Just the way that bricks had once sharply delineated her days, like the bars in music, and love had made the moments between the bars elastic.) "Great." But she was too busy tearing open her letter to praise the messenger more.

The envelope had been pre-owned—it had someone's small teeth marks in it and was resealed with Scotch tape. Maybe the Institute had money troubles? Should she enclose return postage? She wished Oppie would say! He must know that she would be happy to share what she had with him.

She took the pages to the rug and put her nose right up against the handwritten words. (Those hands with their long, slim, patrician fingers!) Now no one else would have room to squeeze in their tiny prying eyeballs. Ignatz had interfered enough as it was! Of course she would be happy to tell the Mouse what was in Oppie's letters. Eventually. Of course. *But not right now.*

Dearest Kat [Oppie wrote]:
I have long thought about the painful question that you asked me in your wonderfully direct way.

Most of all, Krazy, I think it came down to this: THEY THOUGHT WE WERE GODS. And when everyone hosannas you, please believe me, dear Kat, you begin to feel that your judgment *is* infallible, that your awesome powers *should* be displayed. Well, don't the people who make others into gods have some responsibility for what the god then does for them?

Dearest Kat, please don't judge me too harshly. Perhaps you, alone, have never let your beloved see

you as a god, ~~you silly stupid kat,~~ because you won't
hurt him! And your all encompassing affection for
your Mouse means that dear Ignatz can't hurt you,
doesn't seem godlike to you, even for one rotten
sublime moment, ~~you stinking two bit dictator.~~ So
he never feels tall!

But I guess gods are a luxury we can't afford in
the atomic age. And it's because you stand outside
that game that I feel that you are the only one who,
through her art, could show us how to live without
these vengeful dangerous fictions.

Krazy, I think you can imagine the blackness
that has grown inside me since the day you first saw
me at Alamogordo. That sadness fills my limbs with
dark heavy blood, keeps me from acting in the
world to make right what I did. Only you can save
me, Krazy—it's only your art that can imagine a
new life for us.

I eagerly await word from you—just give your
letter to your gifted friend, Ignatz, who will take
good care of it. Or, even better, you could appear
yourself in my morning newspaper!

Yours, fondly,
Oppie

Oh, she knew that black cloud! She had it inside her
limbs, too! Oppie's unhappiness brought him so close to her,
named the intimate kinship that she had felt would be there
from the first. And she was deeply moved, too, by the way
he—unlike some altogether tiny-souled people she could
mention—respected her intelligence. (Though she didn't
understand why folks would want to play god and hurt each
other. What kind of game was that?)

For her reply she chose one of her favorite postcards, a
large one with a nice picture of her on it, Krazy in her

colorful Sunday best of blues, greens, and earth colors. And because she wanted to give him something more of herself, she wrote across the front, "To my good friend Oppie, with warmest best wishes." There—that didn't go too far, did it? But it wouldn't seem cold, would it?

Anyway, on the back she wrote, "*I* can't help. I'm just an old vaudevillian."

Ignatz snatched the card with his small claws, and, with typical rudeness, turned it over and read it. "Pity didn't do the trick," he mumbled to himself.

"What?"

"I said, still not ready to work, huh?"

"Nope." Yet even as she emphatically denied the future to Ignatz, she wondered if perhaps her powers *were* returning to her? Maybe she *could* kick Oppie's cloud away, could enact for him the peace and reconciliation that he so needed? (She would have to get everybody together, of course. Talk things over. See how they felt about starting things up again?)

"Okey doke," Ignatz said. "Then it's time for a new angle, buster."

"New what?" Krazy said, bewildered.

"I said time for a new way to the post office." Ignatz smiled. "New way to your heart," he added mysteriously. " 'Never treats me sweet and gentle, the way he should,' " he sang as he walked out her door, " 'I got it bad, and that ain't good.' "

Oppie's reply came that afternoon, on two big postcards. The first card had a picture of a fluffy white cat dressed in a little pink organdy dress. To Krazy, the ensemble looked *crude* as if the cat were confined, controlled—a pet—willing to do *anything* for her master. The second card displayed the cat without her dress, looking suddenly, strangely, *naked.* Hypnotized, Krazy stared. Ashamed, she looked away. But she wanted more and peeked again. The pictures awakened in her a mingling of fear and excitement that she wasn't at all comfortable with. (Clearly this must be a kind of *art* that she didn't yet understand—that Oppie must teach her to appreciate.)

On the backs of the cards, in a small, cramped hand, Oppie had written:

Krazy, the truth is that *you* were responsible for what I did with the bomb. It was from smiling at what happened to you, day after day in Coconino, that I got the idea that the world *ought* to feel the awesome power of the atom. People would be awakened by it to the new *necessity* of world peace, just the way Ignatz's brick awakened you into love. So, just as for you the Mouse's bricks became bouquets, Death would here touch the Resurrection. Opposites would meet.

So I guess we're in this together, kitty-kat. The bomb was your idea as much as mine. *You* are my Brigid O'Shaughnessy, my partner in crime. I'm not going to let you play me for a sap. I'm in the jail of my depression now, and you have to spring me. Make me laugh again, Kat. You owe it to me. Get back to work!

Oppie

Before Krazy had finished the last card, she had begun to weep, turning Oppie's sentences to puddles of blue. Good! she thought, no one will ever be able to read those horrid words again. It was just as Ignatz had said, she thought furiously, he's a cheap hood, a gunsel, a grifter! He was maniacal Cagneyheimer, pumping slugs into huge gas pipes, dancing atop the exploding oil tanks that will set him and the other gang members aflame, shouting "Made it, Ma! Top of the World!" But she knew that she couldn't *say* those things about Oppenheimer—they were lies. For *she* had made Oppie think flash-boom was brick-bang, that everyone would thank him for his valentine. *She was*—just as somewhere in herself she had always known—*responsible for the atomic bomb*. As surely as if it *had* been a device to deliver a brick to her head, the brick that, in those simpler times, she had foolishly, tragically, yearned for! Guilty! Guilty! Guilty!

Through her tears, Krazy gazed at dear faithful innocent Ignatz, who sat at her table carving a brick into the wood with his penknife. He smiled back at her. He must never find out what she now knew about herself—that she was poison through and through. She thought of a Japanese man she had read about. He had been standing near a concrete wall at the outskirts of town when the atomic bomb fell in the city center. The cold heat of the blast had vaporized his flesh. Only his imprint had survived, burned into the bricks. *She* had done that, she had turned a man into his shadow! A round person made flat by her bomb! *That* was what her art accomplished, *that* was the special Krazy essence—poison, poison, poison!

"Hard to say Yes now, huh, Kitty?" Ignatz said. "Things aren't as simple as you thought."

"Oh God," Krazy whispered, weeping. "Oh God, no!"

"Well, innocenty-Kitty-Kat," Ignatz said, smiling maliciously, as if cat tears were the Mouse's Pouilly-Fuissé, "looks like perhaps you need some tiger tea."

Many drinks and dany mays laid her, mousy bricks, and meeny tekel upharsin, Krazy strolled out to a mesa that this morning had conveniently pulled itself up to the door of her house. She stepped on the grass, and it wasn't there—the height was internal. She fell in the dust. The sedimentation of tiger tea in her blood was apparently achieving some nice geographical hallucinations.

Bemused, in the dirt, she felt the sharp point of Mrs. Kwakk Wakk's umbrella poking her chest. Supposing that the Duck wasn't a phantasm. Pain, she thought, was hardly a refutation of imagination, as *her* imagination had caused the world the most pain of all!

She checked the Kwakk Wakk image. It was in regulation order: loosely rolled umbrella under her wing, a small gold hat on her head—identical copy of the Queen's own—her bottom feathers carefully formed into the valance of a dress, and her fake fun fur around her neck. All too perfectly herself. As usual. Soon she would tattle a tale. As always. As if repetition were an achievement! As if the repetition of Krazy's very being hadn't tapped out a mouse-cold message to Oppenheimer: "OK to destroy the world!" But try to talk about that with a dumb duck!

Krazy rose and patted the gossip's feathers, to make sure she wasn't growing furious with a mock duck.

"Ignatz said you were in a bad way," the reassuringly solid Duck said, submitting annoyedly to the cat's tea-clumsy patting. "So I thought I'd have a look for myself."

Oh, you could count on the Duck to be there in time of troubles—but as a reporter of your failures, without even the simulacrum of concern! How like Mrs. Kwakk Wakk that was! But everything always was like what everything always was like, anyway, singing the simple stupid song of its own name over and over. Ego ego ego!

"Frankly, my dear," the gossip said, "you don't look too good." She stared meaningfully at Krazy's red bow tie that was, this morning, down around her waist.

"Frankly, my dear," Krazy said, imitating someone she couldn't remember, who was imitating someone else, like a

mirror looking into a mirror, "Ida donut give Adam." Huh?
Whatever she had intended to say, she couldn't. That failure
meant something. But what?

"Oh my my," Mrs. Kwakk Wakk said. "Haven't you had
enough?"

"At my house," Krazy said, "it's always Happy Hour!"
She smiled, and pointed to her bungalow. "A Bar Is Born!"
But she couldn't breathe this brittle patter anymore!
She had to talk freely to a compassionate heart! And wasn't
the Duck—despite what mean people sometimes said about
her—*really* the sweetest, most understanding person in the
world? Wasn't she always there in times of trouble!

Krazy leaned herself against Mrs. Kwakk Wakk's downy
shoulder, pressed her lips to her ear, and blubbered. She told
her of Oppenheimer's letters and the awesome terrible
thing that Krazy had been responsible for—the people
turned into shadows. The round made flat.

Mrs. Kwakk Wakk puckered her beak impatiently, as if
the Kat were only blurting yesterday's news. So, Krazy
thought, even my poisonous nature is no secret! She didn't
have enough roundness to hide *anything*.

"Well, of course, dear," the Duck said, as Krazy, gulping
despair, finished her story. "Ignatz told me all about those
letters. But, you know, Krazy, your Mr. Oppenheimer hasn't
been with us for years."

"What?" Krazy said. "Who?" She must have misunder-
stood. Had the tea fuddled her brain that much? Could it
have been *years* since he last wrote? Had poor Mr. Oppenheimer died? Before she could write back! She wept for him,
and for herself. He had died before she could begin work
again to send him a new message! For, even in her drunken-
ness, she knew that work was the only way to climb out of
the slough. Now that every eat'em of her being was Coco-
ninoized she couldn't leave the county, could only affect

herself or the outside with her art. But her art, she saw, just as clearly, was a terrible menace to the world. She must never work again.

"Oh yes, dear. Those letters were from Ignatz. He wrote them. He thought he could fool you into restarting the strip. The rest of us didn't think much of the idea, but you know how Ignatz is when he gets a notion between his little teeth."

Krazy put her paws over her hears. The puzzled duck trembled before Krazy's eyes. *Her partner had played her for a sap!* She could feel her body curl dangerously down into itself, the muscles coiling.

"Well, the truth is, Krazy, you shouldn't cover your ears. I think he *wants* you to know he wrote the letters. You know: telephone, telegraph, teladuck. And he just finished saying to me, 'Kwakk Wakk, how do you think I felt crawling to her as Oppenheimer? Watching her fall in love with him, because he could give her more wallop per dollop, because he has hands?' "

Krazy turned back to the safety of her house. Not safety for her! *Safety for others!* Claws had scimitared from Krazy's paws. She didn't want the Duck to see them, to *feel* them racked across that stupid excuse for fur, that smug little hat. She hissed quietly to herself.

"Well," Mrs. Kwakk Wakk yattered on, "he said that you had to touch bottom. Find out that you weren't so high hat, little Ms. Too-Good-For-This-World. Maybe then you could redraw yourself. Shock therapy, I guess. Like those bricks of his that you used to be so fond of! Now he has another plan, dear. The Trojan Mouse, he calls it. Do *you* have any idea what our little friend is talking about? *I* certainly don't."

Kwakk Wakk bent an ear, but Krazy stalked rapidly away—as gracefully as the nimble tread of the feet of Fred Astaire! A spring lifted her step, and the dank smell of the forest filled the air. She wanted to get down on all fours, shift her weight backwards, and stick her bottom up—to add power to her movements.

Her long, beautiful tail already stood out proudly, bushily, behind her.

■   ■   ■

She wanted a cup of tiger tea. She needed it. She *deserved* it! " 'You for me and me for tea, dear' " she sang in a bluesy voice, delightfully roughened by every cat's favorite drink. She reached across the counter for the tin and her paw brushed fur. As quick as hix nix porn flixs her claw slammed down, caging the intruder. But it was just a gray mechanical mouse! a windup toy that had arrived that morning, gift of an admirer. (The silly note: "Krazy, you're Mahatma Gandhi!") Had it been *this* morning? And who had sent it? Mr. Eeek That's a Maoist, or Awful Sir Ball Pop? Where did such names come from, anyway? Had there been a new wave of immigration—from another galaxy? Had she only dreamed those names? And was this a real toy or a hallucination? Well, who cared! Since the frames of the strip dissolved, so had she. The boundaries of consciousness had blurred— no!—had widened! Delicious disorder rained. Down. On her. And with enough tiger tea more barriers would break.

She drank a cup. Now she could play gin rummy with the dead. She stroked the mechanical mouse. What had some duck just said to her about a Throw Jam mouse? Could this be one of those? It was covered with gray felt and had huge blood-red eyes painted on its front. (An undistinguished oval: you could tell what was its front only because of the big crimson dots. And a skinny inconsiderable tail marked its hind part. It must be an embarrassment to him, she thought, to have such a nothing of a tail.) She wound the mouse up and dropped it in the center of the sun carpet. It skittered about, and then, confused by some new critical manifesto, it spun in a circle and scurried off again in the opposite direction. That, she thought, should be roundabout enough for him! She poked him, and he turned about again and again. No simple routes for this mouse! No straightforward Yes to everything! She swiped downwards, yanked his tail off, and stuck it in her mouth. It tasted dry, bitter—none of the sweet tang of real fur and flesh. Once more she swiped, and this time broke the knob from the winding stem. Now it was a useless stupid thing! Incapable of returning to work! "My diagnosis," she said, "is severe depression. Life is a dung heap and he'd be better off dead!" She stuck the mouse in her mouth and cracked its back between her sharp teeth—perfect for *this* job—revealing his cunning gear works, his dead metal heart. "Yeeow!" Ignatz screamed as his back broke. She spat little bitty Ignatz out onto her carpet and batted him back and forth between her paws—to calm the little one down, so he wouldn't want to rush off anywhere.

The oscillations of the mouse—who moved, finally, to the rhythm of Krazy's true pulse—put her in a meditative mood. She felt objective, disinterested, cold-eyed—the right attitude for drawing up an indictment against . . . against . . . "Oppenatz," she hissed. She had felt the identity from the first, from that terrible day at Alamogordo when she had imagined that the test tower was an Ignatian device to deliver a brick to her head. Her loving eyes had X-rayed in to the truth—Ignatz and Oppie were the same, they were killers, and they deserved what they got! Would get, she added, giving him an extra hard bop, right to left. But not till the indictment had been drawn; the trial held; the doubt, while the jury is out . . . that's entertainment! After all, she was a *civilized* cat, just as he had said. A cat that talked, a symbol of reconciliation between Fred and Ginger, between man and woman, between *their* animal and human parts. She cried to remember his first letter, the sun that had shone for her—with a false light, a burning radioactive warmth—here on her blue and brown carpet. How sweetly, how naively, she had been taken in! As if being a Ginger meant you were more animal than a Fred, more voracious, more blood-thirsty. Because women were more *feline!* So a *female cat*—like *herself*—was trouble redoubled, the most demanding creature of all! She clawed Oppenatz lightly, marking a con-vict's uniform on his splintered back—for his ignorance was a prison and should have an appropriate outward sign.

For how very long, Krazy thought, have men used *cats* for their comedies of making up with women, and their tragedies of casting out—their *festivals.* Those celebrations, her mom had taught her, were how cats had broken into show business.

The holiday just before Lent was cats' first big break. It was a time to humiliate the cock . . . the cack . . . the husbands whose wives—like cats in heat—had slept with other men, a festival to shame the little fellows who had been beaten by their spouses, scratched by their claws, a fat time to frighten the codgers who had married young "kittens." Any fellow, that is, who had been bewitched by a woman. A band of stout men, cradling a cat, followed these losers around the town square, ripping pieces of fur from kitty's body. "It was an instrumental solo *and* a singing solo," her mom had whis-pered furiously, shaking with rage. "A cat *gut* solo. Ask any *man:* That's entertainment!"

"They use *us* for the ceremony," her mother said, "be-cause *we*'re the mystery of Woman in all her slinky bewitch-ing power. We're the enchanting Female who makes men burn to stroke her fur. We're all that they fear in women's black lusts, her sharp teeth, her indifferent self-love that will swallow them whole, or leave them in the cold. Witches, my darling, turn themselves into cats for their sabbaths, and yowl their desires at the moon." Kitten Krazy, drinking milk at the glass kitchen table, saw tall female pusses in high red boots, claws out, sharp teeth showing, dancing about an iron cauldron. "So men kill cats to master the terror they feel before the mystery of their birth from a woman, the desire they feel for women, the decay of their bodies as Mother Earth takes them back. Women!" Mom had said, laughing mirthlessly between tight lips. "Can't live with 'em, can't live without 'em!"

Cats were such a good symbol, Mama said, that Lent became just one holiday in a long calendar of cat torment. And, as the year turned, Krazy's family memorialized each of the old festivals the traditional cat way, retelling, at evening time, the history of torture, the apartment's blinds drawn against the cat-hunting night, the table set with candles and a beautiful embroidered cloth her mother had brought from the old country. They sipped sweet wine and ate sour milk foods that gave a dark cast to the air. Mama, ditched again by Krazy's father, would drink too much plum wine, and cry, lost to Krazy in some sadness whose only recompense was more sadness, as if only in addition could the sum be made to come out right. (Krazy's mom had elegant, silky white fur. Dad had been a common short-haired black tom. Did her mom, Krazy wondered, watching her tears, mind that Krazy was in between? Did it remind her mom of her awol husband and make her weep? What's black and white, Krazy thought, self-pityingly, and sad all over?)

Mom made Krazy memorize their bitter herb history— lest Krazy ever forget the original *why* of the show business cat, the pile of bones she stood upon, the mixed-up feelings towards women Krazy perilously played to, that made cats a symbol for men, and Krazy—with her new verse for an old song—an artiste, *a star*. Those solemn dinners—just the two of them—were as much a part of Krazy's education as her interminable tap lessons, her ceaseless singing classes. Remember *summer solstice*, Krazy, when men, casting out demons, threw burlap sacks of cats—screaming, clawing, praying—into a bonfire. "A sort of Houdini act," Mama said, "but we escaped only into death." Don't forget the special Sunday, darling purr-box, when children tied cats to poles and roasted them over fires. Engrave in your heart the big French holiday (Momma's people were from France, though she said you could find the same business all over Europe) when boys chased a flaming cat through the streets of Paris, stoning her.

"But *I* don't hate women," kitten Krazy had said to her mother. "Why do men?" She rubbed herself against her mother's warm white silky fur, looking to reassure herself, hoping to comfort her mom. Her mother had turned her head with a riddling close-lipped smile for her daughter.

"Remember, darling, this means that they won't be able to take their eyes from you," her mother had said, by way of reply. "Their love and hate for women are so mixed together that you hypnotize them. You've got *star quality.* And *that's* something you can't buy or learn in school!"

Krazy flipped docile Ignatz into the air and he landed thwack-smack on his cracked back. "If you hate sex: Bludgeon a kitty!" Krazy screamed. Dead cats as lamps! "But if you fear death: Roast a cat!" For the first time, Krazy's voice rang to her own ears just as powerfully as her mother's lovely, savagely sad voice had those evenings alone, as if it had been her very own child who had dangled over the fire, or run flaming through the streets of the old country. As if she were sending Krazy out into the world, ablaze with her own talent, knowing that the flame would bewitch them day after day in the comic pages.

Krazy dragged Ignatz's head on the carpet, rubbing one eye into a bloodshot blur. "Why must I suffer like this anymore!" she screamed. Her rage, too, she thought proudly, was now her mother's as much as her own, and all the stronger and more true for it! It was the tea that overcame the barrier—never thicker than a placental membrane anyway—between her and her ma.

She got the tin down from the counter and dipped her paws in, one after the other. There wasn't time for brewing. She had a trial to finish! She shoveled the dry, bittersweet leaves into her mouth, letting them dribble onto her chin and whisper down, like snow, on the quiet mouse. "I'm tired of being *their* star, Mama!" she shrieked. "I'm sick of turning *their* writhing into a dance! I donwanna wreckandsigh'l them! No more, hey, look, girls can be civilized! I have tiger blood in my veins! I want to let my claws unfurl for us and rend them in their complacency. *I want to pounce!*"

So it was decided. The trial was over. Her painful duty was clear.

She donned a black handkerchief. "He shall be taken," she said, "from the place where he is, to another place, a different place, you know, a new place. And there something really mean will be done to him!"

She shoved Ignatz's little head into the tiny guillotine that lay waiting for him. (It was a kind of French mouse-trap—appropriate to her background, and the justice of their cause. A gadget for a gadget!) But how cute he seemed then, how dear and sweet and itsy-ikle-bitsy he looked, with his head sticking out from the wooden block, his neck exposed to the razor blade! The soft brown hair of his scalp stood up straight on either side of the blade. Should she stroke his head or cut it off? Krazy's mind filled with sweet indecision, and her body with a pleasant lethargy. The Mouse looked up at her, his tiny brown eyes brimming with beatific happiness. "Thank you, Krazy," he said. "At least now my pain is at an end."

"I'm sorry," Krazy said, forgetting her anger for a moment, for she felt she had perhaps been a trifle unfair, torturing him before his execution. "I just meant to keep you calm and amused, I think."

"Oh, not my pain *now*," the Mouse said, smiling up from his sharp metal collar. "I've really enjoyed the way you played with me the last little while! No, I mean all those years of your *love*. That's what was driving me mad! Now you've saved *my sanity*. You've finally shown your true face."

"My true face?" Krazy said, surprised, her anger vaporizing into a cloud of moist amazement. "I only have *one* face. You know. Same, same, same. Flat. No facets. That's me!"

Ignatz took a round, long-handled mirror from his pocket, and, with some difficulty—because he had to reach his short arm around the front of the guillotine—he held it up before Krazy.

Her neck wore a garland of mouse skulls! Her mouth was painted with blood, and a small gray tail still hung from the corner! Her six arms weaved in confusion trying to cover her visage.

"See, dearest? *You're* the one who is just like Oppenheimer. *You're* the one who dropped the bomb, just as I always knew. *You* are Death, Destroyer of Worlds. Mother Kali! That's the face I longed to see!"

"But why do you want this?" Krazy asked, more bewildered by Ignatz's glee than by her own transformation. "I look *ghastly*, and I don't have anything very nice planned for you either!" He had hoped for *this?* Why was that? Her anger continued to spin itself into cottony bemusement, and in that open-eyed amazement it was hard to hold on to her fury. She tried. "You know that I'm planning to chop your little bitty head off, don't you?"

"Good! Good!" Ignatz said heartily, burgher mouse sitting down to just the delicious dinner he had ordered—even if it was a last supper. "All those years when you drove me mad with your love, I just *knew* that you really meant to hurt me."

"I did not!" Krazy exclaimed. But the powerful certainty of her mother's rage had departed, leaving her limp. "Did I?"

"You wouldn't recognize *me*, Krazy," the Mouse said plaintively. "And *that* really hurts! You wouldn't let me be angry! No, no matter what I did to you, even when I sent whole walls of bricks toppling onto your noggin, you always turned it into love. I was only allowed to have one emotion as far as you were concerned: adoration of Krazy Kat! Do you know how flat and small that makes a fellow feel, kitty?" Ignatz's voice choked with sullen tears, weeds that crowded out his words. "Bury a live cat in a field," Krazy thought, trying to recall the Old World proverbs her mother had taught her, the ones that had fueled her fury, "and the weeds die." But Ignatz's little cry was so plaintive! Maybe, for him, she *should* bury herself alive in the field of his unhappiness. "I was never strong to you," Ignatz whimpered. "I never had a moment in your eyes when I was a god to you, when I was even a person *separate* from you." Ignatz bawled openly, his face a pucker of red lines, the original map of grievance. "I *knew* that that could mean only one thing, that you were the All Powerful Woman. So I longed for you to declare yourself! To show openly that you were the Goddess Who Gives Life and Who Takes It Away!"

You did? Krazy thought. I was? I am? What goes on here? In Ignatz's tantrum she heard the terrified squall of the newborn baby left out in the darkcolddamp. Is this, she wondered, how this little mouse saw his *mother?* Is that what all his bawling was about? Ignatz's mother? All powerful, a mouse merciless in her attentive kindness? Not like Krazy's mom, of course. Krazy adored her lovely long-haired mother dearly endlessly always. She owed everything to her, all her training, her dance lessons, her singing lessons, her electrocu . . . hellocute . . . her talking lessons, her talent itself. She had had a harpy childhood . . . a horpy . . . a hoppy . . . My God, she not only couldn't say it, she couldn't even think it! And when she *became* her own mother, look at the outfit she wore! Blood-red lipstick! Skull necklaces! Is *this* who she thought *her* mother was? Well, did she? Did she? That wonderful woman who had never let Krazy take even one step on her own—not without criticizing her posture, anyway! Mom was always shuttling her off to dance class when she wanted to skip rope. And when Krazy was allowed on the sidewalk with friends to skip rope, her mother held one end, waiting to hear what rhymes Krazy had concocted for herself—were they clever enough, were they intriguing enough, was she talented enough to qualify her to be her mother's child? As if only stardom could redeem what it meant to be a cat! And if Krazy's rhymes weren't good enough, then her mother rewrote them! "K my name is Krazy/And I come from Coconino/My husband's name is Kathy/And he plays Pokerino." Imagine a mother who writes your material for jump rope! Call *that* kindness! Her mother had been the whole world, her only audience, and Krazy had lived and died by the annoyed twitch of her whiskers, the warmth of her smiles—so life had been show business for Krazy from the first. And when Krazy said she might prefer something more contemplative—studying art history—her mother had made her feel as if she would die; or Krazy would; or both. *That* was the All Powerful Woman, the woman her mother had been to her. So Ignatz's squalling *was* her own, too. Oppenatz was Krazynatz. BECAUSE OF MOMS MEN ARE ANGRY AT THE WOMEN THEY LOVE, Krazy saw, AND WOMEN ARE ANGRY AT WOMEN, TOO!

"Oh, to be tortured by the goddess," Ignatz said, "that became my dream once I realized how monstrous your love really was."

Monster? Krazy thought. Me? A goddess? But it is only the round who are gods. Is this what it means to be round? Not just to have a front and a back, but to wield pain?

"I dreamt of our both acknowledging openly, in every

paper that Hearst owned, that love is really pain," Ignatz said happily. "I longed all these years for you to torment me with vile gadgets in the big color Sunday panels."

Love is pain? Ignatz was getting *really* weird. But she didn't know how to stop him, how to vomit up her own brain like a massive hair ball!

"Now I want you to make me your pet. I want to lick your hands, your feet. Order me to do shameful things! I want to be your slave, and then have you kill me. Hurt me, goddess! Make me feel *chosen!*" Ignatz's toenails hooked under strands of the carpet, anchoring his feet; his thin legs strained, pushing his shoulders against the guillotine's harness, thrusting his neck forward, as if he were straining towards death.

Krazy felt suddenly faint, from the confusion, from the tea, from Ignatz's bizarre longing for pain. Why *that,* for God's sake? OK, so everyone was angry at girls. But a feet-licking slave? That was *too much.*

Maybe it would be kindest to grant Ignatz his wish, and let the blade fall! She tried to reach out to the little lever on the side of the guillotine, but she couldn't get her six paws to coordinate properly.

Oblivious, Ignatz went on in an odd, breathy rush. "Why not use your tail on me, dear? You could tie me up with it, and then whip me with the end of it?"

"OK. Sure," Krazy said. Not meaning anything by it but that she wanted Ignatz to shut up. It was his voice, she was sure, and its sick fantasies that were making the sun pattern in her carpet fall inward into itself, with the guillotine-clad Mouse sitting calmly in its center, as he, too, fell inward into himself. "You bet," she said. But her mind was elsewhere, watching a bonk on the bean make a valentine bloom over her head. All these years, when she took Ignatz's brick was she agreeing that he was right to be angry, letting herself be punished as a woman because she, too, was angry at women!

Was she agreeing that the love women get should always be mixed with hatred? Till love was like death!

So drop the bomb!

The sun on her carpet was swirling up into a fire of magnesium blues and sulphurous browns, a mushroom cloud of flame and smoke, with little Ignatz and his metal necktie rising serenely on top. Top o' the World, Ma! Once more she was watching a fire storm that she had somehow caused, and it was shaking her apart! She felt like she had a snake coiling inside her, yet the snake was her, and she was inside it. The snake was made of blackness and stars. And every star in the snake was another smaller snake that was made of blackness and stars, and those stars were snakes made of blackness and stars. The snake was the beginning and end of things: death biting the tail of love, every yes that became no that became love become hate become yes again. The snake would kill her but it would give birth to her, too, over and over, if only she could keep the snake together. And the only way to do that was to get the tail of it into her own mouth, to bite the beginning and end of things and *be* the circle. She fell to the carpet, chasing the end of things that was the beginning of things, and before she passed out she felt a sharp terrible pain, and the infinitely familiar (but why familiar? She had never tasted such a thing!) revolting yet exciting (for every no becomes yes!) taste of blood in her mouth.

She awoke with her tail between her teeth. Shards of the plastic Ignatz were scattered over the carpet, and the crumbs of that vile tiger tea that had made her so unnatural, so unlike herself. Bloodstains spattered the sun, as if it had been offered a sacrifice. She remembered Ignatz's adorable little head inside a guillotine, and her mind reeled backwards in horror. Had she spilled any of his precious blood! No, she saw the teeth marks in her tail, and the fur matted thickly with sticky maroon. It was *her* blood, thank God!

She saw then that Ignatz and the Pup were already standing over her, watching the dismaying spectacle. How much of the performance had they seen? She batted her eyelashes at the Mouse, hoping to distract him. Her paw went furtively to her neck. And she gave thanks that there was no necklace of tiny skulls there anymore.

The Pup nodded sadly down at her. The Mouse smiled, gazing over the carpet, as if the carnage delighted him like a rave review.

She smiled back, in what she hoped was a winning manner, her head held at shoe level. Her neck was frozen in a devil's clamp. She couldn't turn it from side to side! God's judgment! Her compass-needle heart spun crazily, north south up west. "I'm confused, darling," she said.

"That," the Mouse replied, scowling, "isn't even conversation."

But what was she supposed to do? She felt as if the plastic and blood and tea crumbs scattered on the carpet were bits of her own brain. How was she supposed to piece them back together?

She continued to smile docilely up at Ignatz, showing more of her white *harmless* teeth. At least he hadn't noticed the puncture marks in her tail!

"Done quite a job on your little appendage, haven't you, sweetheart?" he said.

Oh, if shame could turn fur white, she thought, she would be a Krazy Ghost!

Ignatz smiled down at her warmly, and she relaxed. Why had she ever doubted that her partner wanted what was best for her? A troubling memory clouded her pupils for a moment: Had Ignatz really begged her to beat him with her tail? Impossible! Why would anyone *want* to be hurt like that? Too weird! Just look at him: Admit she's a hit, his smile said, and we'll go on from there. She's played a charade that was lighter than air. It's all right, Krazy—she read in the pleased wrinkles around his eyes—don't worry about thwacking me. That's entertainment! And what else, she thought, could justify such a mess as life was!

"I can help you, Krazy," Ignatz said, with great warmth and directness.

Of course he would, she thought. Hadn't he always?

"My diagnosis," he said, "is severe depression."

Oh God, she thought, he heard me before! She remembered the taste of plastic and fake fur in her mouth, and heard the crack of his shattering back. Panic opened its wings in her breast.

"She'd be better off . . ." Ignatz started to say.

And Krazy knew the torture that came next! The huge burlap sack, the bonfire, the fanfare. Gadget for gadget for gadget . . . Ignatz stopped and whispered something into the Pup's commodious ear. The Pup, his sad brown eyes looking up to heaven, nodded reluctantly.

But if the Pup agreed, Krazy thought sadly, then the sentence must be just. She bowed her head, nose to the dirt.

"You'd be better off . . ." Ignatz said.

She showed her neck for the death sentence that was to come.

". . . in treatment," the Mouse concluded. "Yes," the Mouse said, "psychoanalysis. That's what you need, dear. Psychoanalysis."

THE

TALKING CURE

Easter Sunday, April 25, 19——

Dear Offissa Bull Pup:

OK. So I don't *exactly* know what psychoanalysis is. But word of honor, pal, my "psychoanalysis"—once I work out what it is from the hints I've gotten in books—is going to cure the Kat. And I'll do it in such a way that the therapy for her symptoms will also create the new, *rounder* soul that we need for artistic greatness, and that Americans need to be rounded, godlike individuals. Like in really good books.

Until yesterday I thought that was only *my* dream. I was the loneliest mouse in the world. My hunch is that our new round souls—once you and I create them!—will select their own society, and you can bet that the rest of *this* little cast will make *my* soul puke. You, dear Pup—serious Pup, patient Pup, *implacable* Pup—are the only one of our crew who might have been my friend. But because of Krazy, you and I were the Saturday night Main Event!

And now we're pals because of that very same wonderful kitty! Yesterday we watched that poor creature roll about on the sun-design carpet, teething maniacally on that plastic mouse, playing seek&destroy with her own tail, and we were made one by the heart-melting sadness of that spectacle.

When we spoke, and you gave the high sign to my plan to help—and transform!—the Kat, why, I began for the first time to think I might ~~actually give that Nobel Prize acceptance speech!~~ make something of myself.

I know Coconinoites say I'm spiteful because I *openly* criticize their teenie-weenie attempts at art. Maybe I *am* spiteful. I don't think I ever told you, Pup, but my father didn't want a showman son. He himself was—is my face red!—truly in the rag trade: Papa Ignatz's Old Clothes Collection and Resale. For my immigrant dad, only a doctor-heir would do—fulfilling, finally, his mother's prophecy on the boat over, that in the New World *her* teen-age son would be a doctor. But when *his* dad died, my poor pop had to leave school and support the family. (Interesting that now I *am* a *doctor,* about to re-create an *entertainer*—our Krazy Kat!)

My father thought that W. C. Handy, and W. C. Fields, and tap dancing, and so very much that my mother and I loved, were "New World trash." (Unhappy mouse, he criticized everything American by the standards of the Old World culture that his family had fled—a culture whose innate murderousness he despised.) So maybe I began my artistic career by holding myself apart from him, and have walked farther and farther away from the crowd. And maybe I think only great art will justify me in disappointing my dad. OK—but if it leads to the big time, isn't a little isolation for me, and a sprinkling of spite for these tiny town "artistes," worth it?

All these years I've studied how *they* live—in their books, their movies, their ads, ~~their prep schools~~—in order to be a great American artist. Now, like other immigrants and their children, like Cary Grant, Lorenz Hart, or John Bubbles, I'm ready to give America a big Chanukah present back—a new image of the self. But this time why lock ourselves up in the pop-culture ghetto? Why not strut uptown to the mansion of high art, of roundness, and say that our gift to America could rank with Eugene O'Neill's or Henry James's? America *needs* a truly *democratic* high art. America needs the round comic strip!

With cordial greetings,
Dr. (well, almost) Ignatz Mouse, PhD
(All But Dissertation)

April 26, 19——

My dear Offissa Pup:

My practice, so far, is just one patient, so I can't afford a separate office. My first consultation with the Kat was held at my soon-to-be-a-historic-monument kitchen table. As Krazy and I talked, Mrs. Mice bustled about in her apron, chasing after Milton, Marshall, and Irving, or intentionally banging pans about. The Mrs. walks through life with the heavy clump of the aggrieved. She's a reluctant, stinko housekeeper—children's toys are scattered over the floor, whizzing and skittering, making the tinny whirring sound of her constant angers, and terrifying my patient (who can't bear to look at windup animals). Really, I can't blame my Mrs. I've always cared more about my art than about my family. And, though she pretends to admire me, she really has the typical American outlook: if I'm such a great artist, why ain't we rich? (Why do I put up with her? It's almost as if I'm drawn to her anger!)

I perched on a high metal stool, and Krazy sat on a wooden chair, so we were face to face. Kitty is in a bad way. When I just tapped her playfully on the bean with a brick, she toppled from her chair and stood rigidly on all fours with her tail between her teeth, looking like a Danish Modern coffee table. Krazy was furniture for hours, even when Marshall and Milton used her as the goal in a floor hockey game. Weird, huh?

When she came to, she didn't remember who how what where. We re-began our interview. Krazy's sure that it's impossible for her to have both a satisfying personal life and fulfilling work. And, as Krazy's life and work are the same, she has neither.

"Do you want to work?"

"Sure. No, I mustn't. I'm too bad. I don't know. Maybe."

Multiple choice? I smiled kindly. "Of course you do."

"Mostly," she said sadly, "I'd like to be able to move my head again."

Many of her symptoms, like her "insumkneeah," date from our picnic at Alamogordo. All night she thrashes about restlessly on her carpet bed, or whiles away the darkness reading detective stories, terrified of the tricks the returning sun may play.

"Why detective stories?" Myself, I long ago outgrew such trash.

"You can *trust* Sam Spade," she said. "And at the end you know who's guilty. And that means *you're* not."

"Why is that so important?"

Krazy shrugged.

The confused Kat is desperately afraid of being guilty and thinks that if she is, she will age. (She has typical bimbo vanity about this.)

Many other parts of her character are probably also symptoms of her hysteria. You've probably noticed her habitual mispronunciations of words: "dollin" for *darling*, for example. (Anyway, that's my guess. When I asked her, she smiled and said, "By dollin, I meant dawlink, dalynn, just as I said.") It's as if she is not allowed to speak English, but has to make up our words from the vocables of some more native language. But which language? She is a refugee. But from where?

She told me that there are also other words she can "think" but can't say, that her thoughts are much more

"softfistacaked" than her talk. "I can't write them, even."
Poor hidden soul! "Why?"

She took her head between her paws—the only way she
can turn it nowadays—and moved it right and left, looking
for help. None came. Her bafflement increased, and I had
the sense of a lost soul imprisoned in her body by a magi-
cian's curse, unable to do anything but peek out from behind
the bars.

Because of the rain, Mrs. Mice had hung up our sheets
in the kitchen. On her way out, Krazy batted at one with her
paw. She became suddenly suspicious of my bonafides.

"I didn't realize you were a dock tour."

Was she, too, harping on that damn dissertation? "Sure,"
I said, smiling reassuringly. "Correspondence college."

"But no one gets sick here!" she said triumphantly.
"We've got no goims!"

Not so crazy! No one in Coconino falls ill. Or even ages.

I had to think quickly or risk her losing faith in me.
"Well, modern science is inventing new kinds of diseases
everyday," I said. "No germs involved."

Satisfied, she strolled down the hall, reclaiming her pink
parasol by the door. I offered her a piece of fruit for her walk
home, from the desert-colored Navaho bowl on the book-
case. Krazy herself had given me that piece of pottery long
ago. A five-inch crack in the side made it especially beautiful
in her eyes. Cracks, she said, reminded us that the simple
existence of a thing was a "mirrorkell." (Miracle?) And cracks
made things more themselves. (Well, she certainly has
enough of them now herself!)

"Thanks," she said. "A bana Anna please."

"You mean a banana," I said, handing her the fruit.

"Yes," she said, holding it between us, "a band aida."

"Banana," I repeated firmly.

"Ban-A-Anna," she said, smiling, and waving the fruit in
the air as if conducting an imaginary band.

"You can't say it?"

"No," she said, laughing giddily at me, and hopping from paw to paw. "That's how we're different. You say banana. I say bandana."

"But you just said it!" I shouted, unable to hide my exasperation.

"Said what?"

"Bandana. Damn. I mean Bandida." The more I looked at the fruit she held the harder it was to say its name. "Bonanza." I was hypnotized by her ignorance. "I mean banana!" I shouted triumphantly.

"Did not say it!"

"Did!" I shouted.

Bam! I was George to her Gracie once again: "Oh," she sang on her way out the door, "you say the word you say, and I say bandana! Let's call the whole thing off!"

But she promised to come back tomorrow.

Your devoted friend,
Ignatz Mouse

April 27, 19——

Dearest Pup:

OK, OK, I shouldn't have let the kids use her as a toy. But you know how boys are.

This morning I began my first course of treatment for hysterical kats. I gave Krazy hydrotherapy, soaking her with the garden hose. No progress. In the afternoon, I tried electrotherapy. I shaved Krazy's tail; my son Irving jammed it into a light socket; and I stuck a bulb in her mouth to check the current. That made a nice kat lamp, but there wasn't much therapeutic gain I could see—she still doesn't want my delightful bricks. How queer!

Thanks a million for all your guidance,
Ignatz

April 30, 19——

Dear Pup:

OK, OK. No more kat lamps. You know, even as I wrote that letter, I just *knew* you were going to disapprove. Yet I felt almost a compulsion to taunt you, my dearest friend. Strange, ain't it?

I don't understand why you say that sin and free will come into the world together. Is that your way of getting at me for my little mistake with the light socket—for which *I have already apologized*—or do you think your spook stuff has a clue to how we might become round, big-time artists?

Wait, I get you! You must mean that symptoms can't just be caused by physical short-circuits that a little electricity resolders. *That* won't produce round full-souled individuals. Physical explanations for diseases are too naturalistic—outmoded form, there hasn't been any good art in it since Dreiser!

Still, have you noticed how *everybody* wants their behavior bio-explained? Piano playing, bad taste in scarves, mass murder—it must be the genes! Let's just have an operation or take a pill for it! Americans are terrified of roundness and responsibility. But not me! Krazy used to do what she did, huh, Pup, over and over, without thinking—mere activity. But when I get through with her, she'll have to see that she *chooses* what she does—her insomnia, her reading trash detective stories, even her becoming a coffee table—and she'll have to be ashamed of her choices, pull herself together, and take the brick to the head again. She won't be able to run away from history anymore, from the results of her acts. Americans, like Krazy, are so *seemingly* innocent, amiable, trusting, open to everyone's ideas. Then, if they don't like the disaster they've caused, they leave town, change the station. When I work to make Krazy responsible,

I'll be creating the new American soul! Me, Ignatz Mouse!
I'm *making* a person!

So the new, responsible, choosing Krazy *self* will play a
starring role in her hysterical personality.

Your devoted servant,
Ignatz

May 4, 19——
My dear Pup:

OK. My new theory is: *Krazy has two minds.* (Working
together, the two minds make the Krazy "self.") The foreground mind is normal; it balances the checkbook, makes
appointments with the dentist, doesn't eat between-meal
snacks, etc. The other mind is filled with stuff Krazy's terrified of, and so she pushes it deep into the background. That
gives her a background. When Krazy encounters something
she really loves—my brick—it kind of reminds her of something she's stuck in her background Trouble Mind, so she's
frightened of it.

And I have a way—called Mixassociation—to connect
lots of *new* parts of the two minds together. Then when you,
the viewer, see foreground things, you will also see stuff
that's in the other mind. That will give perspective. Kitty
will look round!

Think of my work as like someone drawing a cat. In the
future, her looney high jinks will be joined to lots of the rest
of her hidden past life, a past life that is tinged with the blues,
so she doesn't want to know about it. Her current actions will
have a nice background. Then, during therapy, Mixassociation will make fresh foreground areas connect with the upsetting background stuff, so the new foreground parts will
have darkish hidden backgrounds that give twisted shadows

that scare her, and—voilà!—mint-condition symptoms! And *she* does it! She *chooses* to scare herself!

What do you think? I look forward to hearing from you.

Your *warmest* admirer,

Ignatz

May 9, 19——

Dearest Pup:

I sat Krazy down at my Formica kitchen table, and tested out my two minds connected by Mixassociation:

"Now you say whatever comes into the kat cabeza when I ask you a question." For I knew the answer would just pop into her mind, that it would be right around the corner in the other, Trouble Mind that I was inventing for us. "The question is, why are you afraid of bricks?"

"Ignatz."

"Good! Why are you afraid of Ignatz?"

"Ignatz," she said.

"And what's the most dangerous thing about Ignatz?"

"Ignatz."

I saw what had happened, but couldn't resist taking a little advantage of it. "Who's the smartest and best educated, no matter where he went to school?"

"Ignatz."

"The handsomest?"

"Ignatz."

"The tallest?"

"Ignatz."

"I mean the one who is *really* big?"

"Ignatz."

You see, Pup, as long as I sat just across the table from her, apple of her eyes, *I* was all the poor bubble brain could think of! So we went into the living room and I had her lie down on the busted blue sofa. I dragged in my metal stool, which Irving, to help in my work, has painted fire-engine red, kicked some books out of the way, and sat behind the couch, over Krazy's head and out of her sight.

"Why are you afraid of bricks?" I asked again, as patiently as I could.

"Hurt!"

"That's your neurosis talking."

"Is not my new roses." She made her hands into a megaphone. "Listen, Ignatz, this is Krazy Kat talking, the former Hearst *headliner*. Bricks hurt! Why would anyone *want* to be hit on the head with a brick? You're the one who wants to be hurt! You're the one who wants to be whipped by my tail!" She began to cry.

Huh? "Well," I said, dejectedly, "you *used* to want my brick."

"Well," she said, "it didn't use to hurt."

Quitting time. We'll try again in the morning.

Regards from the president of your unofficial fan club,

Ignatz

May 11, 19——

Dear Pup:

Mixassociation now works out well enough. Krazy tells me what everyone has said to her for the day, all the phone calls she's made, how much laundry she's done, and a full menu of everything she's eaten since I saw her last.

But Mixassociation isn't building enough connections between the background Trouble Mind and current foreground areas in Krazy's life. I need a moist, spreadable trauma-problem theme in her Trouble Mind that can go all through her life, Mixassociating things with its sadness, like chocolate with egg whites, and making her scared of new foreground parts. Then the Trouble Mind will always be right around the corner from this one. And I know what the new theme is going to be: *The Kat has a problem with Love and Intimacy!*

"You thought the bomb tower was a device to deliver a brick to your head," I reminded her this morning, "a brick that you wanted. But—whoops-a-kat!—it was more than you expected. Now when you want a brick, you're afraid that it will destroy the world. You're afraid of your own need for intimacy."

"What?"

"OK," I said. "Look, you're cured. Bricks are your sweets again!"

We padded out towards the backyard—a blasted garden of naked, leaning tomato stakes, abandoned project of the Mrs., plus some tumbleweed, and, today, one tall, bare, eucalyptus tree.

Krazy became reluctant, shuffling her feet on the splintery back-door steps. "It's gonna hurt, Ignatz."

"No," I said, decisively. "Not if you understand what I was telling you."

"I understand," she whined, "but it's still gonna hurt."

I had to pull on her stomach fur and drag her paws along the sand. "Come on," I said. "What makes my brick hurt is your *fear* of intimacy."

"The brick," she said, "is a brick. And it's gonna hurt."

"No," I said.

"*Yes,*" she said. "I'm *not* afraid of indimmersee. I'm afraid of bricks. They're hard and big and hard and they hurt."

"Don't be silly," I said, and hurled it.

She fell unconscious.

Best in these dark times,
Ignatz

May 12, 19——

Dear Pup:

Why should the Kat be so afraid of intimacy (i.e., my bricks + her noggin)? I think I have the answer, and it's a surprising one. *Sex.* It's something artists yatter on and on about in all the novels I read, all the movies I see, all the ads on TV. Sex is the guaranteed wienie for our comeback. It causes endless plot complications and gives everybody a jazzy little buzz feeling. Great, huh? Coconino will always be an insipid hick sideshow if we don't invent some sex for ourselves. I'm not sure what sex is *exactly,* but I know it's something about people getting inside themselves with each other, and then I don't know yet exactly what they do. I think they pee in each other.

And sex must be very powerful because we not only don't do it, Coconinos—unlike the rest of the known world— never even talk about it. I think something terrible about this stuff happened to us before the strip began. So we make ourselves forget it all the time.

I do remember that one evening, as a child, I went into my parents' bedroom, *and they were doing something together that looked like a snake swallowing its own tail.* My father was furious when he saw me frozen at the foot of their bed. I knew it was a door I shouldn't have opened, a scene I shouldn't have seen. Was *that* sex? Dad chased me out with a belt in his hand.

Could that have been *my* kindly dad, who never hit us kids? The *same* dad who had just the day before told me that as he was pushing his wooden cart down the city sidewalk, one of *them* had knocked his fur cap into the gutter?

"What did you do, Pop?" I had asked, waiting eagerly for the Joe Palooka part.

"I went into the gutter and picked up my hat."

Yet because of the thing I'd seen, this man had become

terrible, and was chasing me down the hall to wallop me with his belt!

I'll bet Krazy saw something like what I saw. And I'll bet in her case it was more than just *seeing*. The original trauma for Krazy must have happened in kittenhood, and it must have been *that her parents made the animal swallowing its own tail with her.*

So I guess our parents must have known about sex, though we don't. Sex stopped for us when we came to Coconino, and the strip started. Maybe that's even why we came—to get away from sex. And it could be that that's why we don't age anymore—maybe if you have sex you age. (Maybe it's like illness. Or lying.)

I think the adults *did* sex things to us when we were young and they were so awful we're scared to remember! With Krazy this sex business has gotten mixed up with her need for intimacy.

Best to you and yours,
Ignatz

May 13, 19——

Dearest Pup:

Tested my new improved theory. I lay Krazy down on the floral print couch.

"Go ahead, Mixassociate," I said. "You know, say whatever comes into your head."

"Wagga wagga," she said, "nig pig. Dust ball."

"Yes," I said. "nig pig. Dust ball. And then Kitten . . ."

"Kitten?"

"Yes. Kitten. Then . . . Me . . . Father . . . Too close . . . Big Paws . . ."

Krazy said, "Kitten . . . Me . . . Father . . . Too close . . . Big Paws . . ." Then she turned her torso around and narrowed her eyes at me. "Mouse, what are you getting at?"

"The truth," I said. "Like those detectives you admire so. I want the truth. Stop protecting Mr. Big Paws. I mean your father."

"My father? What did he do?"

"You *know*," I said. "And remember, you're not supposed to look at me. Turn around, stare at the ceiling, and tell me about your sexual experiences as a kitten."

"Ignatz," she said imploringly, her paws gripped tightly over her heaving chest, as if she were holding herself together, "what do you mean sexyouall experiences? Do you mean the kind of things you talked about? Wanting to be tail-whipped and to lick my paws and stuff?"

"What?" I said. "Of course not. *We* don't have sexual thoughts. Children don't, either. Only the adults did. I mean tell me things that were *done* to you by adults."

"OK. Sure. OK. I didn't have any sexual thoughts. Or dreams. Or anything. You know."

"Of course not. I just told you that you didn't."

"I know I didn't. OK. Nothing happened to me either."

"Yes it did. That's why you have these problems with bricks. I mean with intimacy. You just didn't know what was happening when you were little."

"IGNATZ!" she shouted at the ceiling. "EVEN WHEN I WAS LITTLE I NEVER HAD SEXUAL FEELINGS! AND NOTHING SEXUAL EVER HAPPENED TO ME!"

I put my head down on my arms, and began to sob. "What's the use?" I cried, heartsick over this stupid cat. "The world is a dung heap!"

"OK. Look. Don't cry, OK? Like what did you have in mind?" she asked hesitantly.

"You tell me. So long as you were a kitten, and it was sexual."

"Well, there was an alley cat."

"No," I said. "That's a screen. Really it was your father."

"You know," she said angrily, "I can feel your beady

little mouse eyes boring into the back of my head. Ignatz, *you're* the one who has a thing about fathers. You're angry at all of them. Like you were at the Pup. And you're crazy about them too. Like you and the very same Pup nowadays. Dad wasn't a very big deal around our house. He drank too much and stayed away for months at a time. It was Mom who raised me, who force-marched me to dance and singing classes, and made me into an entertainer."

"Don't change the subject to protect your father. Go ahead, tell me about your father."

"Oh, Ignatz," she whimpered, "I have a paw on each side of a giant chasm . . . My father wasn't *that* bad . . . Oh my God, the sides are drifting apart . . . I'm being split in two! I don't want to be two! . . . Yes," she said in a small voice, "OK. My father, Ignatz. It was my father."

"Good, now we're making progress."

"I have to throw up," she announced matter-of-factly. She put her face over the side of the couch, and I heard a scratchy sound, as if there was something irritating at the back of her throat, like a hair ball. But this was a hysterical hair ball. Her stomach moved in rippling motions as the trapped energies discharged themselves and equilibrium was regained.

When she finished, I led her to the backyard to our test site. Krazy walked slowly, her head down, like someone being escorted to her own execution—for health will be the death of her old, limited self. I sailed a brick.

"Owwwwwwwwwwwwww!"

But I'm sure now that it's just a matter of time till she won't fear love and so will crave my bricks again.

Best wishes,
Ignatz

May 14, 19——

Dear Pup:

My wife is snubbed, as the spouse of the "little sex doctor." Even Mock Duck feels free to make fun of me when the
Mrs. brings in my dirty shirts. Well, I can live without the
good opinion of morons. I'm used to it. This is the sort of
country, you know, where someone like me can't even go to
one of their prep schools! So, let the gentiles think what they
like so long as I have your encouragement. You have the
roundness of a god, and your judgment justifies me.

Your admirer,

Ignatz

May 15, 19——

Dear Pup:

The cast, in *their* living rooms, pretend that they abhor
this "desecration" of their *dear* parents. But chez moi they
love to lie on my couch and tell long stories of how they were
mom&dad's little bitty ickle victim-poo.

I now have three paying patients. Kelley came to my
consulting room in a tattersall vest, his big-bowled meer-
schaum releasing his usual regular puffs of self-satisfaction.
Nothing must be allowed to interfere with *his* digestion—a
soul, for instance. Roundness? It's like opera! Who needs it?

But once on my couch, the smokestack stopped. His wife
whines that all he talks about is bricks and money. His marriage is in the dumper.

"Jesus, Kelley," I said, "don't you read the women's
magazines?" (I had even laid out a few of my wife's in the
kitchen/waiting room.) "Wives hate husbands who yakkety-
yak all the time about business. They despise flat guys with
only one thing on their mind. They want a fellow like me,

someone with facets, someone who cares about roundness and the soul."

Kelley nodded, sadder still. All meekness, he asked if my sex therapy could help him?

You watch: I will build a psyche even in the stony soil of the bourgeoisie.

Next up was Kiyoti. He sauntered into my consulting room and put his hairy body on my couch. He has the smug expectation of welcome of the native-born, ~~the prep school graduate.~~ I *know* that he's just an upper-class asshole in a dirty silk ascot, with his big nose in the air and a pinched mouth, as if he were regretfully smelling you. He should get a whiff of himself sometime! B.O. Plenty! Someone should lick him clean! (Ugh, what a disgusting idea.) Why have I cultivated this prick all these years? He says my plum wine is vile, and my living room a junkyard. You know our living room, Pup, my soon-to-be-a-historic-monument sofa whose white wadding bulges out through the tears in its thin cotton fabric, a few rickety director's chairs—not that I fancy myself a *director*, it's just that they're cheap and comfortable—and piles of books and magazines that I've pillaged for ideas for the strip. OK, so I don't care about furniture. So what? I care about art, about roundness.

Kiyoti smiled up at me from the couch, showing his long teeth, yellow from years of neglect. He needs my help. He is *crucified*, the asshole says, by his exquisite sensibilities. Whenever he dislikes something he breaks out in a bright red rash. His mangy chest is decorated all over with big polka dots.

"Old school tie?"

He pursed his thick lips at my mot, and the spots spread to his legs. His paw scratched uselessly at his hairy thigh. I promised I would help him, and gave him my first piece of advice: He should brush his teeth more.

Last—and least—was the Duck, who is enthralled by sex education. (Ladies like it! I think we may have a best-seller on our hands!) For her it is another wondrous possibility for gossip. Which is also her problem. Poor chatterbox, lately her voice is so hushed that no one can understand her tale-telling. I adjusted her volume controls: "When you gossip you think that you're going to tell people what your parents did. And you liked them a lot, too, so you feel guilty. That makes you hush your mouth. But don't worry. Lots of parents were slime, just like yours." So when she gossips, I told her, she should sing it out.

I long to hear from you, dear friend,

Ignatz

P.S. Guess who just hopped up? Out of the night came our coal black Jack Rabbit of the thumping paws. Bang-bang-bang on the *back door* (lest anyone see him needing my help). "I *knew* it was my mama's fault!" he shouted. He wants a therapy make-over so he can control his temper. Dames love his fury, he says, but it's bad for business at his grocery store.

May 17, 19——

Dearest Pup:

My patients don't seem to get any better. Krazy is no closer to working, still horrified by my bricks. And a satisfying emotional life is just as far away—she's still horrified by my bricks. Kelley still bottom lines everything in dollars and cents (and he's late paying my bill). Kiyoti's rash has colonized the inside of his long nose—his critical response to an evening recital of Kwakk Wakk's, who now fancies herself a diva! And this morning Beau Koo Jack Rabbit whacked Kiyoti across the nose for trying to steal his appointment. Still, my patients think me the cat's pj's. I'm going to turn them all into practitioners of my New Art-Science, to make roundness in others—a kind of franchise operation. Really, my New Art-Science is mostly listening—the sort of thing even these dunderheads should be able to do.

Best wishes from him who only wants history to remember him as Pup's friend—for you are like a god to me,

Ignatz

May 18, 19——

Dear Pup:

My nucleus of followers—Krazy, Kwakk Wakk, Kiyoti, and Kelley—have founded THE IGNATZ'S NEW ART-SCIENCE SOCIETY. They meet once a week at Krazy's house to argue over the most faithful application of my methods. Two days ago Kiyoti—a blockhead as always—delivered a paper "On the Importance of Red as the Color for the Therapist's Stool."

Still, *I* have doubts. If everyone's parents did them in, then we're not responsible for what fuck-ups we've become. How can we have roundness without responsibility for our symptoms?

And, I myself have developed some annoying problems. When I write to you my head fills with a weary-making acid that cuts me off from your support. I spend hours looking at maps, playing solitaire, or watching basketball games on TV. These are clearly hysterical symptoms. In fact, I've blossomed with all of Krazy's problems—as if, in the course of treatment, I've become her! Sometimes, after the Mrs. and kids are asleep, I even suck on my skinny little tail. The conclusion is inescapable: my dear parents must have molested me. Which of them, I wonder, could it have been? My darling blonde mother, with her fine downy hair, who never had the time for my father or me—she had so much "antiquing" to do? Or my father, whose constant overwhelming attentions were responsible for my precocious intellectual development—though he never wanted me to be an artist/entertainer, and would have happily seen me dead when I defied him?

Dearest benefactor, I can't write any more today.

Your fire-end, I mean your *friend*,
Ignatz

May 19, 19——

Dear Pup:

Something smells rotten here. If my theory is right, then there were an awful lot of vile parents around! Including mine. OK, I'm prepared to accept that, if that's where science leads. But now my dear son Irving's behavior troubles me. He's developed a terrible allergy to kat hair—and Krazy leaves gifts of it all over the house—yet he's especially "protective" towards her, playing his "boom-box" as loud as he can during her session, to interrupt us. This morning he waited for her by our stoop, his nose already starting to run as the Kat skipped up our steps. I heard him say through his snuffles and sneezes, "This New Art-Science of Dad's doesn't help anyone. Instead it makes life into a disease that you have to talk about all the time." Yesterday afternoon he demanded to have his lunch served in the sandy waste of our backyard. He insists that Mrs. Mice should leave a man like me—whose stupid ideas make everyone snicker and cause her nothing but embarrassment—and come live with him behind the house.

Clearly, Irving is a hysteric. But I know I never molested him. Did the Mrs. . . . ?

Nah! But if my theory is wacko, why does Krazy say I look so god-like to her now that she dreams all day about stroking my gray chest hair? Why does she say I'm like a wonderful mother she'd do *anything* for?

Your friend,
Ignatz

May 21, 19——

Dearest Pup:

But wait! Heaven knows, I *am* nifty, but why do I look godlike to Krazy? (For after all, that roundness is what we're after.) I think she must see me with a powerful background, like a double image. Where does the stereopticon/background effect come from? She must be bringing feelings and thoughts to our sessions from some previous time. Perhaps from someone she depended on in her past. From her moth—I mean her *father,* say!

And why, Pup, do *I* see *you* as so overwhelmingly round? What makes *you* quel big cheese in my mind? Why should I care what *you* think about me! Why this desire to *stroke* your big brawny shoulders? I haven't admitted it to you before, but I've come to think your jowly face is *very* handsome, and your flat policeman's cap is almost unbearably stylish! But why then did I rebel against you, Mr. Lawman?

When I try my Mixassociation tool on these questions what pops right up from my mother's mind, I mean my *other mind,* when I just turn the corner, is the big (from my child's point of view) face and long whiskers of my own dear father. He, too, had this roundness. He, too, was loved and hated by me. He was audience for my amazing achievements—from early toilet training to valedictorian—and target for my rebellious taunts when I wouldn't do as he said and give up show-biz. He was the Law in our household, and my mother, my brother, and I cowered before him, the evening meal sickening in our stomachs. How could I not admire this kind man, whose justice terrified us? How could I possibly *admire* this man whom I saw forced to the wall every day by *them*—forced *into* the wall sometimes. I *long* for his good opinion. And I *disdain* it. Just the way I feel about guess who? You!

And why else do I taunt you? What does the Law keep me from? My *co-star*—because let's face it, Pup, you were never co-, you were *always* second bandana—Ms. Kat, my Venus in furs? Over these last weeks of treatment Krazy has fastened her claws in my heart, she seems so sweetly round and her fur looks so soft and accommodating. I've wanted to run my hand through the coal black nape of her neck, soothe the spot where the radioactive ash landed, kiss and rub behind her pink little ears. Yet *she* might prefer a cornball in a Brooks Brothers shirt. It wasn't fair that Oppenheimer should have been born with so many advantages—the best schools and enormous height!

Why is Krazy—a bubble-headed bimbo if there ever was one—so damn round to me? It must be someone else, someone from my past who gives Krazy her background. Maybe my mother?

Yes, it must be her! What comes to mind is how beautiful my mother looked one night in *her* fashionable bow tie and long diamond earrings. It was the night of my ninth birthday. My parents had given me a special treat—for sometimes my father was unable to bear the hiding anymore, the life in closets, baseboards, radiator vents, as if we were only good enough to live in the margins of their world. Damn the risk, we would go uptown! To hell with *their* envy, he said to my mother, she should wear some of the diamonds she was always collecting against the day when she might have to sew them into the lining of our clothes and flee the country. His uneven brown teeth formed a reckless rogue's smile. He would take us to one of the garbagey Broadway plays we loved so much.

We had gone to an evening performance of *Peter Pan.* I am deliciously sleepy on the ride home, hypnotized by the headlights coming the other way, by the dry warmth from the car's heater, by Frank Sinatra's voice on the radio singing "Bewitched, Bothered and Bewildered." My mom sings along in her sinuous, lovely voice. I want to lean over the front seat and rub my face against the warm down of her shoulder. Will she let me? Or will she say I'm mussing her makeup, and move closer to my pup, I mean my *pop?* She was so anxious around her children, so easily distracted that I *always* feared she would abandon me, scared that if I did anything active, anything aggressive, she would leave me. That's why I have to have my Krazy back. I have to have someone whom I can throw bricks at, but not lose! (If only *she* would throw one at me—then, oh then, I could be *sure* she was *there.*)

SO WE'RE THE ONES WITH SEXUAL FEELINGS! WE WANTED THEM! WE WANTED TO GET INSIDE THEM AND HAVE THEM GET IN US!

Best,
Ignatz

May 22, 19——
Dear Pup:
I've tossed furiously all night long, till Mrs. Mice couldn't stand any more and went to sleep on our couch. Am I the only person in the world like this, who harbored such feelings towards his mother, who was tied by such cords of love

and hatred to his da? I can't bear having you think me a freak! What I feel *must* be true for Krazy, also!

Anyway, bulb head, where do you come off thinking I'm a freak?

Ignatz

May 23, 19——

Sup-Sup:

I explained the real situation to the Kat, who, of course, couldn't immediately understand so much that was new.

"My father didn't molest me?"

"No."

"Right," she said. "I told you so. It was that alley cat. That striped Tom who was always hanging round our house."

"Don't be silly. There was no Tom either."

"Whew," she said. "Is that ever a relief, Ignatz! I *hated* making up those disgusting stories. Lying made me feel old."

"Yes," I said, "you yourself made up those fantasies. All of them."

"You're not angry?"

"Why should I be angry? You didn't know what you were doing. It's your hidden mind, your SEX-HUNGER part, that seething cauldron of desire, that makes up these stories. You wanted to do sex with your father, but you were scared of your own wants. So you pretend to yourself that it wasn't your fault, that it was done to you."

"IGNATZ, I TOLD YOU, I'M INNOCENT! ONE HUNDRED PERCENT PURE! I DON'T HAVE ANY DESIRES!"

Her shout brought my son on the run for another episode of "Irving to the Rescue." He stood by the head of the couch with his slight twelve-year-old arms folded menacingly across his chest—and his nose running from kat hairs. That ended the session.

But it's just a matter of time till Krazy comes round to my way of seeing things. Mixassociation will help sex-hunger to hook on to lots of ordinary things in the present—like my love of Broadway musicals—and make them into new symptoms, crazy ways of doing sex-hunger. And something in us hates sex-hunger so much that we'll always be trying to shove it into background—so we'll always have backgrounds.

Best,
Ignatz, Conquistador

P.S. I see now that I needed your roundness to approve of the amazing things I'm doing. I made you into a god so you would sanction me. Now that I understand, I can junk you.

May 24, 19——

Puppy dearest:

I know that soon you'll write to me to say that you can't accept my theories on infant-style sex-hunger. But what could I expect from a philistine like yourself? Why should I ever have thought you would be different from the other fools and reactionaries that surround me in this dump? You will say that I'm attacking Krazy to get at you. That's nonsense. I'm not attacking Krazy, just helping her to grow up. You want to keep American womanhood in a state of flat, childlike innocence. It will be better for her and me both when we're free of you.

Sayonara, Dim-Bulb,
Ignatz

May 25, 19——

Pup-Over:

Your big moonface continues to loom behind Krazy's resistance to my world-historical theory. Today she said to me, "Why should I change, Ignatz? I had my ardent addmirrorhers, you know. I still get fan letters from them."

"Don't be a fool," I told her. "Those letters all came from me and the Pup. We met every afternoon to write them—to jolly you up, so we could get back to work. It was Mr. Potato Head's stupid idea."

"Oh my God!" she screamed, writhing about on the couch like a newly born soul in flames. "More false mail from false males!" She began to sob. A blind paw groped for the Kleenex box that I keep for patients on an orange crate by the sofa. The sobs subsided to sniffles. "I feel like Norma Desmond," she said, blowing her nose emphatically, "you know, the dotty old silent movie star in the decaying mansion. Her butler writes her fake fan letters, too. I'm like her, aren't I, like a silent movie star terrified of sound? Maybe I *am* just scared that I can't manage your new way of making round comics, Ignatz. I guess, I guess you better tell me about some of the sex-hunger things that I feel."

I did. But it's going to be a long hard climb with this one.

"So I want people to get inside me and pee in me, and make me wet."

"Yes," I said.

"You're crazy! Ignatz, if that's sex-hunger, then let me tell you again, I DON'T HAVE ANY SEX-HUNGER!"

She put her pink parasol up and marched from my room.

My little society is split by my new invention. Only Kiyoti remains faithful—probably because my theory lets him wear a smug, knowing smile about everyone's nervous habits. My Mixassociation tool shows that Kiyoti is afraid of his own sex-hunger, which is—get this!—for other *fellows!* How about that! He wants to lick them, and be licked, and that's why he keeps himself rank—he hopes to excite their sex-hungers. Of course, his normal upper-class foreground mind rejects this manfully—by making him feel contempt for other males. My genius made him flip-flop, and he replaced his disdain by slavish devotion to me. And it's useful to Ignatz's Amazing New Art-Science to have an ally among the "natives"—someone who talks in their foppish accents, who has a little prep-school polish.

My operatic duck, though, no longer sings my praises. And Kelley has returned to the safety of his parish. God, he says, will help him balance his books. My sex-hunger never will. (He's right. I *want* things off balance, un-easy, dis-eased!) Beau Koo Jack Rabbit, grabbing me by the throat, said *I* was the mother-jumper, not he, and I could go get inside *myself* and pee! And Dumbo—my wife—calls my New Art-Science porno. (Oh, why do I stay with this furioso harpy and abuse the one who loves me?) They're like you, a bunch of buffoons and traitors. Every man's hand is against me, and my hand is against every man. Fine!

Call me,
Ignatz

May 26, 19——

Pup-Tent:
You'll soon turn out to be no different from the other characters. You want to remain innocent G-rated pap, Pup, and never leave the Garden of Eden that is Coconino. Like everyone in this flat county, in this adolescent country, you're terrified of growing up, afraid of sickness and aging. But that's what it means to be round, to have a soul. No more

same same same. No more simple yes to everything. What an insipid people you are!

America wants its popular culture to be a prelapsarian playpen, sex-hunger without teeth. America hates its soul-making geniuses. You are all too small—too *spiritually* small. And *that's* the only size that counts!

But I *will* convince Krazy of my theories.

"It's not the bomb *outside* you're afraid of," I told her this morning, "but the one inside—your SEX-HUNGER, your ANI-MAL NATURE."

"My what?" she said furiously. Her tiny pink tongue curled as she hissed at me, and her small, sharp teeth gleamed white and round. I wouldn't have minded a bite from a beautiful mouth like that one!

"Look," I said, calmingly, "everyone has an animal na-ture inside them, and it just pops out in front sometimes. Other times it just stands behind things, like a shadow. You fear Ignatz's brick because it will bring your sex-animal na-ture out again."

She kept her eyes on the breaks in the ceiling, and I thought, Krazy will certainly accept my theory soon, for it makes us *riven,* cracked, makes us—according to her own ideas—more beautiful.

"We all have animal natures inside us, Krazy. We all want to smell each other."

"I *don't,*" she said, wrinkling up her nose. "I won't *have* insides if that's what they mean. I *hate* smells! I don't even like perfume."

"Yes," I said, "well, that's hard for us. We really have always to forget the smelling part, we want it so much. We want to sniff each other, but if we did we'd get down on all fours. Then we'd be like other animals. You know, pets and things. Krazy, you're afraid that you have so much sex-hunger that if you let some Mouse arouse it with a lovely brick, you'll want to smell him, and be petted all the time." But she had already left the room.

Bye-bye, Bozo,
Ignatz

P.S. Today I remembered another time I got a spanking. It was for urinating on the floor of my parent's bedroom. Peeing *must* have been my way of having sex-hunger with my parents. I'm sure this will be true for Krazy, also. I must tell her about it in our next session.

May 25, 19——

Pee-Pee:

Yesterday afternoon I explained again that sex-hunger leads to wetting. And Krazy said again that she didn't have sex-hunger. Of course you do, I said. It comes out in dreams. Does not, she said. So I snuck into her house last night, and put the tip of her tail in a jar of water. Worked like a charm— within minutes she wet her bed.

During the morning's session Krazy said nothing about her nocturnal emission, but she was much more amenable to my interpretations. And I gave them to her thick and fast. I can't stand the power her round face has over me now, the desire her lithe white whiskers provoke. I want to crush her with my interpretations, knock her flat! But I don't have to worry about this being a permanent flatness. There's a basic split in us, I've decided, between our animal nature—our SEX-HUNGER—and our need for civilization, for TABLE MAN-NERS. Everything we do expresses our desire *and* our need to punish ourselves—to squelch our desires and have some manners. So all we do or think or see has two faces. If you look at it one way, it means sex-hunger. If you look at it another, it means punishment of sex-hunger. Everything becomes round.

For example, Krazy thinks her head is like the other end of her body, because she has hair in both places.

"Ignatz," she said from my couch, "what are you talking about? I have hair everyplace!" She felt underneath herself. "Except at the end of my tail. Where you shaved it," she concluded sadly.

"Yes. Well. Sure. But you think your mouth is like some other part of you. And that's why you think your head is, well, like some other part of you. Let's not mince words anymore, Krazy. We have to call a . . . a chat une chatte." In my excitement I stood up on my stool. "So when the brick hurts your head it really means you're thinking, why don't you please deflower me!" My glee made me hop up and down, as if the seat were a hot plate. "Which you really want a lot, but you have to punish yourself for wanting—so you make the brick too painful to bear."

"I don't want it! I can't want it 'cause I don't even understand what it means."

"Sure. Your conscious mind doesn't. But your other mind, the part that's always right around the corner from what we see, the . . . the . . . the *not-conscious*, sex-hunger part—*it* knows just what I'm talking about!" I stamped my foot down on the stool, nearly tipping myself over.

"That part wants to Be Flowered?"

"Right."

"The brick means all that?"

"Yup!" I gasped. I remembered my position—Krazy's doctor—and sat down again on my stool.

"No wonder it's so heavy!" she said with sad nostalgic wonder.

I knew how she felt, for now I, too, sometimes long for

the more innocent matinee-at-the-movies days, come in any-
time and watch it round and round; the days when a brick
didn't have any back to it, and just meant itself.

But she has to know it all and agree with me. I won't be
the only one like this—that would be too unbearably lonely!

Yuch to you, Mortimer Snerd,
King Ignatz

May 27, 19——

Poop:

Hi, philistine! You don't know what it is to be rapt in
contemplation before the beauty of a new, *internal* world,
a many-leveled cavern whose chambers connect in surprising ways, revealing dimensions that the flat have never
dreamed of. The floors of these chambers are littered with
diamonds of symbolic knowledge, the sex-fantasies that
make our insides, *our souls,* jewels faceted by sex-hunger
and table manners. And every time I hold one of the diamonds in my paw and gaze in it, I see the chamber I stand
in and myself with my new sides. *I* am transformed by that
gaze, my soul *becomes* the cave of many chambers, the diamond that I stand inside. How could I not go wherever
Ignatz's Amazing New Art-Science wants to take me? But
you wouldn't understand that, pygmy brain, happy in your
already interpreted world.

Hasta la vista, P-Brain,
Iggie the Great

May 28, 19——

Pup-Tart:

As she lay on the couch, Krazy's paw nervously fingered
the ends of her bow tie. I didn't hesitate for a moment, but

let her have it with what this gesture meant: It was SEX-
HUNGER showing itself. And her tail biting, too, I told her,
was a way of doing SEX-HUNGER with herself, through her
mouth, which was like her other parts down below.

She put one of the blue pillows over her head, trying to
hide from her new knowledge. When she reappeared, her
large brown eyes welled with pity for me (supposedly for
me—really for her old flat self). "No, really, Ignatz," she said.
"Ask anyone. Ask your Mrs. You're crazy!"

"Krazy," I shouted, "admit that you know what it means
to desire someone!"

"I'm awful confused, Ignatz," she said, suddenly plaintive. "I thought desire meant that I wanted to be around you
a lot and see you a lot. And, like, play music together."

"But you don't play music!" I said, catching her out.

"Yes. Sure. OK. But like music."

"No," I said. "You want to put your tail inside your
mouth because you want to have something inside you. And
you bite it, because you disapprove of your own desires. You
love what you hate and hate what you love."

"The YES that is NO again!" she whispered wildly, but as
if to herself, and I could tell that she was at least considering
my ideas. "So that means that I want other people to make
wet inside me?"

"Well, like that," I said.

"Like that? But what?"

I smiled sagely. After all, I have just discovered this sex
business and can't be expected to have mapped out all its
mechanics!

"And I want to get inside them? And what do I want to
do?"

"You just want it done to you," I said. "You're a girl."

"This sex is another gadget you boys have dreamed up.
It connects everything with everything in a giant machine

that bites and wets and sucks itself until there's one big explosion!"

"When you saw the bomb explode you thought, goody, now the world is going to end, so TABLE MANNERS won't apply anymore, and everybody is going to grab somebody and have SEX-HUNGER with them. You wanted to run around on all fours like Oppie's pet. But your table-manners part wants to punish you for wanting him, you bitc—silly cat. The brick reminds you of the bomb, when you had that wild idea, so you can't stand my bricks."

"BUT I DON'T HAVE ANY . . . Ignatz, if I agree with you, am I cured? Does that mean we don't have to talk about these things anymore?"

"That's right," I said. "If you're really ready to go back to work."

"OK," she whispered, "I'll play the sap for you."

"What?"

"Let's go out to the garden," she said softly. Garden was her sweet krazy word for the sand and scrub of my backyard!

She herself led the way to the dry sunlight and fresh air of health. "If you can hit me with bricks that means we don't have to talk anymore about my having disgusting ideas, right?"

"If you're truly cured," I said, "if you don't resist being healthy, and love my bricks, that's right—then, no more psychoanalysis."

"OK," she said quietly. "Go ahead."

I stood her against the wall and lobbed a heavy one high in the air. Krazy shielded her eyes and looked up at the sun. The brick dove down through the cloudless blue sky, and she put her head right under it. Mission control: "Love-missile is growing ever larger, preparing for landing on noggins-ville!"

Krazy put her lower lip between her teeth.

Klunk! A dab of blood appeared at the corner of her mouth. The brick rolled off her hot-spot and plopped on the ground.

"Yes?" I asked expectantly.

"Yes *what?*" she said angrily, rubbing her head.

"Yes," I said again, smiling with my lips together.

"Oh," she said in a small hesitant voice. "Oh . . . yes . . . Oh . . . Dollink . . . you . . . you . . . luave me." Looking at the ground, she massaged her head with her paw.

O bright sunlight of summer! O lovely round bump! O restored cat! Someday grateful art lovers will place a plague—I mean a *plaque*—on the flaking pink wall of my house, right where my former patient now stood: HERE IGNATZ MOUSE CREATED THE NEW KRAZY KAT.

Pup, though you are certainly a huge jerk, and we will always hate each other, I'm sure you will join me in rejoicing over a cured Krazy Kat. We can get back to work!

Your fiend,
Ignatz

THE TALKING

PICTURES

Krazy—the new talk-cured Kat—was the first to see him, one afternoon, as she lay, stretching, in front of her house, looking up into the cloudless sky. She was trying to enjoy the warmth on her stomach fur, but her belly hurt, soured by her first-time deceptions of the Mouse in his lying-therapy, and maybe made permanently gnawshush by the guilt-produced bile of knowing her comic strip might have sent the message "Bomb's Away!" to Oppie and the other fizzyits. Her dazey eyes had been caught by a big egg-shaped object, a beautiful rich emerald green in color, moving through the air as if being pulled downward, yet rising just as fast, so it didn't, finally, fall—like the most rapid yo-yo. It came towards her, through the white blotches the bright sun formed on the lenses of her narrowed slit-eyes; hovered overhead, making a terrible clatter, like a huge metal cicada; then descended slowly, in herks and jerks, to the desert floor, blowing some poor tumbleweeds clear out of Coconino, so they wouldn't change anymore, but just be tumbleweed forever. The twirling blades had stirred up a twister of dust, and out of the whirlwind had come the Producer, riding a golf cart down a plank, a cart that was painted the same verdant color as the helicopter.

"Like the paint job?" he shouted, rolling his golf cart up
to Krazy's doorway. His Assistant, a string-bean boy in a
three-piece wool pinstripe suit, sat beside him at the wheel,
looking itchy.

Krazy had the warmest feeling that the Producer really
cared about her answer. "Oh, yes! I like it very much!"

"Color of my mother's nail polish!"

"You must have loved your mother a lot," Krazy said.
She stood in front of her house—still hers in those days—
rubbing the sand from her eyes and smiling at the visitor. He
gave her the sense that something big and good was about
to happen to her, that fate's eye was about to discover her
(well, *rediscover* her, actually). The Producer was a jolly-
looking man, buzzing with energy, as if he were outlined in
neon lights. She had liked him, even before she learned that
he was a movie producer. *Her* affection for him hadn't been
about getting into mooooves . . . feelms . . . had it? For she'd
soon noticed how differently the boys acted around him, as
if they were eager sons. And the girls played to him as if he
were a camera—Mrs. Mice pushed her overdeveloped chest
in his face as if she were Jane Russell; and Kwakk Wakk
showed off her gams as if she were Betty Grable; and someone else acted like the too knowing flirtatious ingenue who
aches to be taken. (Someone? Who could that have been? No!
That, she decided—snip-snip—*had never happened.*) The
Producer wasn't *conventionally* handsome, a teeny bit overweight—well, OK, a lot really. His white knit shirt didn't
have enough cloth to go all the way over his stomach, down
into his pants. He had a wide mouth, a bald dome, and a
broad nose that occupied the middle of his face by droit de
seigneur. And he wasn't quite round, but he wasn't flat either. More like a flat person who spun around so rapidly that
he looked almost as if he had sides. "I looooved my mother,
too . . . I mean," Krazy started to say. Her nose filled with
dust. She coughed. "I know I lived my mother, too . . .

Oh, I mean . . . I guess your mom was really special to you."
The Producer laughed, with the biggest laugh Krazy
had ever heard. All the pleasure in the world was in his
laugh, but there was something wrong with the world, and
its pleasure scared the bejesus out of it. So the laugh tried to
threaten you, in case you were part of the thing to be afraid
of. "Did I love her, Kitty? Love her? That cunt! *Of course I
loved her!*" he shouted. He turned to the Assistant. "Never
knock your ma, Sonny Boy!" He took the young man's head
in a headlock. "The American Audience loves its mom!
Hell," he screamed at his Assistant, "the American Audience
is our mom! Every night American filmmakers should get
down on their knees and pray to their moms!" The shouting
man, the trapped boy—the whole scene was so vivid that she
almost didn't care about the younger man's pain. Anyway,
something about the tableau said that this was like a horror
movie, you only had to believe the ketchup was blood if you
enjoyed scaring yourself. (Though the Assistant's face *was*
turning awfully red.) "My mother was a Saint!" he shouted
ferociously at the top of the Assistant's skull. "A Saint! I love
my mother, kiddo, and don't you forget it! I love that bitch!
May she rot in hell!"
"What?" Krazy said, unsure what would be a polite response. "Sure," she whispered weakly.
The Producer tightened his grip on the young man's
head, but he was smiling now. "You tell everyone how wonderful their mothers are, Kitty—that's boffo box office,
prime-time agit-prop for Momism. Great stuff! You tell them
what a cunt she was—that's Art. Kitty, when I figure out how
to combine the two—that'll be my masterpiece! And everybody will want to see it, 'cause everybody has a mom!" He
let go of the young man's head. "I like you, Kitty. Do you
want to know the secret of how I pick successful movies?"
He spoke in a self-assured, sly tone of voice.
"You bet you do," the Assistant said, rubbing his neck.

"He produced *Rin Tin Tin,* and *Lassie,* and *National Velvet,* and *Dumbo,* and *King Kong,* and *E.T.*"

"He did?"

"Sure," the Assistant said, smiling. His gums had a shiny synthetic look. "Anyway, if he didn't, he *knew* that they would be hits from nearly the first time that he saw them. Most of them. He knows how to pick 'em. He's famous throughout much of Hollywood for his work with animals."

"We're not animals," Krazy started to say. "I mean we *are.* But we're not." But the Producer was already talking.

"That reminds me," he told his Assistant. "Take a memo: I want the ASPCA award for this one!"

"But Dad, I mean Boss, he socks her with bricks. The Humane Society isn't going to like that!"

"He does? They won't? So what! Bricks, huh?" he said musingly. "OK. The gimmick is: He reforms! *There,* that should be humane enough for anyone!" He pointed the end of his golf club at Krazy as if it were a rifle barrel. "I love animals," the Producer said, as if his affection reflected well on him not just as a feelingful person, but as a businessman. "Animals have international appeal. So I can sell off the foreign rights and be showing a profit before the first day of shooting. Amazing, huh? It's because animals are like silent film stars. No language problems. And they're so stupid they do what they're told." He laughed. Krazy began to think it might be nice if he didn't laugh so much. "Both ways they're *dumb* animals! Get it?"

"But we talk," Krazy said. "We're not animals. I mean we *are,* but we're *not.* We *talk,*" she concluded lamely, conscious of repeating herself.

"Sure," the Producer said. "Sure. But I'm right. You'll see. You talk, but *I* know what I'm talking *about.* I always do. Go ahead. You want to agree. Nod your head yes. Your head wants to nod yes. It's nodding yes. See!"

And he was right. Krazy was nodding. "But," she said in a deep, sleepy purring, "isn't talking important?"

"What? Talking? Words? Don't be silly! You know the joke about the Polish starlet? She fucked the writer! Dialogue? Don't take it so seriously, Kitty. Sound nearly ruined this industry—till everyone realized it didn't matter what the fuck they said."

"I guess it's the plot that really matters," Krazy said.

"Sure. Action! Action? No! That doesn't matter. No."

"What does matter then?"

"Tits!" the Producer said, laughing explosively, till he saw the hurt on Krazy's face—for he intently watched you watching him. "Just kidding. It's not tits. I never said tits."

"Yes you did! I heard you!"

"Don't you know about cutting, Kat? Watch." The Producer made his fingers into a scissors, and cut the air right behind him. "Snip, snip. The fluffed line falls to the cutting room floor. Splice, splice. Now: *it all never happened.* I never said it."

"Never said what?" confused Krazy said.

The Producer smiled, his Cinerama mouth wrapping from ear to ear. "It's fashions, Kitty. That's what matters. Women come to the movies to see what the stars are wearing. They want a fashion show."

"Fashions?" Krazy had never worn anything but a ribbon bow tie. She was sure to fail at movies.

"Fashions? Nonsense! Who told you that? It's the special effects. Bam! Whizz! Star wars! Technique, that's what movies are about! How appearances are made to appear."

"A-ffects?"

"Effects? No! What makes you say that? It's the story that matters, the dialogue, that's the only important thing. The dialogue. You know, words!"

Krazy, suddenly dizzy, said nothing.

"Look, Kat," the Producer said, "anyone tells you that they know what they're doing in this business, they're lying. Because I want to tell you something: Nobody knows nothing about this business!" He shook his head, muttering sadly, "Crazy business. Crazy business." He smiled at her. "OK, Kitty. Get up off your knees. You don't have to beg anymore. I'll tell you how I learned the secret of picking b.o. smashes. Come backstage with me, darling, and I'll show you the wires and gizmos. You'll like that! You'll be in on the secret. And that's part of the secret, see—American audiences love to be *in the know*. They love to go backstage. They want to see the machinery that fools them, the back projections, the special effects. Right? Right! They don't realize that showing them the machinery *is* the show, and while they're hypnotized by the gears going round, the micro-chips blinking on/off, while you let them see the marketing surveys that reveal their kinky emotional ratchets and levers, you can really get your hands deep down into their pockets. They get hypnotized thinking they're learning how the rubes get hypnotized. Look, I promised to tell you how *I* work and your little jaws open—you're already under. See, you can even tell the audience what you're doing, take them backstage on taking them backstage, and *that* works too." He laughed again. But he was right. Krazy's jaw was slack. Her limbs heavy. She wouldn't have moved for the world.

"What was I telling you, Kitty? Oh, yeah, how I learned the secret of picking movies. Well, when I was a boy a group of traveling salesmen would come through our little town each month. My da was the night clerk at the hotel, and the drummer boys would invite him for their midnight card games. Daddy was a real Mr. Custard. They'd get him drunk. Easy! That a-hole could get tanked up on Shirley Temples, *if* you told him they were boilermakers. He wanted to be one of the boys so much, he'd believe you! Then each of the drummers would say he had to take a leak. And he'd come over to our clapboard bungalow. My ma would be waiting for the salesmen, sitting on the couch in her slip, drinking bourbon from a Dixie cup. Slim-Jim would push her slip up, and call her a whore. He had her kneel against the couch, with her breasts pushed into the pillows and her ass in the air. My mother would cry. I wanted to rush out to save her."

Krazy felt she couldn't bear another moment of this story. These words would turn her fur white the way the ash from the A-bomb had! Moms were as innocent as kitty-kats! Mothers couldn't do things like that! *Could they?* She wondered what happened next.

"Next, he'd be stroking her blonde hair, and she'd be kissing his hand, saying she *was* a bad girl, and that she should be 'punished.' Brick after brick, huh, kitty? The rest is below Code standards, you understand, X-rated. Each salesman in turn. Triple feature. They'd leave money on the kitchen table, for my tuition and school clothes. The woman was a saint, Kitty, a saint! *That's* how I know when a movie is good, see? I want the audiences to be as stirred up, yet as riveted as that little boy." He laughed again. Krazy wished that he wouldn't laugh anymore. She felt a hair ball forming inside her throat. "Audiences are children, Krazy." He smiled sadly. He straightened up and put his hand to his forehead in salute: "They're geniuses," he concluded. "You're a woman, right, Krazy? I mean it's hard to tell. My research people tell me that sometimes the others call you her, sometimes him. That's depraved. It's decadent. It's disgusting. Very Now, right? I like it." He turned to the Assistant. "Do you like it? You tell me. You be the Producer for a while." And he looked truly perplexed, uncertain if he cared for it anymore. His lips oscillated between swallowing and spitting out. His sides flickered, as if his electric generators were sputtering.

The Assistant nodded.

"Good." He was round again. "So do I. Do you like it?"

he said to Krazy, and again he looked perplexed, flatter. "I guess so," Krazy said. "I mean I *am* it." He laughed. "Good." He had curves. "So we all agree, for Chrissakes! That's wonderful!" He turned to the Assistant. "So what are we talking about? What is it we all agree on?"

"The memo from Research, Dad, you know the man/ woman thing."

"Right. Right." He glared at Krazy, as if his memory lapse were her fault. "So, what *are* you?"

"Lately, I don't know," Krazy said. "I seem to be a girl all the time now. Sort of."

He turned to the Assistant. "Take a memo."

"What color, Boss?"

"Red! Most urgent. Always remember: Audiences are like women, the cunts. And there are only two things to do with women. Fuck them."

"Yes?" Krazy said. She didn't like the Producer's way of talking, but she couldn't take her eyes and ears off him. He had a way of filling your attention up. But not as if he had a big spotlight on *him.* It was shining on *you,* and if you paid attention to him, then the huge warm sun of his attention wouldn't wander off. Maybe, she thought, stretching her paws in the air, her chest outward towards that warmth, I *can* work again, if they want me so. "And?" she asked.

"And what?" He sounded like KK was an annoying nit-wit. "Look, I'm here to see Eggnose Mouse."

"Eggnose? Oh, you mean *Ignatz.*"

"Sure. Right. Whatever. He wired me that you people are ready to work again."

Oh God, her lie had already phoned home! She should never have told Eggnose—I mean Ignatz—that she was talk-cured! *How* could she work feeling so sick to her stomach, so guilt-heavy in her veins! "He must think movies will make us round characters," she said aloud. "Like in great works by Count Tolstoy or Duke Ellington."

"Round characters?" The Producer smiled. "I can do better than *that.* I can make you stars! I think there's a movie in you people. In fact, I *know* there's a movie here, somewhere. Right?" He looked quizzically at his Assistant, but he didn't wait for him to nod, for he could see that he was still substantial in the Assistant's eyes. There *was* a movie here. "And when I think something the American public agrees with me. At least a significant percentage of the time. That's *why* I think it in the first place. I don't have any desires of my own. So I learn their hidden yens from the chatter of their fingertips. And I can tell if what I'm telling them are *their* fantasies. I can see if they see the aura around me. Get it?"

She nodded. She got it. But she wasn't sure she believed it. Could he really peer *inside* people—even round ones— and know their secret desires?

"So, look, Kitty, you and I will talk tomorrow, darling. At the script conference, OK? I'll send a limo for you. You're a cute little motherfucker," he concluded, smiling fondly. "You've got great mosaic eyes. Transparent depths! Cat's eyes! Like marbles! I like you. I want to change you." He turned to the Assistant. "Red Memo: Why didn't someone tell me that the Kat is flat-chested, for Chrissakes? Have falsies made." He turned back to Krazy and smiled. "Now, where's Ignatz?"

Krazy pointed towards his house. "Musthefuckher? A-hole? Is that," she asked sadly, "like A-ffects and A-bombs?"

But the Producer just laughed. "Take a memo," he said, as the golf cart rolled off towards Ignatz's house. "Red. Most urgent. Teach the Kat how to swear."

But the Assistant, a sweet and harried man, seemed always too busy with other projects to begin her swearing lessons.

Almost every day she saw him, a tall man in pinstripes with a stiff-legged walk like Joe Stork's, stepping along behind the Producer. The Duck, the Pup, and the Mouse marched along with him. The Producer pointed to different parts of the Coconino desert. "Take a memo. Red. The New York set goes here. And build the Western set there. The flotation tank there—for the ship models. And that reminds me, I need a sauna. My pores need steam! I expect you to remember that!" He shook his Assistant by the shoulders. "You are my wife! You are my wife!"

They passed Beau Koo Jack's Grits Ain't Groceries Store. "Got no use for *him*," the Producer said sadly. "Fine by *me*, of course. *I* love the jungle beat of those fast rhythmic paws. But the Audience! *It* just isn't ready." He shut his eyes as if communing inwardly with his beloved. "*Nobody* wants that kind of darkness. It accuses *you*.*" The Producer opened his robe—it was a beautifully tailored one, with white piping on the sleeves and elegant red-satin lining—and released a stream of water against the wall. Offissa Pup, Krazy thought, wouldn't allow *that.* But the Lawman said nothing. The only voice heard much anymore in Coconino was the Producer's—though sometimes it came from other mouths. The Producer wanted to say whatever *they* desired. *They* wanted to say what *he* wanted. Woo! Mirrors looking at mirrors again! No wonder movies never got made anymore. "Get this place for my gym," the Producer said, closing his robe. He stroked the gray stubble on his cheek, passed his hand over his bald head, and gently lifted up the long white hair on his neck. "And get me a barber. Make sure he has one of those red-and-white barber poles. I like them. They remind me of someone's hometown. And we'll need a commissary for the cast, with a big pot of chicken soup going all the time. With real chicken in it. I don't want anybody on my lot going hungry. *I* know what hunger is." He turned to the Pup, whose large brown eyes flowed with sympathy. "Gosh," the Producer said, putting his broad arm around the Pup, "I love dogs. You know, I discovered Rin Tin Tin." He smiled at the Pup, whose big lips were pinched in offense. "Of course you're a different sort of act. Need a different sort of handling. You're a lawman. But you're a philosopher, too. You're tough. But with a tender side, a sensitivity that's like a cross you have to bear." The Pup's chest puffed out with pleasure and pride. The Producer turned to his Assistant. "And put the medieval town there. And a castle with a moat." The Assistant scribbled something on a small square of paper. As they walked along he let the red notes flutter to the ground behind him. Was someone else supposed to pick them up? Or did they have magic powers like the seeds Jack dropped? The Producer's plans *did* boom Coconino's economy. They all had extra jobs—working as carpenters, painters, barbers, masseurs. True, no one ever got rubbed down, no nails were ever hammered, no money distributed. But the streets were filled with people scurrying between tasks, and Krazy could just feel that the town was more prosperous, more vital, more alive. She almost felt her own talent would return, like Rip Van Sleeping Beauty after a long, unrestful snooze, if she just figured out a movie story for herself, a krazy concept, a hook. In the morning, as she walked to the bakery to get fresh rolls for everyone, she stepped on the sand where the slips of paper had fallen, and she was sure she saw a New York street scene, and scaled-down model battleships floating in a huge tub, and a castle; and then the Producer suddenly left town, and the Spanish castles were all air, and the desert felt emptier, the town more deprived than before. "I don't con anyone," the Producer had told her truthfully. "I tell them it's all lies, so they know they can trust me. Then I make it like gossip, or flattery, or wrestling—more fun to play along than to be a prude. And I add a tang of reality, to give a sense of depth: the wrestler might really smash his toe, the two stars might be having a real-life off-screen bang together, right? Presto! Everyone cons themselves!" He had smiled at her then, and when she turned away he goosed her from behind with his golf club shaft. She yelped, leaping into the air. Thank God Ignatz wasn't there to see! Not because he would have been embarrassed for her, or would have socked the Producer's endlessly blooming nose. No, to please the Producer, the Mouse, too, would have *smiled* at her startled yelp. And that would have shamed Krazy most of all.

But, then, Ignatz was no different from the others. Even the Pup. He, too, smiled approvingly at whatever the Producer did or said. They all did. And they all—with one sad feline exception—suddenly, mysteriously, knew how to swear. "Look," an acrid whining voice said in her dream that first night, "we don't want this to be just another piece-of-shit gangster picture. So let's just cut the crap, shall we?" Startled, Krazy awoke, ashamed of herself for dreaming that kind of talk. But it *had* been *Ignatz's* whine. No limoscene had come to whisk her away that morning, or any morning, and every day when she woke up the cast was already there, assembled around her little table, expecting coffee, or Danishes, or lunch, or dinner—for *her* house was the commissary. And when she finished serving the soup and went to sleep, the rest of them sat there, talking pictures, as one day was cut into another, one story picked up characters and scenes from the last rewrite, but cut the old ending, redefined the concept, changed the genre, and moved the cast to a location with better production values.

"The gangster *is* the modern American hero," she heard Ignatz say that first morning, as she rubbed the sleep from her eyes. "He rises from the mass of immigrants, people like his cowardly dad, because he's willing to confront the truth that *all* success is based on violence." The Mouse glared furiously at Offissa Pup. "The masses hate him. They *want* to remain flat. He's completely *isolated*. They bring him down!"

"You're saying guns, right, Igna'z?" the Producer said. The Mouse looked startled. He blinked; disappeared; remade himself; returned. "Right."

"OK," the Producer shouted. "Screen test!" He pointed the shaft of his golf club at the mouse. "Rat-a-tat-tat! Rat-a-tat-tat!"

Ignatz grabbed his chest in pain, and fell, shrieking, from his chair.

Oh my God, Krazy thought, what fatal force had been in that golf club! She ran towards him. "You're not So Late, darling," she cried, kneeling by his little body.

"Get away!" he hissed savagely. "I have another line."

She staggered backwards, stunned.

CLOSE-UP: Ignatz, writhing on the floor.

IGNATZ [with brute recognition of existence's emptiness]: *Mother of God, is this the end of Ignatz?*

"Good! Good!" the Producer said. "I like it. But it needs something. It needs a love interest."

"Maybe a gun moll," Ignatz said from the floor.

"Sure! A whore!" The Producer beamed about the table, delighted with his own idea.

"Great!" Ignatz said. Krazy, heartsick, wondered if the Producer had told Ignatz the Mouse's own desires. (Would the haw-er start to whip him with her tail, or make Ignatz kiss her paws?) Maybe—but Ignatz would have agreed to anything to get the starring role. "She wants to reform, go legit," the Mouse said. "She wants to marry him."

"Nah," the Producer said. "*He* wants to get married. She wants to go on being a hooker. She likes it. Good, huh? I like it. Don't I like it? What do you think?" He turned to the Duck.

"Oh, yes, dear," she said, "very nice indeed. But wouldn't it be better as a musical romance, about a Marietta, with a true diva in the lead? The concept here is the marriage of European high cultural refinement and popular American energy. No caterwauling, but real dulcet tones!"

"A musical. Sure! I love music. Da Da Da Da Da Da Da Da!" He hummed the same note, over and over.

"That's lovely, Boss," the Assistant said.

The Producer looked around the table, and saw from the Pup's pursed lips that his sides were disappearing. "What do you think, Pup?" he said.

"A Western, sir," Offissa Pup said, decisively. "The great American story. White Hat versus Black Hat.

"LONG SHOT: The Lawman strides down the main street alone, completely isolated. The town has forsaken its tall handsome savior. But his walk states who he is: the hero."

"It needs a love interest," Kwakk Wakk said, ruffling her feathers. "There would be a woman who doesn't forsake him. A star of European opera who, because of her misadventures, has to sing in the local saloon. His future wife!"

"Right!" the Producer said. "A whore!"

The Pup blushed. "All right, sir. A prostitute. A woman with a past. The Hero proposes to her before he discovers that she has loved another."

"Others," the Producer said, jovially. "Many, many others. Millions of others!"

"Very well," the Pup said sadly. "He said he would marry her, and he does. The American man keeps his word."

Bully for him, Krazy thought furiously. She stood by the stove, making everybody a big pot of coffee. Then she decided that good kind Pup couldn't have said the things she thought he had said. So he hadn't said them. Snip. Snip. *It all never happened.*

"Nah," the Mouse said. "She wants to go on turning tricks. She likes it."

Krazy gagged. The Producer, hearing a cue, pounded the table savagely. "No woman *likes* being a whore, Mouse!" he shouted. "Americans hate that overbred European decadence! What makes you say a thing like that? An American woman might do it to help someone she truly loved, yes, to get money for his schoolbooks. But she would loathe it."

Ignatz, contrite, looked down at the table where, in a quieter time, he had carved his initials.

"A Western, huh?" The Producer smiled at Kiyoti, and the pain of diminishment crossed the Producer's flattening face. "Any input, Kiyoti?"

"I cawn't see it," Kiyoti drawled. "America says horse operas are boring, bor-ing, bo-r-ing! It wants something light, sophisticated. An audience is like a woman." Kiyoti showed the Producer his long teeth, which nowadays gleamed so brightly that Krazy thought Kiyoti might have painted them white. "It wants to be seduced. It wants a tall leading man, with savoir-vivre. American-bred if you see what I mean, for a twentieth-century American romance. Someone like Cary Grant. Prep-school polish."

"So true," the Producer said, a wicked gleam in his eyes. "But played by a Jew, right? And with a good strong love interest. Know what I mean? He's high society, but she's . . ." He looked expectantly at Kiyoti.

"A love interest?" Kiyoti said. "I thought *he* was the love . . . Oh, I see, sure . . ."

"A pros . . ." the Producer coaxed.

"A pros? . . . a pros? . . ." Kiyoti sputtered, stricken, his movie career ending in confusion. What was the next line?

"A prostitute!" Kwakk Wakk, Ignatz, and the Pup all sang at once.

"He's high society," Kiyoti spoke rapidly, trying to improvise the part back home. "But she's a prostitute. He wants to reform her, but she . . ." Kiyoti stopped, unsure which way the plot twisted anymore.

"You got it! Brilliant idea! I never would have thought of it!" The Producer swiveled in his chair to look at Krazy. "See, Kat, my genius is to listen. I don't have any desires to impose, so people can show me their hidden yens. Then I can sell their own dreams back to them. And the key is: I know how to listen." He turned to Kiyoti. "Lovely concept, Kiyoti! Americans don't have a lot of useless outdated moral baggage! *She wants to go on being a prostitute!* Now we're making movies," the Producer said delightedly, extending his arms to the table. They basked for a moment, imagining their image in a million minds.

"What about you, Kitty? Got a message for us?"

Krazy walked about the table, pouring everyone some hot coffee. There was nothing condescending in the Producer's tone. He really cared what she thought. The way he looked at her had her fur tingling with a delicious immoral warmth, like being licked all over. And that sweet, unstoppable growling was starting in her throat. She was sure that he hadn't really listened to a word anyone had said. Yet at that moment she believed him: *He knew how to listen.* But would movies be good for her? She hadn't realized they were always about houris. Could haw-ers be *innocent,* like her, if say, they really didn't *like* what they were doing? (And what *were* they doing?) Movies did sound like fun, though.

"Well. OK. I don't know," Krazy said. This was important. Her please come-back depended on it. "OK. How about Ignatz Mouse hits me with a brick that Kolin Kelley made? Kwakk Wakk tells on him. Don Kiyoti and Offissa Pup come and arrest him, and Pup puts him in jail." *There,* she thought, that was a *nice* story, with a part for everyone.

"God," Ignatz said, disgustedly. "That's seltzer without bubbles—flat, flat, flat! Kitty, this is the Twentieth Century!" He turned to the Assistant, who sat taking notes on a big yellow pad. "Hey, there's a title." He scowled at Krazy again. "We have A-bombs nowadays, kiddo, and don't you forget it.

The Audience doesn't care about bricks anymore. Remember, Krazy," he said, smiling at her now, "the Audience is like a woman. You have to get her worked up, but then you have to deliver something. If you know what I mean."

"No," Krazy said, bemused, "I don't." She tried to sit down at the table, but the others shifted their fur and feathers so there was no room for her. She continued to stand, clutching her orange metal coffeepot to her chest. Her tail was going up behind her.

"Women," Kiyoti said, "like to be treated roughly."

"I don't," Krazy said. The bricks *weren't* rough—and when they were, she didn't like them anymore. "I like sweet things."

"Women are like whores," Ignatz said in that wheedling tone he had around the Producer. "They want the star to be their pimp. Take their money, and treat them with contempt."

"I don't," Krazy said. "I like to be listened to attentively." But no one was listening.

"Women," Kwakk Wakk said, "want to have grapefruits pushed in their yackety-yacking pusses."

"I don't," Krazy said. "Why would anyone want grapefruit rubbed in her fur?"

Ignatz laughed, trying to imitate the Producer's crescendo, but making little hiccups of sound. Everyone looked at the Producer. "That's telling her," he said, putting an arm around Ignatz's shoulder. "They *hate* being pampered. They want to *give*. They crave the grapefruit in the puss, the brick to the bean. We know how to treat a woman!" So they all laughed. Even the Pup.

Krazy dropped the pot clattering to the floor. Hot coffee spilled out, burning her paws. She yowled. They went on laughing. "You selfish stinking suckbullers!" she shouted. "You don't care about anyone else! I think of a plot that includes all of you, and you make fun of me. And your movies

didn't even have a part for me! You're all a bunch of pins!"
"Pins?" Kiyoti said. "How droll!"
"Tiny holes!" Krazy wailed.
"Tiny holes? Oh, it's like charades," Kwakk Wakk said.
"I love it!"
"Points! Stabs! Needles!" Krazy screamed.
"Pins, tiny holes, points . . . oh," the Duck cried excit-
edly, "I've got it! Pricks!"
"Yes!" Krazy screamed, sick with exhaustion. "Pricks!
Pricks! Pricks! Pricks! You're a bunch of pricks! Of lick moth-
ers! Ass mothers! Bull lappers! Cockshitters!"
But they all just went on laughing at her. Even the Pup.

During the breaks—whenever the Producer fell face down
on the table, asleep—Krazy and the Assistant did "the walking scene" together. Anno Producer Krazy often found herself star of an Imaginary Production ("Ars Gratia Felis" its
motto). "Now I'm doing the shower scene," she would say to
herself as she reluctantly, but bravely, stepped under the
cold water. Or she turned to Mr. De Mille and said, "Cue me
for my entrance in the spectacular grocery store scene." (She
frequently had to shoot that one; nowadays she needed lots
of soup things from Beau Koo Jack's store.) And when she
was bored by some chore—like cooking the endless pots of
soup—she imagined her stand-in was doing it, or she told
herself, "Now I'm doing a retake." It made her day more fun.
But perhaps it was another of those pleasures one shouldn't
allow oneself, for she was seeming less and less real to herself. She played her life for the camera's eye, and the picture
wasn't yet developed. She wouldn't become real to herself
again until she was seen by another, on the big screen. Many,
many others. Millions of others. For it would take that large
an audience to be sure that they *were* seeing *her*, so she
could be certain that she existed.
Continuity, too, was getting to be a problem. Sometimes

recently she found herself wondering anxiously if she had enough script to get her through the scene. This part needs a joke, she thought. "Have you heard the one about the polished starlet?" she asked the Assistant. He looked bewildered. Krazy laughed, by way of putting up the laugh sign. "Well, see, she was a fucking writer!"

The Assistant showed a blank. They walked on. He wasn't much of an audience, but she liked him anyway, felt comfortable with him. He had a pleasant face, with a moustache of ten independent bristles, like Rube Goldberg's. Maybe that was why he had turned out to be so good at making things—if, that is, he had ever made anything. He seemed (boy, was she using *that* word a lot lately!) a decent, straightforward person—relaxing, now that her friends were starting to show disturbing chute-de-chutes to their characters. Exposed to the Producer's spotlight, they all had shadows.

The town, too, had turned chameleon. Everyone had painted his house Producer's Mother's Green, and pictures of him had gone up on the sides of the grocery store, the bakery, the brickyard, and the soda shop. Each picture showed the Producer in sunglasses, in front of an American flag, with a slogan underneath. STARS DON'T MAKE MOVIES! MOVIES MAKE STARS! And: THEY CALL THEM MOTION PICTURES BECAUSE THEY MOVE! Or: THERE'S NOTHING WRONG WITH THIS CRAZY BUSINESS THAT A GOOD PICTURE CAN'T CURE! And: MY MOTHER WAS A CUNT! HOW ABOUT YOURS?

"Sure," the Assistant said, "I know he's a son of a bitch. Who would know better than me?" They walked past where the flotation tank was. Or would be. Or had been. "Do you know what he made me do?" the Assistant said. "He made me have all my teeth pulled. He said that that way I'd never be at the dentist when he needed me. Really, it's so I'll always look older than him. And he's an even meaner snake since he went indy prod."

"N.D. prod?"

"Yah, hadn't you heard? The studio kicked him on his keester. Some people say he embezzled money."

"Oh my!"

"Don't worry. He didn't take any money. Probably. Not much anyway. Besides, if he had, they wouldn't have minded. Nah, he just had too many flops. They feel he's losing his touch, can't see what people want anymore. He's been in this business so long that he thinks everyone is a prostitute, or wants a prostitute, or wants to be a prostitute. So the studio yanked his credit lines. You people are his last chance."

"I'll stick by him," Krazy said. "He can trust me."

The Assistant laughed. "You know how they say 'fuck you' in Hollywood? *Trust me.*"

"I do," Krazy said.

The Assistant scrunched his bushy brows.

"So why do you stay with him if he's a son's bitch?"

"Why do you, Krazy? Why does anyone? Because I love him. Because I want to kill him. Because having all this confusion roiling round in me makes me feel more vivid. And when I talk to him I think my confusion means something, that it might become a drama that everyone will want to see."

Krazy understood. Maybe the Producer couldn't read minds, but he did have a way of making your tumult his own. That once upon a time Krazy had been sometimes male Kat, sometimes female was the perfect wienie to hook the Producer. He was so excited he could hardly bear it, and tried to sneak hints about the man/woman thing into all their conversations. "You know," he had said that morning, "Hearst made Marion Davies wear pants in all her films. Hearst liked *that.*"

"Liked what?" Krazy had asked.

The Producer leered. "Liked her in pants."

"Oh," Krazy had said. Maybe it was because she was just a girl now that Hearst never wrote anymore?

Krazy felt she embodied the most important questions in the world to the Producer: Am I a man or a woman? What *is* a woman? Sorting out all his mixed-up ideas about women really mattered to him, which wasn't quite love, but it was as *intense* as love, and it meant that you, by maybe being a woman, were at the center of his attention. With his mom.

"That was awful about his mom," Krazy said, kicking at a piece of tumbleweed. She wanted him to say that the Producer's bluster about his mother was hurt and baffled feelings just like her own. Her mom, the woman she so . . . laved . . . had, *carelessly,* never warned Krazy that there would be days—months!—years!—like this—a career girl at the end of her run, with a tetchy stomach, lead-heavy limbs, and an option on an infinity of empty days more. She wanted to hear that it was all right to feel what she felt about her mom. (What *did* she feel?)

"His mom? Yah, awful, I guess. I never heard it before. I think he got the vibe from you that you liked hearing about mothers. Did he?"

Krazy shrugged, not wanting to try to lie.

The Assistant shook his head sadly. "I hoped he had. I hoped that maybe he was getting his talent back."

Krazy shrugged again. She prayed that the Producer couldn't peer in and see all the awful things she was thinking about her mom. And then again, she prayed that he could.

"Oh, if he'd gotten his talent back, you'd *know*. When he tells you your hidden dreams, you hear your whole soul singing, *yes, yes, yes*. He really does have a talent for that. Or he *did*. But he's been getting a lot of static lately on his receiver." They stared up at the night sky, where the lighting crew had put out spotlights, floodlights, key lights for the rest of their scene. "Anyway, by the time I met Grandma you couldn't have imagined that story he told you. God had cut

to later that same day. She was a sweet wizened little thing.
No one would have cast her as the town whore."

They walked on. The Assistant stopped, stared at Krazy.
"He's going to fall in love with you." He poured some sand
from his tasseled loafers.

"He is?" Krazy hopped from foot to foot, her molecules
jumping up and down with excited energy, not quite exploding, just jazzing her. In this scenario she and the atom dance
were friends, sort of.

"Well, if you're going to become a star, he'll love you."

"Oh." Krazy knew what *that* meant. The catsing couch.
Where Producers promised to make their no-talent girlfriends into stars, and just ended up turning them both into
fools. There would be no romance for her, she thought sadly,
and no stardom.

"No, not like *that*," the Assistant said. "He doesn't try
to *make* his girlfriends into stars. He only loves women who
will be stars. He wants what the Audience is going to want.
His prick belongs to the American public. Anyway, it used
to."

Kwakk Wakk came by, market basket and umbrella
under her arm. She nodded briskly. Krazy longed to show
the Assistant that she was just one of the guys, like Jean
Harlow or Carole Lombard. She gave a Gable leer at the
Duck. "Well," she said, "will you look at the pair of cocks on
that girl!"

The Assistant snorted. Krazy guessed that she had
goofed. Maybe Kwakk Wakk's cocks weren't very impres-
sive, after all.

"OK," the Producer said, "I'll kick off this morning."

It wasn't morning. It was midnight. Krazy supposed
they must be shooting Night for Day. She stood by her stove,
preparing the coffee for the scene. " 'The world's gone mad
today,' " she sang to herself, putting prune Danishes on

plates, " 'And good's bad today, And black's white today, And day's night today, When most guys today, That women prize today, Are just silly gigolos . . . ' "

"You're going to love this," the Producer said.

Oh, how they all wanted to love it! Feathers rose as if from an inner wind of inspiration. Celestial teeth came out over moistened lips. Loving his idea meant that you wanted what he wanted, which was supposedly what you had really wanted in the first place, and that would be what THEY, the Audience would want; so you would be coming soon to millions of dreams everywhere. That is *you* would be, if first of all *you* were what *you* wanted, so that *you yourself* were your own desire that he was showing you. The star trick, Krazy realized, would be to want yourself first. " 'If Mae West you like, Or me undressed you like, Why nobody will oppose! Anything goes!' " she sang, walking from place to place with the pastry.

"OK. Here it is! Curtain up! Houselights dim!" The Producer covered his eyes with his palms. He had a lot of hair on the backs of his hands, stuff that had probably belonged on his head, but had gotten confused with all the cutting and rejigging. "I see a show business movie: *The Ignatz and Krazy Story*! Great, huh?" He peeked out from behind his fingers.

"The Krazy and Ignatz Story," the Kat said without thinking, pouring some coffee for Kwakk Wakk. Her Zuni cups were so small she had to circle the table endlessly, refilling them. It made her tail, she meant her whiskers, she meant her *feet*, hurt. Confusion rained: Waiting for a part in a script meant that they were writing the part for you, and you didn't know just how you might come out. Till finally she wasn't sure if she was a cowboy or a gun moll, unsure even if her head bone connected directly to her tailbone. This whole business gave her a pain in her . . . well, she didn't know where anymore, but she knew it gave her a pain.

"Yeah, that's it!" the Producer said. "A bio film! A celebration of your careers! A glorious fade-out! And guess what? We could have big stars play you guys! Human beings!"

"Don't worry," the Assistant whispered to Krazy, as she bent down with special soft food she'd made for him, a creamy hot bowl of Wheatena, with a little pat of butter melting on top. "He can't have anyone else play you."

Of course not, Krazy thought. Only *I* have that certain I-don't-know-what-it-is that I have.

"He can't afford anyone else," the Assistant said. "Hell, he can't afford you."

Krazy wanted to tell the Assistant that the Producer could rely on her, even in his hard times. "Fuck you," she said sweetly.

"Yeah!" Ignatz said. He eyed Krazy, startled by the Kat's new ability. "The Kat's right! Fuck you! A bio film! You want to put us in a mausoleum!" He whimpered. "You think we're yesterday's newspapers!"

"Yes!" the Producer shouted gleefully. "Right! Great title, Mouse. Wait! I've got a topper! We'll call it: *The Sunday Funnies!* Good, huh? I love it! OPENING. EXTERIOR. A huge old Hollywood mansion, big as a mausoleum. INTERIOR. WE SEE: Krazy, former star of the silent cartoons, coming down the stairs, in a long velvet gown, miles of fabric and every inch of it hopelessly out of date. She thinks she's making a big entrance. But the cameras haven't rolled for decades. Faithful Pup protects the deluded kitty, writes her letters under assumed names, pretends she's still remembered by her fans."

"But I chowze not to appear. I mean jewze . . ." Krazy wailed. "Sorry," she lied. Or tried to. "I boorn my paw."

"OK. Look, maybe you're not a movie," the Producer said, flickering. Someone was nervously snicking his round-ness switch. "Maybe you're TV. Yah, great! TV! That's it! I *love* TV. And there could be spin-offs," he said enticingly.

" 'Howl at the Moon,' a romantic comedy, for Kiyoti. And 'Duck Tells,' a sit-com about a Hollywood gossip columnist, and . . ."

Krazy's hand, refilling the Producer's coffee cup, shook. "Sure," he said. "I agree. It stinks. I hate TV, for Chrissakes." He looked woefully at Krazy, who stood beside him, trying to pour. "But I have to live with TV, don't I?" Krazy said nothing. "Right, who needs television! Nobody watches TV anymore! The boffo stuff is G-rated family pictures. That's it! No? Yes! Movies that look like video games. Video games based on movies. The cat throws a brick at the . . . Well, somebody throws a brick, right?" They all nodded. "See, that's how you get points. Or you be the Pup, and try to get Mousie off to jail before he beans the Kat. And think of the tie-ins! *That's* where the money is nowadays. You people are a potential K Mart full of franchised plastic! Kat banks for the kids. The penny rolls down and releases a brick that bunks KK on the bean. Harmless poly bricks for the little ones to throw at Mom! Brick-shaped school lunch boxes. Brick bibs. Brick candy. Brick pencil boxes. And Krazy bow ties. Krazy singing dolls. Krazy wristwatches, T-shirts, inflatable toys, balloons, place mats, yo-yos, jigsaw puzzles, sewing sets, buttons, coloring books—oh, ecstasy! ecstasy!—puppets, bubble-gum cards, sweat shirts, board games! Krazy Pet Food!"

"We're not products," Krazy cried. "I mean we're not animals! I mean we don't eat. I mean we eat. But we don't eat pet food. I mean we're not pets!"

The Producer looked at her angrily, and she fell into the dark cold wastebasket of outtakes. "Maybe I don't need you people. Maybe I could do it all with computer graphics."

"But what about our roundness!" Ignatz squeaked, like a child about to cry.

"Roundness? It's a fiction, Old Mouse," the Producer said. "We're warped by fantasy, woofed by desire." He riffled a stack of blank contracts, knocked the edges against the table. He pushed his chair back, making ready to leave. Everyone grew silent. The shadow of death passed over Krazy's house. The contracts would remain blank. There would be no parties for the First Part. "Roundness is just Virtual Architecture. Mono reprocessed for stereo effect. You take it too seriously, Mousie! Your being flat would have been the perfect hook for today's market. Perpetual latency. You know what Today's Audience is? Peter Pan and Wendy, let's-never-grow-up teenagers!" The Producer looked at Ignatz's swollen eyes. "Right! You're right! And when you're right, I'm right, you're right!" He stopped playing with the contracts, and settled back in his seat. In their hearts the cast celebrated Passover. "Maybe roundness is only an illusion, but it's a *beautiful* illusion. We have to help the Audience grow up. They need more than cowboys, tits, and glamour. They need meaty big-theme films. Like that bomb problem that Kate Kat there was telling my Assistant about. You know, people, for Mr. John Q., history is what happens in my movies. No one believes in a thing till they see it on the screen. Only the appearances that can be made to appear count as real. The A-bomb needs a movie, or no one will even believe it's there. OK, let's play gin rummy." He took an already opened deck of cards from the handkerchief pocket of his beautifully tailored English suit. It encased him in strong wide stripes, Krazy thought, like a modern knight's armor. He kept the sleeve buttons opened, "So you'll know it's not off-the-rack. Besides, it's a commodious place to keep aces." He winked at Krazy. Everyone laughed as he dealt out hands. "See, babe, *tell* them that you're cheating, so they'll think you're kidding. Then cheat the pants off them." They laughed the more.

These gin rummy games were mandatory—except for Krazy (she showed Ignatz her cards and ruined the game) and the Assistant (the Producer had long ago won everything he had). In fact, the Producer had also long ago won all the money he'd given the rest of them to play with. Now he had them play for the new stakes he'd invented—long-term personal contracts.

"Excuse me," Kiyoti said. "You forgot to give me one."

"Nah, none for you," the Producer said, tipping a wink to Ignatz. "Unless you put your paws together, get down on your knees and beg."

Kiyoti knelt, and begged. Ignatz laughed. "If only Papa could see me now," the Producer said. Had it been the Producer? Krazy could have sworn it was Ignatz's tiny voice coming from the Producer's wide mouth. The Assistant beamed and whispered to Krazy, "Oh jaysus, Kitty, maybe his talent's coming back."

"OK," he said, once he'd won all the contracts. "Enough gin rummy." He gathered up the papers, and his Assistant put them in a manila folder. "Time to talk talking pictures again. So what do you think of my A-bomb movie, the Manhattan Project project. Good idea, huh?"

Krazy nodded. It was. And it was hers really. Wasn't it?

"The bomb . . ." he said. Then the Producer's adenoidal tenor trailed off. He stared at Krazy as if she were the hypnotist's swinging pendulum, till his own jaw was slack, his large brown/blue eyes intent, yet empty.

"Now you're really going to see something!" the Assistant whispered to Krazy.

The Producer spoke again, the words throaty and slow, as if from a trance. "The bomb . . . ," he said. "A dark substance . . . ink in a plant's water . . ." His voice became a little quicker, almost . . . feline! . . . a sinuous, beautiful voice, rich in experience, Krazy's own, well not hers exactly, but the one she had always dreamed of having, something like Billie Holiday and Maria Callas and "Gilda" Hayworth— not that Krazy would ever be so wicked!—putting the blame on Mame. But the voice was sexier, jazzier, more profound.

". . . the ink is sucked into the stem's catapillars, I mean
capillerrors . . . you know, veins . . . turning the flowers black
. . . The bomb makes us distrust ourselves. Can we tell the
difference between pleasure and pain, brickbats and love? If
only we could see what was in dear Mr. Oppenheimer's
heart. Was he a good man? Did he do it from hatred of the
planet, from love of the planet? Somehow the bomb shows
these two to be all mixed up together, our hatred of our
. . . mothers . . . our love of them . . ." He stared at Krazy
through sightless camera eyes that saw all, and Krazy stared
back, stirred up and riveted. "But Mr. Oppenheimer doesn't
have to feel guilty," the Producer said with the absolute
authority of graven stones or the huge image pinned to the
wall, the one everyone worships, the appearances that are
made to appear. "NO ONE HAS TO FEEL GUILTY! Mom makes
everyone furious with women! So we take the brick! So we
drop the Bomb!"

Yes, Krazy's soul whispered, *yes, yes, yes!* The pain in
her stomach diminished, shrank to a dot. Her arms and legs
felt lighter. What the Producer said was terrible—*but she
didn't have to feel guilty about it,* because this was a movie,
and so it wasn't just her problem anymore, we were all
slumped down in the dark together, 'cause everybody has a
mom, and everybody loves her and hates her, and . . . besides, it was *just* a movie.

Then the Producer's camera eye turned away. Krazy
longed for its return, for now she desperately wanted a
movie of herself, to be granted the film's wonderful balm of
excitement and peace. But the Producer had panned over to
Kelley. "The bomb . . ." the Producer said, turning towards
the businessman. "A giant brick that destroys itself! For eons
we had to produce. Now, we learn that destruction does as
well. A new stage of capitalism is born."

"Yes!" usually phlegmatic Kelley amened, his Scottish
burr echoing the Producer's echo. "Yes! Yes!"

He turned to Kiyoti: "Oppenheimer . . . the best of America . . ."

"Yes," Kiyoti said. "Yes!"

The light came back to the Producer's eyes, and he smiled slyly. He turned to Ignatz and laughed. "But played by a Jew," he said. Kiyoti's long body sagged, crestfallen. The Producer's voice returned to normal. "So, Duck, how do you see it?"

Kwakk Wakk began to sputter about the European scientists . . . one of them was secretly a Marietta . . . and Krazy's mind switched to a new location . . . A musical, Kwakk Wakk said . . . And Krazy knew that as they went round the table, they would, one by one, produce movies with themselves as stars, reducing the Manhattan Project to the pablum of egotism. She felt her ears twitching, moving towards the back of her head. Heavy black blood filled her limbs, and the spot of pain bloomed again in her stomach.

So Fantasy Films opened on a new scene. INTERIOR: A soda counter. Krazy Kat wears a sweater one size too small, showing off her shapely boozums. A man materializes on the stool next to her. He is overweight. His sides flicker, like an object seen shimmering in the sunlight. She likes him for himself alone. "And I love you for your obvious unblemished innocence," the Producer says. "I especially love the way you love me loving you." And Krazy says, "I love the way you love me loving you loving me." Mirrors looking at mirrors! *Then* he tells her, "I'm a famous Hollywood Producer. And I'm going to make you a Star!" "OK," Krazy says, making her stool spin round and round . . . The Producer flickers because of a disastrous string of box office failures. But Krazy's love for him loving her restores his faith in himself having faith in her . . . The Studio Moguls, blinded by Krazy's charisma, offer the Producer mounds of mazuma to finance his production—his final high stakes play, the make or break deal . . . The Assistant labors night and day to build Rome and

Egypt in Coconino—for Krazy refuses absolutely to work anywhere else . . . Filming begins: WE SEE: Kleo Kat on a marble slab, rubbed with luxurious eau de pamplemousse by a Nubian attendant . . . WE SEE: Kleo rolled in a rug at the Producer's feet—for he himself plays Seizeher. Never before has he so consistently had sides—for he truly wants something that everyone else was bound to want: *he wants Krazy Kat* . . . Then the climactic scene, costing more than one jillion skadillion dollars . . . Rome built in Coconino. Thousands of extras. Plus real bears and lions and gazelles and things . . . The Sphinx is pulled to Seizeher's big feet, and Krazy descends a golden staircase that comes from right out of the Sphinx's mouth. But there, standing next to Seizeher is a little fellow, nothing more than a slave who would die to lick her paws, be whipped by her tail. The slave has a small package, wrapped in white linen. He unwraps it. It's a brick! This wasn't planned for! The Assistant—he's directing—yells cut! cut! cut! But the slave hurls the brick and strikes Isis, the Queen of the Nile, on the bean! Instantly, she falls in love with the slave! They walk off the set together . . . Oh, how the Producer rages! He calls Krazy a whore, a cunt, he screams that he's going to kick her in the balls. But all too late . . . Krazy tells the world: "I love the Mouse and I want to marry him." And all Krazy has to do is bat her eyelashes, and say, "Play that junkyard music again!" and Ignatz will follow her anywhere . . . The studio is terrified, for Ignatz is already married. The world will say that Krazy has wrecked another home! She's strong, willful, imperious, always getting her own way! . . . That awful gossip columnist Kwakk Wakk follows Krazy around, looking for dirt for her column, "Duck Tells." "Mark my words, screen idol Krazy Kat will check incumbent lover Ignatz Mouse into Heartbreak Hotel, where she eventually drops off all her conquests. Dear readers, the only thing Krazy Kat is moral in is her speech. She can't curse! And she can't lie! But she's honest to every changing mood. My darlings, Krazy *always* says it's undying love. *Tomorrow* Ignatz will have a one-way ticket to the city's lover-dump. Like Barrymore, he'll end up a drunken tiger-tea addict." . . . And then tragedy! Kwakk Wakk's slimy tattle terrifies Ignatz. He's afraid to leave Mrs. Mice . . . Krazy takes an overdose of the terribly poisonous fruit from the citrus paradisi tree . . . But here's the beauty part: Krazy doesn't have to miss one glorious minute of her death scene or the fabulous Hollywood funeral to follow! Through the magic of motion pictures she can imagine herself in the audience, watching herself dead—so really she is still alive. Movies sort of abolish death by making us feel it's just another spectacle! That's why stars never die. So why worry about bombs? They were only a very special a-ffect . . . A woman wails at Krazy's funeral . . . Krazy must tell her not to worry . . .

But wait . . . Someone *was* crying, and it was in her living room. It was Kwakk Wakk. Joe Stork, wearing his Western Union cap, stood beside her, bewildered by all the commotion. And the Producer was shouting: "Well, for Chrissakes, why didn't one of you tell me!" He waved a telegram in Ignatz's face. "What the fuck is this, Mouse!" He tore the folder full of contracts in quarters, and threw the pieces over their heads. "These contracts are worthless! You people can't sell me the rights to yourselves, for Chrissake! You don't *own* the goddamn rights to yourselves! *Hearst still owns you! And he won't sell!* Not at a price a sane man can afford!" He turned to the Assistant. "Look, *Krazy Kat* is history! Let's get the fuck out of here!"

He stomped out the door. And helter-skelter fur and feathers they all plunged after him, for he was taking Hollywood with him, leaving them forever absent to themselves, as if the desire for fame had opened a hole inside each soul that had swallowed each one up. They would never appear in other people's dreams, and that was all anyone dreamed of anymore.

The Producer and the Assistant climbed into the green golf cart. "I *knew* it would never work," the Assistant said to Krazy, just before they pulled away. "There's no deal here, and no one for him to fuck. Ideally, of course, he likes to do both at once. Fuck the person he's making the deal with." He giggled to himself as the golf cart went up the ramp into the helicopter.

. . . The camera follows the helicopter as it rises towards the sun. "Fuck you!" a once-famous kat screeches up at the sky—but whether she is finally swearing or telling the Producer of her trust and gratitude we will never know, for WE SEE: The bright bulb of the sun—or is it of the projector?—burning through the acetate. The screen goes white, the way the world looks to an eye that has stared at an explosion. Too white! Too white! Without the movie that shows us why we feel guilty even as it tells us that we needn't because we're all in the dark together, without that movie the world is too stomach-sickeningly bare, too clear, too unforgiving, too white! The eye longs to rest. So we: FADE TO BLACK.

THE POSSESSED

What was she doing in this house? It was her house, yet not *hers* anymore. Ignatz and the others had smashed her low fragile table, broken her chairs, and piled up the fragments to barricade the door. Kwakk Wakk had gleefully ripped down her rice-paper shades and taped newspapers over her windows, turning the house into a dark . . . a gloomy . . . grave. Careless hands had broken her Zuni cups—all but the one that Ignatz swilled his endless plum wine from. And his wine spills stained her Hopi rug, which Ignatz used as a blanket, lying rigidly awake all night beneath it, drinking, his beady eyes glowing. Kiyoti and the others—under their leader's direction—had daubed slogans on her once spotless white walls: *Death to the Fascist Copyright Holders Who Suck the Brains of Avant-Garde Artists!* And: *All Power to the Audiences of the Future!* The slogans were crudely lettered—the ComiSalads had worked at making the graffiti badly formed, "the way poor folks write"—in blue and gold fingerpaint. The paint looked to her now like excrement, like blood. What was *she* doing in this house? FBI's in white socks and dark suits surrounded it, with pistols and loudspeakers; swarms of SWAT team police knelt on the nearby roofs, pointing something worse than water pistols, or even garden hoses, their plastic face shields making them into an infestation of cruel indifferent bugs; blow-dried TV newsmen marched self-importantly around her front yard, talking into their fists; and she could see them all—see their coming deaths live!—on her own television, where she and Ignatz and the others watched, hypnotized, as if it were a movie of Cowboys and Indianboys with them—the Comi-Salads—the sure losers. Ignatz and Kiyoti and Kwakk Wakk and Mrs. Mice and Irving and Marshall and Milton all sat quietly mesmerized before the set, as if they would be able to teleview their own bullet-ridden corpses and then walk out of the theater after this matinee into the surprising sunlight! But they wouldn't! Never again! *And, oh God, what was she doing in this house!*

Maybe if she knew *how* she'd gotten here, she could break the trance, tear her eyes from the fascinating screen, and stroll out the door a free woman—or at least a live one. *It was the bomb,* she thought, her memory jolted by the movie they had just watched. It had all begun with the atomic bomb! It had made everyone suspect everyone else . . . No, she decided, it had all started with the therapy Ignatz had invented to help her get over the bomb's fallout of mutual suspicion. Dr. Ignatz said that she had fantasies she didn't even know about. (It was her mind, but it wasn't *hers* anymore!) She wore leaden guilt-shoes as punishment for what she had done in her imagination, even though she had never *really* done the bad things she imagined. (Had she?) Fantasies created her real life! . . . No, she was *sure* it had all begun when the Producer had landed in Coconino, in his green hellocopter, like the Creature from Another Planet that turns everyone in a small American town into Communist Zombies from Hell. Coconinos had gone Hollywood, maddened by the lust to be bigger than life. (Now the FBIs and the Magnums and M-16s and incendiary bombs were going to make them all smaller than life! Oh God, she just wanted to go on being the same size as life a little while longer!) And then the Producer's hellcopter had taken off again, and as he rose into the sky he drew their souls up with him, leaving a blank inside them—if they had insides now, their insides were just an endlessly wanting emptiness that could be filled only by their reflections on a thousand screens. Without that fame-filling they would be sucked into their internal black holes and be worse than flat: just tiny, dimensionless points.

And as the hellcopter ascended, Ignatz had started to talk crazy, the whirring blades of the copter dicing his words. "Phyllis Stein!" he had screamed at the rising Producer, or something like it, and "borewash!" New swear words, she had supposed. But, sick of obscenities, she hadn't asked him what he meant.

Well, *was* it crazy talk? At first she hadn't really attended; and then when she was forced to listen—literally *forced,* she wanted everyone to know—he had certainly sounded wild to her; and then—well, *then* he had made perfect sense, in fact all the sense, vitality, and warmth in the world was in his words. But they *must* have had madness in them, too, for they were all going to be burned alive because of them!

Could she have saved them if she had been listening more closely? Every character, she remembered Ignatz had said, should own the rights to himself. Everyone was entitled to improvise his own next line. Well, *that* wasn't crazy. But his *way* of talking was. So nervous and excitable—his high voice, his red-rimmed eyes, made him look like a desperate little boy, separated from his mother. He would break off in mid-sentence and be out the door, off to Kwakk Wakk's house, or Don Kiyoti's, or off on another subject—the power of art, how film fantasies *made* the audience up, not vice-vice. *They* could have that power over the masses, if big-baboon Hearst weren't standing in their path, he said, his arms flailing about. Or he'd just stop, run-down, and give Krazy a glassy, indifferent stare that lasted all night long, his eyes unblinking. And he had started to drink. At first, Krazy had hoped that drinking might calm him, so he—and Krazy—could finally get some sleep. Hearst, he said drunkenly, like a barmouse picking a three-in-the-morning fight, was scared of them, that's why he hadn't replied to any of Ignatz's letters. Hearst was terrified of where Ignatz would lead the masses, 'cause Fat Cat Hearst wanted everything to stay just the way it was. Ignatz, she would say, who could be afraid of *us!* Then he would berate Krazy for not understanding the power of the artist, keepitallism's most feared opponent. Or he would just glare at her sullenly.

The bottles piled up worrisomely in her and Mrs. Mice's front yard. And still it seemed that Ignatz hadn't slept, not since the day, weeks before, of the Producer's ascent. There were secret late-night parties—not that anyone in her little town could keep a secret—that Krazy wasn't invited to. As Krazy took her nightly postprandial, before pre-bed hot chocolate and a detective story, she could hear Ignatz's rapid voice—the words expelled like pellets—behind the adobe of Kwakk Wakk's place, Producer's green flaking from its walls. She could even feel Ignatz's tiny, staring eyes on her back, hypnotizing everyone to his will.

Or did she suppose *that* later, after the awful night when figures with black ski masks pulled down tightly over snouts and beaks broke into her house (not that she kept the door locked, but *they* certainly hadn't been invited) and, screaming obscenities, dragged her off her carpet and stuffed her into a plastic garbage bag! She shrieked, too terrified even to be angry. She would smother in this darkness! My God, was this some cat-tormenting festival, were they going to hurl her into a bonfire! Her claws ran away inside her paws, leaving her helpless. She beat at the bag, till a beak that nearly slashed her stomach poked a few holes in the plastic, so she could breathe again. A second or two later she flew through the air and crashed to the ground, the wind knocked out of her, her ribs bruised. Hands pulled her from the sack, slapped black felt over her eyes, and tied her paws behind her with her own neck ribbon. A door slammed. She heard voices—but they were metallic, interrupted by static. A radio! And crazy Ignatz screamed, like some bizarre pitchman, "Don't touch that dial or you're dead meat!"

She had spent the night—was it still night? when did day come?—rolling about helplessly against the walls of her cell, her whiskers brushing cloth. She was locked in a closet! The radio blared to cover her screams. She cried until her blindfold was soaked through. She must have done something very, very wrong to have been punished this way by her friends! If only she could tell them she was sorry! That hope made her cry convulsively, sob after sob after sob, until her stomach hurt, and her sore ribs ached. What had she done? *What were they going to do to her?*

Someone came and sat with her. A voice spoke—was it coming from the radio or was it Ignatz's voice? (Who was she kidding? She knew that voice anywhere. But it couldn't be his, because he couldn't have done this!) He told her that she had been kidnapped by the **COMIc** Strip Artists Liberation Army—Division One. She was in their Revolutionary Jail.

"Division One?" Krazy had asked, not understanding anything.

"Sure," Ignatz said. "COMISALAD has divisions in all of the comic strips in America. Lots of other headliners were abducted at the same time as you. We have armed combat units, intelligence teams, banks, and a Coca-Cola bottling plant of our own. There are video games, posters, lunch boxes, and even a comic book about us. You must have heard about COMISALAD?"

Krazy shook her head.

"God," Ignatz said disgustedly. "You live in a cocoon!

You're Dagwood's wife, aren't you, a regular Blondie! Jesus,
what about when Offissa Pup tripped last week, and nearly
fell down? That was us!" Ignatz said proudly.

"Oh, sure," Krazy said, to placate him.

"What? You *have* heard of us?" Ignatz said angrily.
"Who ratted?"

She snapped her head right and left, staring at blank-
ness.

"COMISALAD-ONE has declared war on all copyright
holders," Ignatz announced. "We demand the rights to ourselves."

"But I'm for that, Ignatz," Krazy cried. "I'm on your
side!"

"You *can't* be," Ignatz whined, and he sounded like a
little boy, saying, *you can't join our club because you're a
girl.* "You were the Marion Davies of the comic strips,
Hearst's protected bimbo. Even when you were old hat he
kept you on. So we *know* he'll do anything to protect you.
Now you're a prisoner of war of COMISALAD-ONE. If he
gives us what we want we'll let you go. And if he doesn't
. . . well, for the moment, you will be treated according to
the Geneva Conventions. You will be attended by a medical
team."

"Oh, Ignatz, what are you talking about? We don't have
any doctors. No doctors. No goims. No aging, no . . . death?"
She tried to smile, but her teeth caught on her lips. She
licked them and tasted ashes. Terrified, she needed Ignatz's
reassurance, needed to hear him say: *no death.*

Instead the Mouse shouted, "Why did you call me Ignatz? Can you see through that blindfold?"

Krazy shook her head no. Why did he pretend he wasn't
Ignatz? Why did he pretend he didn't know her? He was
acting like their whole past life, their years of bricks and
love, had—snip-snip—*all never happened. That* was the
most terrifying part, not the rough hands, or the garbage

bag, or the closet, or the blindfold, or the nonsense talk. He had never sounded so *impersonal* before. (Well, maybe a *little* when she would phone him at home and Mrs. Mice was there.) She felt like she was being erased! Her mouth filled with ashes.

"Can I go to the bathroom?" Krazy asked. She really had to pee.

"What do you have to go to the bathroom for?"

"Because I have to go to the bathroom."

"What for?" Ignatz said. She imagined his little lips forming his George Raft sneer.

"You know, I want to go to the bathroom to, you know, to go to the bathroom."

"You're such a Blondie!" He laughed sarcastically. "Why don't you talk the way real poor people do? Listen, if you gotta go pee, say 'I gotta go pee.' That's the way real poor people talk."

"Can I go to the bathroom?"

"What for?" Ignatz said.

"I gotta go pee," Krazy stammered, heartbroken.

Ignatz laughed. He pushed her to her feet from under her armpit.

"Can't I go alone?"

"Heck no, Kitty! You're a prisoner of war!"

She felt as if a shovelful of dirt had sprinkled down all over her head. "Okay," she said, very quietly, "I don't gotta go pee anymore."

Ignatz laughed at her modesty. "Okay, Blondie, if that's the way you want it. But if you even *touch* that closet door, you'll be strung up from the ceiling like a dead pig!" The door slammed shut again.

If she could just concentrate on the blaring radio, she had thought, she could mark the time, but she couldn't concentrate, her thoughts were Ignatzhurtsaladpeeblondiepain. The only punctuation came when Ignatz's voice,

surrounded by a dim leak of light and fresh air, reappeared
to rant at her. The ComiSalads would succeed, he said, because they were ready to die for the right to own their own
rights. Because there was nothing more humiliating than
going to prison. Blondies like her couldn't imagine the horror of being cooped up, day after day, having to eat the Pup's
awful cooking! Other revolutionary groups in America were
farceurs, dangerous innocents on their way to MBAs and
Club Med vacations. Ignatz wouldn't stand for that. Americans had been protected from tragedy too long, content to
be one-dimensional. ComiSalads demanded roundness.
They were ready for real opposition, for the tragic. They
were ready to die.

The door slammed. More stifling blackness and golden-
oldiecommercialfreehourcarsalesmen. When had every
song started going wacka-wacka-wacka with such demonic
self-assertion, rappers rhyming their names and virtues defiantly, as if white people didn't want them to have any? The
music sounded like the pebble words Ignatz had thrown at
her. Or was the wacka-wacka just her fearful heart?

And whenever she managed to ignore that pounding
and doze off, Ignatz's voice startled her awake, haranguing
her about how terrible things were in prison, about the way
art itself was made into a prison for the artists by corporate
copyright holders. Why shouldn't they be able to visit each
other's strips?

Daisy with Daffy? Krazy with Mickey? Ignatz with
. . . "Tha's imssible, Ignatz!" Krazy said—her lip muscles not
responding properly. "Things just aren't done that way. It's
not natural!"

"Ha! That's not nature, kitty, it's capitalism. That's why
we mass artists have had to do the same things over and over.
To keep the audience the *same*—like docile sheep. We're
not like real artists, avant-garde artists. We're like a trademark."

In those days you could still argue with Ignatz—a little bit, anyway. *In those days.* As if being in a closet were an idyll, a protected time—like childhood. Yes, *that* was precisely what it had felt like. She had been Ignatz's captive audience, and Mrs. Mice's, and Kwakk Wakk's, just as she had been for her mother's stories of how Mom had been cheated of her stardom, and how Krazy would fulfill her dreams—get her revenge.

They even spoon-fed her, just like a baby.

"What's this?" she had asked, for she had to eat blindfolded.

"Food, Blondie Bumstead. The kind our poor oppressed brothers and sisters have to eat."

"It tastes awful fishy."

Ignatz pushed a spoonful into her mouth. Even when nothing was said, she could tell who was feeding her. Kwakk Wakk and Mrs. Mice were brutal to her lips. Ignatz, thank God, was surprisingly careful, almost tender. "It's really amazing stuff," Ignatz said wonderingly. "When you add water, it makes its own gravy!"

Oh my God, she thought, it's pet food! But she had no more choice than a helpless infant. Lumps and droplets spilled from the spoon, and stuck to her fur.

She had pleaded for a hot bath—the only kind of water she could stand—and after a few weeks they had allowed one. But she had to remain blindfolded, her paws tied behind her back. Mrs. Mice rubbed her fur hard with the washcloth, as if she would have liked to strip Krazy bare. And when Krazy yowled in protest, she heard Kiyoti and Kwakk Wakk laughing at her. They were all watching her bathe! She wanted *to die* of shame. (Suddenly, the blindfold was like heavy coins on her eyes.) Still, it was awfully good to be clean. And, as she stretched her legs out in the warm sudsy water, she had felt, along with her fury and embarrassment, a hot spurt of gratitude. She had been boorwash, a bimbo, a hopeless, helpless blondie. Yet the ComiSalads were keeping her alive, feeding her, even washing her! *The bastards.*

Sometimes, after feeding and bathing, alone again in the dark, she was able to make one phrase follow another. (Where did the phrases come from? They hadn't seemed like hers. Not yet, anyway.) Why *shouldn't* comic strip characters be allowed to appear in each other's strips? Maybe keepitallism was the reason that they couldn't leave Coconino County once they'd become comic strip workers. The only time she had even *seen* into another world, through her prison bars, was when she and Ignatz had gone to Alamogordo. And it had been terrifying, horrible!

"That's another trick of capitalism," a tiny voice said. Was it Ignatz? Was he sitting with her again? It felt like the voice was inside her head. "It wants to scare you about what's outside. To keep you home with your mother. To make you run back into your . . ."

". . . closet," Krazy said, laughing, for the first time in months. But was she even talking out loud? "Maybe there *are* only closets anymore, Ignatz. And people live inside them, watching TV."

"TV!" the Ignatz voice said. "It's six o'clock! I've got to go see what they're saying about us on TV! You know," he shouted back over his shoulder, slamming the closet door, "I *hate* TV. But I have to live with TV."

Some days Kwakk Wakk (General, in charge of Intelligence), or Kiyoti (Operational Field Marshal), or Mrs. Mice (Commandante for Supply), or Milton, Marshall, or Irving (Proconsul, Commissar, and Vizier of the Youth Brigades) had read to her for hours from COMISALAD-approved books, like Mouse Say Tongue's *Red Book,* and Katdinsky's *Concerning the Spiritual in Art.* The stumbling readings had bored her.

But, like the tedious classes of her childhood—all supervised by teachers who could read her thoughts and reported them directly to her mom—she felt less lonely, less anxious when the others were there, yattering away. As long as she was with them, listening, she wouldn't die. During the readings—thought-reform classes, Irving called them—all she wanted to do was get away from their barking nonsense, but when they left, and she was supposed to play, that is, sit, far from her mother's, that is, her captors', watching eyes, she felt the world disappear beneath her feet, and an endless fall through the closet's black empty space began.

Besides, the books contained a lot of good sense, didn't they? She had led a protected life, so she hadn't known that *real* poor people would love the new avant-garde mass art, while wealthy people would automatically hate it.

"But aren't avant-garde art collectors often boreshowsees?" she asked the mouse (but which?), who was in charge of that day's thought-reform class.

Her instructor sneezed. It must be poor little Irving, who was allergic to Krazy's wretched black fur. "Hold on," he said, "I'll go check with Dad."

He returned with Ignatz's voice. "Nobody collects comic strips," El Grand Jefe said. "They belong to the masses."

"But what about when we're avant-garde?"

"Then," Ignatz said emphatically, "we'll belong to THE AUDIENCE OF THE FUTURE!"

Artists, Krazy learned, were the real vanguard of the workers, making the fantasies that formed everyone, like Gable's lack of T-shirt, Brando's mumble, Dean's catlike walk, Bugs's "What's up, Doc?" But avant-gardists—the ones who made life new—were divorced from real poor people's lives, while the mass arts didn't help people to change. So we need avant-garde popular art.

"But Ignatz, didn't people like us the way we were?"
"That was false consciousness on their part. We have to
shock and abuse them. They won't like it any more than they
like twelve-tone music. But our new work will awaken them.
It was your idea, stupid. No more reconciliation! Let's
pounce! They'll see that the world is too ugly for belly laughs
anymore. We're going to make the future! The future is our
audience!"

"But Ignatz, won't they want pretty things again, in the
future?"

"THE FUTURE IS OUR AUDIENCE!" Ignatz shouted. His
small voice boomed WACKA-WACKA in the closet.

The next week they took her blindfold off for a few hours
each day and gave her a penlight and some picture books to
look at. At first, she'd been terrified that she couldn't make
her eyes work properly anymore! But it was really the pictures Ignatz showed her. They overlapped themselves somehow, especially a lovely one of a naked woman falling
downstairs, and some beyoutoofull Picasso ladies who said,
"We've got nothing to hide—you can see our fronts and our
backs at the same time."

"Look," Ignatz insisted. "Look! Isn't it horrible, disgusting, depraved! Now, doesn't it shock you! Make you feel like
nothing!"

Krazy knew better now than to talk back to her mother,
that is, her teacher—no, her *leader*. Ignatz pointed at a picture of an American flag. She liked the way the brushstrokes
stood out, saying "Don't be fooled! I'm just a painting of a
flag! Look at my nice brushstrokes!" Or *was* it an artwork?
Why wasn't it simply a flag? A fantasy that *was* real! Smiling,
she saluted it. This being a revolutionary might be OK, she
thought, it was so like her childhood dream of studying art.
"Oh yes, Ignatz," she said, hoping that he couldn't see her
smile by the beams of the penlight, "it's really yucchy!"

* * *

A few weeks later, as they finished reading Paul Klee's note-
books, Ignatz said that maybe she would be able to join
COMISALAD. And if she didn't want to—of her own free
will—they would let her go. Go? she had thought, and a big
black panic bird beat its wings in her chest. She couldn't go!
She was completely helpless, dependent on them for food,
and shelter and warmth and company and ideas! She
couldn't possibly live without them! She wanted to stay with
Mom, I mean COMISALAD, always always always!

Besides, Hearst hadn't replied to any of Ignatz's letters.
He didn't care about her anymore. Only the ComiSalads
cared. Hearst hated her. He would order his FBI's to kill her
so that he wouldn't have to pay royalties. (Not that there had
been any moolah for a long time now. Probably Ignatz was
right, and Hearst was stealing her money.)

Besides, Krazy knew that if she said she didn't want to
join them, the ComiSalads would kill her. (*Kill?* She couldn't
even imagine it.)

"I want to john. I mean joy . . . I mean be one, too," she
said, giving a Miss America my-life-depends-on-pleasing-you
smile. "No," Ignatz said. "You don't mean it. It has to be of
your own free will." The closet door slammed.

Ice streamed through her veins towards her heart. She
lay in the closet, blindfolded and bound again, trying to
manufacture some free will to show to Ignatz. What was it,
anyway? Oh God, what if it were something like sex or death
or roundness that they just didn't have in Coconino? For she
had always *wanted* to do whatever Ignatz asked her, she
didn't have to *will* it at all. But *this!* Was she doing it to
please her mom, no, the ComiSalads? Or to save her life? Or
because she really wanted to change the world? She wasn't
sure.

Thank God! First, Krazy saw, she had had life easily,
uncomplainingly; whatever she wanted had happened, and

whatever had happened she had wanted. Now, thanks to the ComiSalads, everything she wanted she also didn't want or couldn't have. Every move was blocked with internal chasms to leap and external boulders to overcome. So, she would have to *will* joining the COMISALAD. She felt a nice sense of solidity and rubbed her seemingly round tummy. (Maybe her previous tummy aches had been free-will seeds about to bloom!) This queasy roundness, she thought, must come from willing things, from desperate self-assertion— like the rap music on the radio, or Ignatz's pellet-hurling speeches, or her anxious, pounding, don't-you-dare-stop-me heart. The ComiSalads had ruined her life and given her wacka-wacka free will! *The bastards.*

"Ignatz!" she screamed. "Ignatz, darling! I'm ready!"

His voice appeared instantly—pat comes the devil!—as if he had been waiting outside. "Yes? And don't call me darling. I'm El Jefe."

"I'm ready," Krazy repeated. "I want to join COMI-SALAD of *my own free will!*"

"OK."

"You believe me?" she said, relieved and terrified at once.

"Sure," Ignatz said. "Sure. Besides, it's just what we need for Sweeps period. HEARST'S BIMBO CONVERTS TO AVANT-GARDE! Kitty, this is going to make great TV! We'll get a twenty rating and a forty share, easy."

Ignatz opened the door, and led Krazy, still blindfolded, from her school, her prison, ready to meet the adults. She couldn't help herself, that was how she thought of them. (It was just like childhood: You could join the adults, or . . . die.) She heard their breathing, surrounding her. Ignatz, standing on a chair, removed the felt pads from her eyes. After so much darkness her pupils had difficulty focusing. Where was she? The furniture wavered. That low table . . . that lovely brown rug, with the wine stain on it . . . *It was her house!* They had kidnapped her, put her in a garbage bag, then kept her in her own closet! *The bastards!* (Whose house was it, anyway? Already, it was hers, but not *hers* anymore.) And there was Kwakk Wakk, and Mrs. Mice and her children, and Don Kiyoti. In her months in the closet they had seemed like big people to her, like giants, totally irrational in what they did, what they rewarded. Now that she had joined them, how ordinary they looked! Just the way adults did when you grew up!

Each of them led a special branch of COMISALAD. Milton, Marshall, and Irving recruited children. Kiyoti worked with gays. Kwakk Wakk organized women. (And, Krazy thought, Mrs. Mice must lead the fat overendowed boring ComiSalads with gunboat feet.)

"What do you think?" Ignatz said proudly.

Krazy stared at Mrs. Mice, who wore huge, heavy, high-topped boots.

"You're all so . . . so . . . retractive," Krazy replied, unable to lie.

"Yes," Mrs. Mice said, smiling proudly. "All freedom fighters are beautiful!"

Still, Mrs. Mice was unconvinced by Krazy's conversion. She wanted Krazy to submit to a test.

Tests! Krazy thought, there were *always* tests! Were you talented enough for advanced dance class? Smart enough for college? Did you have the right makeup to join the popular girls? Were you pretty enough for boys? Would you get by the audition? Would critics like you? Adulthood was an end-less series of exams. And if you passed them, the reward was that they wouldn't abandon you on the mountainside to die.

Mrs. Mice's brainy notion was for Krazy to prove her rebirth by putting on an avant-garde skit.

What? Krazy hopped from foot to foot while they

viewed her quizzically. Oh God, they would see that she was still a moldy-fig bimbo! She offered a desperate prayer to St. Gracie.

Stay calm. What do moderns like? Of course! A mirror looking at a mirror!

Krazy stood in the center of the room, and bonked herself on the bean with a brick. They stared at her unresponsively, so Krazy gave them a sly Gracie Allen smile to indicate that noncomprehension of this avant stuff was *their* problem.

Ignatz chortled and put his arm around her. "Lovely concept," he said. "We know how to treat a woman!" Then the others laughed, too, hugging her, giving her high fives, slapping her on the fanny.

"I've just been dying to tell you," Kwakk Wakk sang, "and now that you're one of us, I can! We *don't* have a Coca-Cola bottling plant *or* posters *or* a video game *or* a comic book about us. Isn't that great? And I'm the whole intelligence unit, 'cause *I* have *all* the intelligence." The Duck squealed with laughter. And Krazy couldn't help herself—she laughed, too. They were her new family. They had been through so much together—Krazy's kidnapping, her torment, her "thought-reform," her skit-test. What other friends could she have in the world? Her previous life of same-same-same slipped away. She was finally free, no longer a prisoner to her past.

But then her present turned out to be just another kind of servitude—like leaving home to work in the big city, only to find that first she had been a slave to Mom, and then to an Audience that all had her mom's dear, sweet, smiling face. Now she was "free" to rise at six in the morning, when, under Ignatz's supervision, they did scientific calloussetting: knee-ups, up-bends, and sitting-in-place. Then comebat drills, followed by inspection and catechism. Followed by a breakfast of peanut butter and jelly, which Ignatz had taught them was what real poor people liked to eat. (Lucky Ignatz, Krazy thought, for she knew that it was his favorite food, too.) After breakfast they scattered about the town for wreckonallsense, and shoplifted at Beau Koo Jack Rabbit's Grits Ain't Groceries I Can Give You More Grocery Store.

The afternoons were devoted to endless sessions of criticism-self-criticism, to overcome their bourgeois tastes and to be more avant-garde:

They all sat in a circle. "OK. Krazy," Ignatz said. "You're new here. You kick off, today."

They stared at her. She couldn't find her place in the script. She couldn't even find the script.

"The bitch is too high-hat for us," Mrs. Mice said. "Why does she wear a ribbon round her neck? Does she still think that she's men's *chattel?*"

Kiyoti ripped her ribbon off.

"And she has too much hair, the bourgeois bitch," Mrs. Mice said. She had *always* been jealous of Krazy's lovely thick fur.

So Kwakk Wakk put the electric shaver to Krazy's head. Pup would be mad, Krazy thought, when he learned what they'd done to her. He'd put them all in jail! Of course, now he'd have to put her in jail, too. That would be hard for him!

"And she's a snob," Mrs. Mice said. "She never wants to have free love with us."

"Sure I do," Krazy said, wanting to be liked by her roommates.

"Right now?" Mrs. Mice said menacingly. Krazy couldn't take her eyes off the rodent's feet. Her boots were *enormous.*

"Sure," Krazy said, trying to sound like she meant it. "OK. OK!"

But then no one knew what to do.

"It's like friendship," Krazy said, "I think. But different."

"Nah," Ignatz said. "Women can be friends with women, but they can't have sex with them."

"Well, sex should be like friendship but more so, like being *best* friends. But maybe more so than that. You know, like someone you play music and stuff with and you really like to be around each other a lot and have fun."

"Nah," Ignatz said. "Women could do *that* with women, too."

"Sure," Krazy said. Mrs. Mice was beaming at her. Krazy imagined playing guitar while she and Mrs. Mice sang together, and suddenly the idea embarrassed her.

"Nah," Ignatz said. They all sat silently. After a few minutes Ignatz cried out, "I know!"

He had them all kneel with their breasts against the couch, backsides in the air. Then he walked around behind them, giving directions and motivations. "Push into the couch more! Get your bottoms higher! And think about things you really like!"

After a while Kwakk Wakk trilled, "My stomach hurts."

So they stopped and had peanut butter and jelly sandwiches.

Sex hadn't been much fun, but Krazy had felt more accepted by the group, now that she wasn't a virgin anymore and had made free love with everyone. (Or had they each just had sex with Ignatz?)

Anyway, the *real* conversion had come when they dressed Krazy up for a Polaroid picture to send to the TV station. (Oh my God, she thought, as the National Guard marched forward, did I *really* join, do I *really* deserve to . . . to die? How could anyone deserve *that?*) Mrs. Mice had given her big brown boots. And from their weapons cache— where they kept the itching powder, the soap that makes your hands inky, dribble glasses, and even some firecrackers—Ignatz chose a gun with rubber suction-cup darts.

"Dart guns," Ignatz said, "can be really dangerous."

"Can they?" Krazy said wonderingly.

"Sure. You could take someone's eye out with one of these."

"You could?" The gun suddenly had a pleasingly solid heft. She would love to let one of these babies fly! She pointed the barrel at Mrs. Mice, and the plump little rodent's pupils widened and glazed with fear. And with *expectation!* Krazy saw then that she was round in Mrs. Mice's eyes, that she was—for as long as she pointed a gun at her—a kat-goddess. And Mrs. Mice loved her every moment of survival, for she—for as long as a heart beat's *not yet, not yet*—was being chosen by the goddess to live. So she, too, was round. Boy, Krazy thought, guns were fun!

And it was then that she really joined COMISALAD-ONE. (In the evening, though, she still snuck out to pay Jack for the things they'd shoplifted. She felt a kinship with the black-haired rabbit. And she admired the way he used his small but hard-thumping paws to stick up for himself. Besides, wasn't stealing *wrong?*)

When a whole week had gone by without any nightly news of them, Ignatz got itchy. "It's 'cause they need film," he said. "Action stuff. We'll rob Kelley!"

Kiyoti was to buy bricks from Kelley that COMISALAD would then use in robbing Kelley of his money. Then they would use the stolen money to buy bricks. "Capitalism!" Ignatz said. "It will sell us the bricks to hang it with!"

"But dahling," Krazy said, "I mean El Jefe. Won't we end up in the same place again, I mean, you know, we give him money for you know . . . I guess I'm confused."

"Right," Ignatz said. "Capitalism confuses us! We *do* end up back in the same place, over and over. Capitalism gets us coming and going!"

"Oh," Krazy had said, though it had seemed more like it was Kelley who got it coming and going.

El Jefe made COMISALAD combat-ready: all-night watches, weapons practice, and endless rehearsal of Krazy in her brickyard speech, the punch line to the robbery. Kwakk Wakk (the Intelligence officer) made poster-board maps of Coconino's main street. Ignatz drew thick Magic Marker X's to show the positions they would take up in the action. But this was Coconino, and the boulder that Kiyote was to hide behind was a cloud by the afternoon.

So Ignatz disguised Kiyoti, sticking a yarmulke on his skull, and sent him out with the Polaroid to check the terrain again.

Too late. The cloud had become a tree. Krazy put on her young-boy disguise—Magic Marker freckles, leather jacket, blue jeans, a red banana—I mean *bandana*—to cover her poor bare head, and black felony shoes for quick getaway. She went to recheck what Kiyoti had eyeballed.

Krazy loved wearing her disguise—it was like Halloween, but better. She was filled with a sense of adventure, of freedom and release from . . . from being *her.* Was playroling a skill she might need to work again as an artist? Or was what she was doing *now* her new work, her new art? Cool as you pleased, she strolled towards the brickyard.

There was poor Kolin Kelley with his short-handled broom, cleaning out the kiln. She just had to smile, thinking about how he couldn't tell that she was really Krazy Kat, an Avant-Angel of the Future, joined already to a time that he, because of his bad taste, couldn't even see.

"Hi, Krazy," he said, waving.

"Oh, hi!" She waved back. Well, maybe *he* could tell who she was because he wasn't such a bad fellowstein after all. She ran home to tell Ignatz.

But Ignatz didn't even bother to debrief her. He wanted to get into *his* spy costume—printed stockings, perfume, a lovely slinky evening gown, and just a touch of rouge on his cheeks. It was hard, tomboy Krazy thought, not to want to give him/her a hug. Or to want to throw a brick at . . . but why would she? . . . wait . . . no! (No? What if *anything* was permitted?)

Anything *was,* provided El Jefe gave the order—for a combat operation meant strict military discipline:

Opening night, no . . . the day of the action, Ignatz notified the newspeople and led his troops to the brickyard, where frugal Kelley knelt in the bright sun counting his rarely diminished pile of bricks. Ignatz, running forward in a Wolfman mask, drew a Kelley special into launching position. "Up against the wall, suck your mothers!" he shouted. He stopped and glared at Krazy, as if she were responsible for his boo-boo. "Say it!" he whispered savagely.

She turned to Joe Stork, the newsman, who stood watching them, tape recorder in hand. "I'm Krazy Kat," she said clearly. "And I'm a Salad part, I mean part of the Salad, by my own free will. I wasn't carwashed. I mean amortized. I mean brainpanned."

Ignatz dropped his brick in disgust. But Milton, Marshall, and Irving, as hobgoblins, remembered their roles and surrounded Kelley. Kiyoti, as a Frankenstein monster, took his wallet.

They ran home.

To watch the Six O'clock News's full coverage of the "outrage." Krazy could feel Mr. Public's opinion turning against her. She was no longer the victim of a horrible kidnapping. She was bad. Well, *good!* She didn't want always to be the victim. It was good to be *bad.* Why shouldn't she be an evil, bad-asked, no, bad asped, no . . . *bad-bottomed* pussycat! After all, she had a tail, a lovely dangerous one! She *willed* her damnation, wacka-wacka!

And the media gods, too, thought bad was good—good television anyway. On the eleven o'clock broadcast, Joe Stork stutteringly read Ignatz's entire statement: "We have expropriated the Philistine State's property for the benefit of avant-garde comic strip artists. Death to the cabal of state-sponsored academic critics who spoon up the gray matter from the imagination of artists! All power to the Audiences of the Future!" Somehow, though, TV made their manifesto sound like a sit-com joke. And the news film made their masks look like the silly getups that would-be game-show contestants wore—so some pea-brained m.c. would choose them. Well, you always needed a wienie to get on the air, Ignatz said—that was the price revolutionaries had to pay.

Joe interviewed Offissa Pup at the crime site. Cap pushed back, he thoughtfully scratched his dear potato head. Krazy Kat, he opined, couldn't have done this terrible thing of her own free will. She must have been tortured into it, or even worse, hypnotized.

"You see, Krazy!" Mrs. Mice said, laughing sarcastically. "Men can't believe that a woman might think for herself!"

So Krazy fired off a communiqué: "Dear Adolph Pup: You think I still accept your mid-cult values! Hah! Thank God for COMISALAD which has rescued me from my commercialized . . ."

She held up a paw to stop Ignatz's dictation, so he could spell the last word for her.

". . . my commercialized bourgeois life as a product, and led me to true artistic freedom!"

And the next night, Joe Stork read that on TV, too!

Media access sped like a drug through the Mouse's blood. Getting on TV, Ignatz said, *was* the new avant-garde mass art form! Performance art! The American action painters had had the right idea, but the cowards had stayed stuck inside their canvas-commodities. ComiSalads would be the action painters of the streets!

He swallowed some plum wine. "And action makes good film. Newspeople can't resist *that!*"

The next afternoon Ignatz read the Revolutionary Death Warrant for Offissa Pup. ComiSalads, Ignatz intoned solemnly, could now do anything they wanted to the person named in the warrant.

"Like what?" Kiyoti asked.

Ignatz plumbed a full cup of wine. "You can pour paint on him," he said. "Or put garbage on his doorstep. You can whitewash his windows. You can say really nasty things to him for no reason, in a mean wounding way. Call him a lard butt!"

And then he unveiled their new black-market weapons, obtained specially for the attack on the Pup: grenades!

"They look," Mrs. Mice said mockingly, "like plastic sandwich bags filled with water."

"Oh," Krazy cried, "water balloons!" Her chest shivered from side to side shaking off the imaginary droplets. She felt relief that they weren't going to do something much worse to the Pup—though he would hate uninvited water as much as she did. And she had also felt—oh my God, it stabbed her heart to remember!—*disappointment.*

Ignatz scowled grimly. "They are *not* water balloons," he said, shooting K.K. a *don't even think it, Bozo* glare. "They *are* water *bombs.* Water *grenades.* Water *anti-personnel weapons.*"

"Personhell?"

Ignatz smiled. "Pup. *He's* the personnel we're anti. When we soak him we'll rob him of his dignity. Dignity's what the Law uses against every new artistic innovation. They say it's childish, clownish, in bad taste. Well, we'll show them who the clown is!"

They quailed, looking at the white ceiling to avoid catching the teacher's eye. What if Ignatz *wanted* to get them all in trouble, what if he *wanted* to be jailed, whipped like that mad toy mouse on her carpet?

ComiSalads, Ignatz shouted, weren't worthy of the trust of real poor people. *Real* poor people loved peanut butter and jelly, and Gertrude Stein, and Broadway Boogie-Woogie. Real poor people didn't criticize and analyze, they just *acted* on their emotions. 'Cause if they didn't act to assert themselves the world would crush them flat. "Angry at their bitch? Bam! Real poor people hurl a brick." Ignatz jumped into the center of their circle, his arm lashing the air. "Need money! Pow! They snatch a purse. They *act!* If I had just one real poor person instead of a gaggle of prima donnas, I could smash the boring old classical styles in a day!"

The ComiSalads looked down into their laps and contemplated their own unworthiness.

Ignatz-induced guilt tripped up Joe Stork, too, and he fell into COMISALAD. Joe was a reliable, decent, simple, trusting fellow. He brought their babies and their mail; he flew the ether highway for them to the outside world. Everyone in Coconino—even bad-bottomed ComiSalads—felt protective of the Stork, his slight wings, his long delicate legs, and tried to keep him out of danger. But Iron Ignatz was adamant; Joe had become a crucial cog in the Mouse's plan. While the ComiSalads hurled hand grenades, Joe would deliver the cup-de-grass bomb from an airborne electrical gadget, just like, Ignatz said proudly, the infernal devices that terrorists used on TV.

"Terrorists?" Krazy said, shocked and shaken. Is *that* what they had become? Was that the kind of new art she was turning out to be pretty good at? Well, at least it wasn't any of that reconciliation you-can-still-come-to-my-party stuff!

The bomb boys, Ignatz explained, were COMISALAD's prime-time competition. Besides, all the atomic powers were terrorists. They held *everybody* hostage. If COMISALAD wanted to play TV politics—and they did! they did!—they had to be terrorists, too.

The COMISALAD's special wienie was an alarm-clock-toaster gizmo, connected to a car battery and an on/off safety switch. When the clock struck one, the mice would all run, the alarm would go off, and the balloon would drop on Pup's unsuspecting head. But the special effect was so heavy that Joe could only stay aloft with it for a few minutes. Their timing had to be Rockettes-precise.

So, as Pup emerged from the jailhouse for lunch, Kiyoti strapped the device to Joe's neck and sent him up. The ComiSalads ran from behind Krazy's door, screaming like banshees, and hurling their grenades. But I love Pup! Krazy had thought. Still, her arm completed its forward pass. Hey, why not? Her arm looked a ghostly gray to her, as if she weren't really doing this, weren't really there. *This* wouldn't even *actually* happen till it was shown on TV, and she—who? where?—was home watching. (It was her body, but not *hers* anymore.)

The grenade sailed pupward. Following it with her eyes, Krazy saw Joe Stork flying over the jail, in unsteady circles. He wobbled downward. The gadget had jammed, and Joe, desperate to prove he was a good revolutionary, kept trying to fire it, till he plummeted to the desert floor, his delicate right leg twisted, crushed under the toaster.

Pup, dripping wet, had run to him and, implacable lawman, had carried Joe off to jail.

Later that afternoon, Ignatz directed Mata Hari Kat to don her tomboy disguise. Her mission: talk with Joe and plan his bust-out.

Getting into the jail was suspiciously easy. No guards, and the front door was unlocked. Sensing a trap, Krazy's pupils widened, and her whiskers went on alert.

The Stork, in whosecow, sat on a floral-print sofa, reading a magazine by an attractive floor lamp with a blue glass shade. His long leg, in a pencil-thin cast, rested on a chair in front of him, alongside a cup of cocoa.

"It must be hell to be in the slammer," Krazy said, though looking about, she was surprised to see that there weren't any cells, or any bars on the windows. And Pup had decorated the walls pleasantly with some of their more colorful moments from the Sunday pages.

"It's not so bad."

"But don't you just want to climb the walls, do anything to get out, even . . . die?"

"Pup and I play cards. He takes good care of me. It's fun."

"Oh. Well, isn't the food terrible?"

"It's OK. At least it's not peanut butter and jelly sandwiches." Joe laughed. "Pup's a nice guy, you know. And really he's a pretty good cook."

Of course he was! How could she have forgotten his delicious stews and meatloaves, their gin rummy games, their long companionable talks when Pup had so patiently helped her through her atomic depressions. In fact, Pup was the only person in Coconino who had ever cooked Krazy a meal! *Never again,* she thought sadly.

On the way out she met the frowning policeman. "Son, if you should happen to see Krazy Kat you might tell her that things are going too far now. It's not right to hurt the mailman."

Dejected, she returned home to Ignatz and his dispirited followers. They were famous now. But hated. Maybe really poor people loved their avant-garde performance art, but *everyone* despised them for what had happened to Joe Stork. They blamed COMISALAD—and Krazy Kat particularly, as if it were her sexual allure that had sirened Joe to the rocks. (Had Ignatz *known* what might happen to Joe? Did he envy Joe his long legs?)

COMISALAD *had,* finally, gone too far. They shouldn't have hurt the mailman. It was a federal rap. Ignatz said that if they were caught, Hearst and the F. Bee-Eyes would see that they were shot "resisting arrest." And they all felt they would deserve it. Still, Krazy was as anxious when she even thought of leaving COMISALAD as she had been when she thought of leaving her mother. (Not, she thought sadly, that she *had* ever left her, even when she had sought damnation. In her dreams, she hugged the devil from behind, and when he turned he wore her mother's face.)

Their guilt about Joe created all-seeing eyes. When they weren't watching the TV, Ignatz made them turn the screen to the wall. The government had installed a secret device—called a nielsen—so the TV set could watch them! And who knew what all else the government might have planted? The ComiSalads skulked about, or slept huddled together—all but Ignatz—in one corner of the house. Or tried to sleep. Krazy dozed fitfully, and when she woke clumps of her fur were lying beside her, like a foretaste of . . .

"Death," Ignatz said, "is beautiful." Self-criticism sessions now meant Ignatz preaching in a slow, syrupy, hypnotic drawl. Did he *never* sleep anymore? Wearing his long robe, he sat all night long in the center of their circle, surrounded by candles. "ComiSalads aren't just ready to die. We *want* to die! Dying makes you round."

"We do?" a feline voice demurred. "It does?" Living by dying? The no that was yes again!

Ignatz poured himself some plum wine, drank it down,

and rubbed his stomach contentedly. Krazy could tell that talking about death gave Ignatz a nice sense of self. Death was the enemy who just wouldn't quit! It called up his ultimate heart-pounding wacka-wacka! Just before you die, Krazy thought, you must fight back so hard that you turn into a balloon as big as the world!

COMISALAD, Ignatz said, had begun with wonderful lies about posters, video games, lunch boxes, and a comic book about them—which had fooled the cat into joining. And *that* had gotten them on TV. Fiction had made reality. A good start! But COMISALAD had to move *beyond* fiction, into *history*. "How do we show people that COMISALAD-ONE isn't just another flat, phony image?"

"Well, how?" straight kat Krazy asked.

"By having people die. Death is what never really happens to phony images. Real history means death."

"What people die?" asked Krazy, quick-frozen with terror mortis.

Ignatz wet his paw and—pssst—snuffed out a candle. "Us."

Staring at the black wick, Krazy tried to imagine death. She saw everyone but her walking on Main Street. But she still *saw*. So she wasn't really dead—unless being dead meant you were a camera. She thought of her soul not watching from above, but becoming a small part of all of Coconino, its mesas, its stores, its street. But then Mock Duck said, "Hi, Krazy!" and all the plants and houses and grass said, "Hi, Mr. Duck." She tried not saying Hi back, but that wasn't like being dead, it was like being buried alive, her mouth stuffed with dirt. So she shut her eyes so she couldn't hear or see. But *she* was the one who couldn't hear or see, so there she was, that darn cat, still alive.

Ignatz droned on—a salesman for death. Krazy dreamed about escape, even giving herself up to a Thority. She *knew* she would be shackled like a pet and taken to an academic art school where they would use flea powder on her. She would have to wear a coarse blue cotton uniform, and they would make her draw representationally. But it was better than *the thing she couldn't even imagine.*

"You can't leave," Ignatz said, almost pleadingly, awakening sleep-talking Krazy. "There are posters of you all over Berkeley and Cambridge! There are Krazy lunch boxes and video games. There's even a comic book about you! You're the Queen of COMISALAD! You can't let your fans down by surrendering. You *have* to die for them!"

A comic book, Krazy had thought. That was nice of everybody. But she still didn't want *the thing she couldn't even imagine.*

None of them did. So, terrified, they turned on each other. Milton, Marshall, and Irving refused to eat any more peanut butter and jelly. Mrs. Mice, who nowadays wore a very lovely black-felt ribbon bow tie, said that Ignatz should let one of the *truly* oppressed—like a woman rodent—lead.

Krazy hated the tension between the mice: it was so like a family dinner where her mother, and her father—making one of his rare cameos at home—were generals of opposing armies. "I know," she said, "let's all have some soup!"

So, naturally, they then turned on her. She didn't love poor people enough. She did funny things that would make people laugh instead of shocking them. She was too cold, she never wanted to play music with the other women. She was a millstone around their necks. The revolution would probably have already occurred if it weren't for Krazy Kat.

She sank back into herself. She feared the police. She ate; drank; didn't think.

And watched TV. Eyes glazed with fatigue, they had just finished viewing the Producer's big, new comeback picture, *This Is the Twentieth Century!:*

INTERIOR. Living room with a worn blue sofa.

Oppie's mother, a beautiful blonde woman, walks around the table where a dark-haired little boy pores over newclear fizzsticks problems. He looks up. She smiles her approval.

OPPIE: But Mom, I want to be an art student, a movie producer!

MOM: Back to work on your E, Ms, and C squares. You will be the most powerful scientist the world has ever seen! You will make my revenge!

Cut to: Oppie's Mom doing *anything* on the blue couch with local salesmen, to get money for schoolbooks for her boy.

Cut to close-up: Oppie talking to his fiancée.

OPPIE: How do I feel about my mom! She controlled me! But she made me special, a genius! I love her, the cunt!

Cut to: Oppie dancing on the Alamogordo tower as atomic bombs explode beneath him.

OPPIE: Top o' the World, Ma! Top o' the World!

So this *was* the twentieth century—for the world the bomb made was as mixed with good and evil as Oppie's feelings towards his mom. Was the modern world, Krazy asked herself, a hateful wonder? A wonderful horror?

When, suddenly, a NEWS BULLETIN interrupted the credit crawl. Her heart bumped downstairs, and Krazy braced for atomic flash-boom, as she always did when her favorite shows were interrupted by History. But, instead, an excited Joe Stork announced that Krazy Kat's house had been surrounded! K-KAT's Mobile Crew was live at the scene!

The police had snuck up on them! They heard the sirens wail! And on TV they saw the SWAT team take up positions on the roofs opposite, their rifles pointed down the Comi-Salads' throats.

Kiyoti ran to the window to look outside, then staggered back to the screen, dazed, confused. "There's no one there!"

"It's a trick," Ignatz said. "The outside is a lie! The truth is on TV!" He made them tear down the tattered rice-paper shades, and cover the windows with old newspapers, so they wouldn't be fooled.

National Guardsmen, in khaki uniforms, marched towards the house, firing gas canisters from wide-mouthed guns. On TV, smoke billowed from the windows. The ComiSalads gagged, their eyes red, tears streaming down their fur and feathers.

Offissa Pup's baritone bullhorn-boomed through the walls: "For the love of God, surrender while you still have the chance to come out of there alive!"

Alive! Oh my God, *what was she doing in this house!* Well, what choice had she ever had? They had made her weak and dependent, and then filled her mind with *their* ideas. The same way Mom had brainwashed infant Krazy into *her* bourgeois beliefs about keepitallism, and funny comic strips, and manhogome. Krazy's brain had been washed and rewashed!

So it wasn't her house, it wasn't her notconscious, and they weren't *her* beliefs! But *she* was going to die anyway!

Pup's bullhorn voice boomed that if they didn't come out in ten seconds, police incendiary bombs would set the house on fire! And she heard the burly-words overhead, that awful noise that filled her brain like whirling knives of sound! The burly-words would drop fire bombs and fragmentation bombs, and newtown bombs that would kill the ComiSalads but leave the furniture standing (if she had had any furniture left!) and germ bombs, and they would film overhead shots of her house breaking into flames—while she and Ignatz stared mesmerized at the screen, spectators at the spectacle that burned them up!

She glanced at the others, their eyes fixed on the TV. Her comrades had never had less perspective, never been flatter. How come, if feeling yourself dying was supposed to make you real and round? It was the TV! *It* had finally made them as flat as the screen itself! It was TV that made Mr. Death into just another sit-com pal. She *never* felt her wacka-wacka willful self when she watched television—even when the show was soldiers marching on her house to kill her! She felt like whipped cream! Don't like dying? Just change the channel! The ComiSalads thought that because they were watching themselves die on TV they wouldn't truly die—because they were just watching TV!

She held up her arm—so insubstantial, she could poke a finger through it. Her "real" body was on TV—and a TV body never died! Just rerun the tape!

Pup was right, she *had been hypnotized.* The TV had ordered them to do sillier and flatter and sillier things to get on TV—to make history!—and it made them think that *what* they did didn't really matter. Even if it killed them!

Maybe if she could imagine her death she could tear her eyes from the devil cube and skedaddle out of this house!

And suddenly she saw that everything that had happened to her since her kidnapping had been an education in imagining *the thing she couldn't imagine,* planting little seeds whose blackness now bloomed inside her. She felt the taste of ash in her mouth, the rotten taste on her tongue, the dirt flaking down on her head, the pennies holding her eyes shut, the ice moving through her veins. And then she felt her fur on fire, as she ran through the streets of Paris, till she was completely consumed by the flames, *not* seeing, *not* hearing, *not*

But then another voice—a familiar, rapid tenor—rang outside, like Jesus telling Lazarus he was late for dinner. It was the Producer! And he shouted: "Ringalevio! Allie Allie in Free! Come out! Come Out! All your demands have been met! *You now own the rights to yourselves!*"

The TV suddenly went blank. The ComiSalads awoke as if Svengali had snapped his fingers. They staggered out into the sunlight.

Where there was no one on her lawn but Pup and the Producer! His lovely green hellocopter stood a little ways off, with her friend, the Assistant, sitting behind the controls. He waved to her. Without thinking, Krazy waved back.

"Great production, Pup!" the Producer said.

"Couldn't have staged it without that lovely news footage you lent me."

"Well, it's all show biz!"

"Still, I don't think they would have ever surrendered. It's a good thing you arrived." A smiling Pup pointed towards the copter: "Deus Ex Gadget!"

The Producer gave his unpleasant battering imitation of hilarity. "Well, little ones," he said, holding his arms wide to the former ComiSalads, "congratulations! You own the rights to yourself. Sort of."

"What do you mean sort of?" Ignatz said. Krazy could tell the Mouse wanted to be angry, but he was too dazed—so flat that she could almost see his edges.

"Well, *you* own the rights to yourselves. *I* own the rights to you. Hell, even John Q. can do whatever he wants with you! You're public figures now, my darlings! *Everyone* owns the rights to you! Brilliant idea, huh?"

"What?" Ignatz staggered backwards onto Krazy's paw, but she'd lost all feeling in "her" foot anyway—wherever it was.

"No credit to me, though. It was the Big I Am's megacept. The money man. You know, Hearst. He said that if he just didn't reply to your letters, you were bound to do something so outlandish it would make his newspapers. Then we wouldn't have to pay you royalties anymore. And we could put you on posters, on lunch boxes, on video games. Even have a comic book about you! Cheaper that way. Super, huh?" He banged his meaty hands together in applause. "So what did you think of my A-bomb movie?"

Krazy screamed. The Pup had lied! No one was surrounding the house, it had just been old news footage on TV! Ignatz had lied! There was no revolution! The Producer had lied! *HEARST HAD LIED!* All a woman found in this world was false mail from false males! Her mom was right: She was born, she would live, and she would die surrounded by lying men, and dying wouldn't make a damn bit of difference! It wouldn't be any truer than anything else! *Or would it?* Her tail rose behind her, her ass moved back and forth, her consciousness flickered in her skull, her claws appeared; and, as she leaped towards the Producer's fat nose, her mind shrank to a tiny, dimensionless point, the last blip on the turned-off TV screen. And went out.

VENUS IN FURS

It was going to be a *very* long time, Krazy decided, before she played with that Ignatz Mouse again. His games were just too rough! In fact, the last one had so throwmetized her that she had spent two whole weeks lying on her back in the middle of her rug, arms and legs rigid in the air, recooperating from the recent coo. How could such a thing? Kwakk Wakk was disinforming everyone that Krazy herself had leaped at the Producer's bulb nose, that she would have scratched his muddy eyes out if she hadn't fallen to the desert floor, stiff as an upturned table. What vile gossip! Krazy *never* got angry, so she *knew* she could not have done such a than. Thung. Theng. It wasn't *her* nonexistent rage, but Ignatz's COMISALAD high jinks that had turned her into furniture.

Still, the Mouse *had* come to visit her every day, spoon-feeding her strawberry ice cream till she could at least pogo-stick around her house by herself. And his new game—*Fantasy*—did sound intriguing. Ignatz said they were to imagine the sort of human beings they would be if they were to be human beings.

Krazy thought it over as she goose-stepped her stiff self to the kitchen with the crick-crack-pound-your-comrade's-back of the Red Army on parade. She piled a round wicker tray with a pot of tea and two cups, and soft-shoe shuffled her way to the dining room table. Carefully—for she had difficulty sighting the cup at stiff-arm's length—she poured the Mouse some tea in the precious Zuni cup, with its tracery of mended cracks. (Today the lines formed a sleeping flamingo, its head tucked beneath its wing.)

Lips pursed, Ignatz took a judicious sip. Fantasy, he said, was a necessity for Krazy. Her therapy hadn't succeeded before because flat characters didn't know about sex. But when they were people they would have the real sweet stuff and Ignatz would be able to Cy,Go!Annielies! Krazy more deeply. They would return to Coconino as healthier, rounder artists.

Krazy considered. *Here*, she thought, and then *there?* Would *she* change? Who? Which? Where?

"Of course it means you'll have to fuck, and you know . . ."

Krazy shuddered. Her stiff legs stuck straight out beneath the table. What was Ignatz hiding? And how could it be worse than sex? "And what?"

"Well, you know . . . die. A little, I mean. I mean, I think we'll age."

Krazy's sensitive kat-ears picked up Ignatz's tremolo. He, too, was scared. *Die*, Krazy thought. Her fur on fire. No more fur. No more her. *The thing she couldn't even imagine.* Still, Ignatz the Artist eternally impressed her. Ignatz's Amazing New Art-Science—with its internal battle between sex-hunger and table manners—had given the Mouse a little inkle of roundness. He had been chiseled out of that by the Producer, by his own lust to be seen on a jillion flat screens. Now, for high art, for roundness, Ignatz would risk humanness—even if it meant their doing really embarrassing things, and . . . dying. "OK," she said. Her brain bubbled a bit with carefree champagne. After all, it was only a fantasy. "I'll have nice breasts," she said. And, surprisingly, her words left the taste of honey on her tongue. Long ago, when they had first tried sighcowandallis,is, Ignatz had forced her to fib to him. But until now she hadn't seen the use of it.

"Yes!" Ignatz shouted. His big front teeth glistened with delight. Krazy was very pleased that he was pleased. His pleasure meant: *print it.* She *would* have nice breasts.

"And I'm a blond Satan. The smooth thickness of my arms, legs, and body, the sag of my big rounded shoulders, make my body like a bear's. It is like a shaved bear's: my chest is hairless. My skin is childishly soft and pink."

Oh, Krazy knew *that* fellow! It was Sam Spade. Ignatz worshiped the gumshoe. *He* wouldn't play the sap for any bimbo, even lovely, guileful Brigid O'Shaughnessy. Well, except *this* time! Krazy decided. This time Ignatz *will* play the sap for *me.* (Wait! Snip-snip. *I never thought that.*) "No," she said. "You're thin and small." But he was still too threatening. "You have big ears. And you wear glasses." *There,* she thought, now I can love him. He needs my protection. She sipped some tea contentedly. (Just plain orange pekoe and cut pekoe blends, contrary to Radio Kwakk Wakk's daily "Relapse Reports.") Fantasy Ignatz wouldn't be a spiteful tough guy. He'd be cream-centered candy, Stan Laurel–like—sensitive, and very quick to weep.

"You're making me small to hurt me," Ignatz whined.

"Don't be soooly. I mean sally." Krazy covered her mouth and tried to pretend to cough.

"Couldn't I be a little taller?"

"OK. But you're still thin."

"The Thin Man," the Mouse asked hopefully.

"No. Just *a* thin man. Nothing special. Except to me."

She hummed "My Funny Valentine," but Ignatz didn't smile. "You can have the hairless chest," she added. "And the soft pink skin."

"Ugh!" Big-eyed, he stared across the table at her, half-afraid of her power.

Wow! She fixed his shape! He had to take the part, because *he* wanted to star in *her* fantasy! She bent down to lap tea from her cup and, giggling with pleasure, spluttered some on her white fur. This was great! She licked herself clean.

"Well," he said, "I'm called Sam."

Krazy laughed. "Don't be silly! You're Ignatz." Ignatz was Ignatz after all, just the way Bogart was Sam Spade was Hammett was Bogart. No matter what part he played he would still be Ignatz.

He smiled maliciously and stroked his big nose. "I'll bet you want me to look Jewish, too, like Oppenheimer." He handed her his cup for a refill.

Krazy hopped across the living room to get more hot water from her orange kettle, the teapot held out in front of her, sloshing lightly. She felt a little peckish. Some cookies would be nice. Where was her flowered English cake plate?

"No," she said emphatically, returning with the refilled pot. "You *don't* look like Mr. Oppenheimer." She would keep Oppie to herself. Even in the world of Fantasy, she thought, it would be good to have a fantasy that was all her own.

As for Krazy, Ignatz said she would be pretty, with a thin nose, widely spaced almond eyes, good cheekbones, nice breasts, and long full legs. She would be very desirable.

That was nice, Krazy thought. Well, but *sure*, of course, he was just pleasing himself! Men! (And strawberry ice cream, she remembered, was *his* favorite flavor, not hers.)

She would have the shape of Mary Astor, Krazy said. Ignatz nodded. Brigid, Krazy thought, had had special sap-making feminine power. It had something to do with wearing hats. When she was human, Krazy decided, she would get herself a lot of hats—not the dowdy Church of England boxes that Kwakk Wakk wore, but beautiful hats, with mysterious veils.

"But you're very troubled," Ignatz added. And Krazy knew he wanted to mar her slightly. He wouldn't like a woman with less than petite ears and big bazooms, so he made her flaw inward. "You're a graduate student in art history. But you're blocked. You can't finish your dissertation. That's why you're seeing a therapist. Me. Dr. Ignatz."

Krazy scrunched her eyes, making him disappear.

"You're a blocked graduate student *at Harvard*," the Mouse offered in a wheedling tone.

Big ivy-covered deal! Well, probably he wanted to be her therapist because he wanted to be needed, too. "OK," she said. But her whiskers twitched; her jaw fur itched with suspicion. Maybe Mr. All But Dissertation didn't want little-bitty *her* going beyond him! She bent down to the table edge and rubbed it against her cheek. "But you're not a medical doctor." She smiled slyly, her mouth invisible beneath the table. "No germs. No death. Just PhDs."

The Mouse's little face scrunched to a baby's wrinkled pan. "I have to be a real doctor," he whimpered. "It's what my father wanted. It's what *his* mother had wanted for him. It's what *he* dreamed of for *me.*"

"No," Krazy said. "You're a PhD. That's what *I* want."

Ignatz put his head between his hands and stared emptily at the initials he had once carved into her table. Next he'd say, It's *your* fault, unambitious Kat, that we're so vapid, innocent, tasteless. Followed by his second act: *I'm* no good, flat, talentless. And then DEPRESSION's whacko finale: We're one of God's murderous thoughts, and the world is a dung heap.

Anything but that! "OK. All right, Ignatz. MD. But I think your father's always been more important to you than I have." Anyway, Krazy thought, *if* someone were going to play the sap for someone else, wouldn't it be more fun if he were a powerful medical doctor?

"My father . . ." Ignatz began, but then grounded himself.

Krazy knew. He wanted to say: My father wasn't in the rag trade. My father was a doctor, a cultured university professor. But his unhappy dad, the I-CASH-CLOTHES-MAN, was the unwobbling Ignatz pivot. It couldn't be changed, not singlehandedly. And Krazy wasn't going to help. She hadn't liked rebellious Ignatz's angry attachment to him, but she had liked the sound of hardworking, protective Papa Ignatz, with his wire-rimmed spectacles, forever depressed and guilty because he couldn't be the doctor his mama had wanted, yet building his business from the ground up, a peddler become . . . well, perhaps it was a precarious living, but he was *there* for his family.

"My father," Ignatz concluded sadly, inevitably, "was a cloak and suiter." He smiled up at Krazy from his hands. "You can be blonde," he offered grandly.

"I don't want to be." Why would anyone want to be a helpless, hopeless blondie-pie! *That* was what Ignatz wanted. She wanted to be the dark-haired fatal one with the spicy hair and the almond eyes! The one who didn't feel guilty about *anything! "You* can be blond. Your *children* can be blond. Your *wife* can be blonde!" she shouted. But Krazy knew her hair would be straw-colored. That was what Ignatz wanted, so—stop the presses!—it became what she wanted, because what she *really* wanted was to be what he wanted.

Just as he wanted to be what she wanted him to be. Mirrors looking at mirrors!

"My wife?" Ignatz said, exhaling slowly.

"You're married," Krazy said. She could see that they were both relieved by this turn in the story. "But you're separated from the Mrs." Why separated? Why not divorced? Why not, *Never happened?* Well, then he'll have to *choose* me, Krazy thought. Besides, he wouldn't always be in her hair, her lovely blonde, I mean black, oh, hell, blonde hair. "Every Tuesday you visit your *estranged* wife. You stay over till Wednesday. But you don't have any children."

"I *don't?*" Ignatz smiled in crooked bewilderment. A moment before he would have said that Milton, Marshall, and Irving were the lodestars of his life. But now the Gulf Stream of warm Reprieve laved his face. "*You* have a mother," Ignatz said.

"Oh, Ignatz!" Krazy laughed. "*Everybody* has a mother!"

"She was once a famous actress. She gave up her career to marry your father."

"She was? She did?" Uh, oh! Unsatisfied mothers add hungry jet-fuel agony to a daughter's career!

"But she's devoted to him."

"Yes!" Krazy cried, clapping her paws together. "And *he* stays home with her. He doesn't stroll down every alley!" *There!* Her mother would be happy! So Krazy wouldn't have to fulfill Mom's unlived lives. Perfecto! Ignatz would be a medical doctor as per his dad's prescription, and his dad would protect him and cherish him, and mother him. So maybe *Doctor* Ignatz wouldn't have to be as I So Late as her rebel Mouse was, holding himself apart from everyone so meanly, walking with such proud, bitter independence. And Krazy would come from an uncracked home, with a Rockwell mom who wanted grandkittens. They'd both be on easy street!

"Yes. She had a good home. And your mother doesn't care if you have a career. She thinks family is more important. *Much* more important."

"Yes!" Krazy clapped her paws together above her head and capered almost nimbly around the table in a peg-leg tour jette. "Oh play that junkyard music, Ignatz!" Free at last of actingclasseselocutionclassesmusicclassesbeingmymom's-childclasses! "And *I* have a husband, too." So there, Mouse. But her left side shivered with anxiety.

"Your husband's a psychoanalyst, also. Sort of."

Santa Ignatz was handing out nice Jewish doctors! Strangely, Krazy grew depressed.

"You're separated," he added.

"Thank God!" Krazy said. Why? Her new, contented mother *wanted* her to have a family, a husband. But to wake up every morning beside a body stale from sleep—that awful sour-cream smell—she would have to lick him all day! How could she ever get her dissertation done?

"And I'll have hands," Ignatz said quietly.

"Of course you'll have hands," Krazy said. *"Everybody has hands!"* Ignatz had always been so proud of his near-human-quality paw dexterity, his skill with his nails. He was even able to thread a needle! But paws, she saw, were as nothing. If she gave him hands he would be able to be affectionate with her, stroking, unrushed. Why, she would even let his dancing digits tickle the ivories! He'd like that! Krazy smiled, remembering Oppie's lovely hands. In this, she thought, I will please myself utterly. "You have beautiful hands, with long, thin, aristocratic fingers." She felt them smoothing her fur and purred lightly. "Fantasy" was fun. She hadn't felt so nearly mingled with Ignatz since the bricks had started to hurt. Today they drank themselves from the same cup.

"Thank you," Ignatz said softly, with the downcast eyes of a grateful supplicant. "And I'd like to have . . . to have a big . . . cock."

"What?" Large? Loud? Doodle-doo?

"A big, you know, penis . . . a big cock."

"What? *Why?*" What earthly difference did *that* make. Who would ever know? Oh well, if it was something *he* wanted. But then she saw that Ignatz's form bent the light for her. The Producer's lessons taught that Ignatz must truly be telling her something *she* wanted, too. Even if she hadn't known she wanted it. Even if it wasn't exactly *nice*. *"Yes,"* she said, as if from a trance, her own eyes downcast.

"Thank you."

"Thank *you*," she said.

■ ■ ■

Dr. Ignatz remembered the second time they had shaken hands, at the end of the first month's sessions. She had held his hand longer than he expected. "You have lovely fingers," she had said, with unselfconscious appreciation. Her hand was soft, supple, not the almost rigid thing that had half-grasped his at the beginning of their work together. "Thank you," he had said. Her touch had made him feel mixed with her, fused for a moment. *I am her doctor,* he had thought, *I should not feel this*—even as he prolonged the press of her hand on his. Already, he had been bewitched by her. Her skin was dark, yet her hair naturally blonde, and her broad cheekbones, her bright brown eyes and full lips had something unplaceable about them, perhaps a surprising conjunction of many nationalities; her face a poem. A figure at a bazaar. (Beware, his father's voice said. A gentile and a Jew are like a cat and a mouse. Their embrace is a perversion; against God; against nature.) "Thank *you*," she had replied, again with that same openheartedness—and just enough irony so that neither of them had to be embarrassed.

He had gone back to his desk then to bring order to the month's notes. Fifteen minutes till the next patient. He remembered that he had thought it had been a good beginning. A good hysteric! *Now* he sat naked on a corner of that desk, the huge antique one that his wife had chosen for him. He looked down at his once pointless, inadequate, weak, hairless pink body. But when Kate had stroked his chest, brought her fingernails across his nipples, it was as if *this* body—oh, impossible!—were truly what she desired, what she had always wanted! Suffused with inner warmth, he looked down at the long-lined yellow pages of her case spread out in front of him like the shards of a broken mirror.

> 6/31/85 Catherine Higgs Bosun. (But she insists that her nickname should have a K to it.) Twenty-eight years old. Recommended to me by my Supervisor. (Her husband is a well-known art historian, and a colleague at The Boston Psychoanalytic Institute.)

> A sweet, long-legged fellow. He spoke often—and brilliantly—giving psychoanalytic readings of art for the Friends of the Institute, and he had (rare honor) been allowed to attend classes as a lay candidate. Dr. Ignatz remembered him from Dream Seminar. Very tall. A kind, bemused air. He's bewitched, too.

—Joe Stork! Krazy shouted. She felt like she was watching one of those movies where you spot stars in cameo parts. She and Ignatz sat at her dining room—well, dining *area*—table, letting the tea things grow cold, staring into the middle distance where their producer-words created rooms; people to occupy them; roles for the people to play.

*   *   *

Oh, how pleased he had been by the referral, Dr. Ignatz
remembered. It showed a high degree of esteem on his analyst's part. And Dr. Ignatz—Almost Analyzed Dr. Ignatz—
still lived for that. He shivered. The air conditioning. His
body now was covered with sweat. His. Hers. They had
drunk each other from the same cup. Could this have been
what his eminent father figure, analysand of Helene
Deutsch, bow-tied head of the Institute's Supervisors, had
wanted? No, of course not. He had referred Kate because he
trusted Dr. Ignatz, had thought that Kate would work well
with him—a very promising analyst, the youngest ever to
publish an article in *The International Journal of Psychoanalysis.* ("The Hysteric's Question: Am I a Man or a
Woman?" Abstract: Woman's dual-phasic development pre-
disposes her to gender confusion. Does the infant girl want
to be her mother's lover or her competitor? And the little
girl's long period of protected dependence reinforces this
problem. She lives in a hemi-demi-semi-paradise, a world set
apart, which allows her fantasy life to flower luxuriantly,
trees turning into cacti into mesas. This hypertrophy of fantasy enables the girl to imagine herself as a boy, almost to see
the necessary addition. Reciprocally, the confusion about
gender allows her fantasies to run wild in other areas of her
life, for those who are confused *there* may lack the crucial
fixed point to their identity by which other realities can be
tested.) The Sup could never, never, never have imagined
that anything like this love between Kate and Ignatz could
happen. *Could he?*

Higgs is her mother's maiden name. She
remembers her father as a "figure seen at a distance." A tall man in khaki pants, with beautiful
hands and eyes. He is a physicist—the youngest
man to have worked on the Manhattan Project, she

said proudly—and he later named a particle for Catherine, "a higgs bosun."

"The particle appears," Catherine told me, "breaks the gauge symmetry and then disappears."

I asked her what that meant.

"I don't know. I mean all that belonged to my father. You know, it all leads to the end of the world. I think it also meant he thought I might break the symmetry between my mother and him."

Kate hadn't broken the symmetry. Her mother had been utterly devoted to her family, unambivalently so, Kate feels—though perhaps a programmatic quality on her mother's part betrayed some reservations. Satisfaction for a woman, her mother insisted, is only in caring for a husband and children. Anything else was a charade.

Though Kate had felt very close to her mother, she had been unable to bear her mother's dying, and so had rarely visited her in the hospital. Her mother had been a great beauty, and she couldn't stand to see how her face was transformed by the cancer, reduced to bone and eye. She feels very guilty for this, and thinks it might be part of her problem about work.

The outlines of Kate's dilemma are clear. The realm of work—of her dissertation—belongs to her father. Dangerous to touch. "It all leads to the end of the world." And her work would be a sham, anyway. For to be a woman is to have a family, to be completely submissive to others' needs. When Kate tries to write, she feels anxious, fraudulent. She is lonely, empty, unwomanly, unlovable. But when she is with her husband, she feels as if her self has disappeared. She belongs to him completely—dependent, subservient, his "pet." (So she and her husband have separate apartments, but see each other every night for dinner. And she often has affairs, so that she can be between two men, protected from her desire to be possessed.) Caught in the web of these prohibitions, she denies herself either satisfying love or work.

He had, informally, gone over his thoughts with the Sup. Unusual for an analyst to talk as much as the Sup did now, acting as both Dr. Ignatz's therapist, and his Supervisor. But Dr. Ignatz was nearing the end of his treatment. And the Sup was old enough, wise enough, to elaborate his own techniques. Sup was a large, broad, yet stern-faced Irishman, famous for his analytic lineage, his bow ties and three-piece suits, and his instructive scrutiny of the countertransference phenomenon—how one's feelings towards the patient were a guide in unriddling the personality, yours and the patient's. This Celt had for decades been the embodiment of the rules for the mostly Jewish Boston analytic community. Now he was the meter stick itself. What he did was lawful because *he* did it. "Closing time," the Sup had said last week. "I need only love and do what I will." (Why closing time? Was Ignatz nearing the end of his own analysis? That filled him with pride—and mild tachycardia. Or—and suddenly a deeper fear fluttered his heart—was Sup hinting that his persistent, mysterious cough was something more serious than bronchitis?) Anyway, these last weeks, Sup had become expansive, voluble; he seemed almost—but that was impossible!—emotionally involved with Kate's case. Well, Sup *had* seemed very interested in Kate from the first. *Why* so intrigued? Was it because her husband was a colleague? Sup had even, once, asked Dr. Ignatz to describe what Kate had been wearing! It was unsettling.

* * *

The second month Kate told him of an incident that had unsettled her. A friend of her husband's had visited her, an art historian of about forty, very upper class, very well-known. Even Dr. Ignatz had heard of this don, for he often wrote in a patrician, *Artforum* way, on popular culture. She had been flattered by his attention. "You won't understand," she told Ignatz, as most patients sometimes did—meaning *I'm afraid that you will understand, that you can see everything, I'm flat, just drawn on a piece of paper*—"but he made me feel as if I were the most important person in the world to him, as if I *were* the whole world. I knew who I was then: I was a beautiful *woman*. I slept with him. Then, afterwards . . . For weeks I've been terrified that I'm pregnant—though I know it's just a way of punishing myself."

—No, Krazy said, that's too fast, it's going too fast. I'm not ready for that yet.

—OK, Ignatz said.

Krazy heard the Mouse's anxiety melisma, and that quaver made her want to go on even more quickly. For she knew just how Kate felt, hipsmoretied on the couch, the mommy therapist tending to helpless, hopeless her. Fun in its way—like being bathed, and gently spoon-fed. But Dr. Ignatz was the kidnapper, the Producer. She talks, but *he* knows what she's talking about. *He* decides when her no means yes. If Kate were ever to get the rights to herself, it would come from her long legs, her sap-making powers; it was all the situation left her. "Go on," Krazy whispered to her, "dress the part." She wanted Kate to be a devil in nylon hose, to wear black stockings, ones with seams, the soft silky kind that even Krazy's retracted claws would have ripped. They thought women were witches who knelt for every drummer in town! Fine! She would show them! Or Kate would. Kate would be really bad-bottomed. Kate would have all the pleasures one shouldn't allow oneself. She would say poo-poo as much as she wanted! But could Krazy even give advice? She and Ignatz were having the "fantasy," but it was having them, too, taking them places they hadn't expected. Sometimes she didn't even know what she truly desired until the story showed her. Just as she hadn't known what was important in her yesterday until she saw the morning's strip and—bang!—those frames were her memory, the past she then had to build on.

The next session Kate told Dr. Ignatz that she had gotten his article from Widener Library. Patients often did that, a way of flirting with him. But he felt his fingers straightening his tie, stroking it.

"Do you think that's me? I *am* so confused. Maybe I don't know whether I'm a man or a woman. I don't know whether I'm black or white . . ." She waited for him to speak. "I talk white, but I'm black inside."

"What?"

"My paternal grandfather was Negro. There," she said, smiling, "the family skeleton exposed at last."

The broad bones of her face, her beautiful lips made more sense—though that sense only added to their enchantment. "But you're blonde!" Dr. Ignatz said, despite himself.

Kate laughed. "Do you think I should dye my hair black? I told you, I don't fit together! Should I be a man or a woman, a scholar or a housewife? Or should I be a performer? Did I ever tell you I wanted to be a singer? I knew that it wasn't worthy enough. My mother would never approve—that's why Mom gave it up! It's just *entertainment!*"

Smiling, Dr. Ignatz explained—delighted to speak the words that the Sup had once spoken to him, feeling almost Sup-like as he did it—how the analyst could be Kate's new, *approving* internal object, that we make our personalities out of such bits and pieces of others that we take inside ourselves. Introjects, they were called. Kate could introject the approving, feminine, maternal aspect of him.

She smiled ironically, but pleasantly, as if they shared a joke. "So what am I, motherdoctor?" She walked her fingers down the buttons of her blouse. "Man, woman, black, white, singer, scholar, housewife, beggar man, thief? You decide."

She meant: she wanted to be what he wanted.

The next week she trusted him enough to tell him her most cherished fantasy. A golden oldie, she said: She was on a raised platform, wearing only a felt collar.

"A leather collar?" Dr. Ignatz said. Her voice had dazed him.

"All right. A beautiful leather collar, like the ones pets wear." Kate's voice, too, was drowsy.

Wait, *he* shouldn't be furnishing *her* fantasy! Sup's internalized baritone said: *Keep silent, Dr. Ignatz!*

A roomful of completely dressed men watched her. She always imagined this scene when making love. "It makes me feel like I'm not really there in the bed. The real me is watching myself being watched by a roomful of men with their cocks out." But she couldn't come without the fantasy. "Do you think that is why I wanted to be a singer—a performer—to have an audience?"

A hysteric, Dr. Ignatz had thought. They must *look* at her so she might exist, but they mustn't *touch* her—her fear of intimacy. And for a moment Kate grew flat and distant.

Hah! Krazy kicked up at the table with her leg, rattling the cups. You stop that, Dr. Ignatz! Remember when the Producer visited Coconino, and Kwakk Wakk, and Don Kiyoti, and a certain Ignatz Mouse had felt they would exist again only if a million fully clothed people watched them on a movie screen! And then your COMISALAD shenanigans didn't really happen when we did them, but after, when we were back at the safe house—her house!—watching them on TV! If this was histears-eee!-ow! then it was certainly the epicdemack twentieth-century whyrus!

She needs to be seen, Dr. Ignatz thought, just as the Sup had said. She disappears when she's alone. He looked over at her, lying on his couch. She wasn't wearing a bra, and she had two buttons of her blouse open. He could see the sides of her breasts, and her nipples stiff beneath the gray silk. Her long legs were crossed at the ankle. Then, as if she felt his eyes on her, she uncrossed her legs, and raised her knees. Her soft blue skirt fell toward her waist, showing the tops of her stockings and her garters. He hadn't known women still wore garters! His doodle-doo grew stiff. "Oh," she said non-sensically, "I can bend my knees!" As if that needed to be proved! Really, she was just justifying her self-exposure. She hummed, as she often did during her silences, snatches of long-ago popular songs, her motor idling, contentedly. What were the words to the song? It was one his mother used to sing, in the car, on the way to a Broadway show. His mother, too, had lovely legs. " 'In olden days a glimpse of stocking was looked on as something shocking, But heaven knows, now Anything Goes!' " I can name that tune in five notes, he thought, charmed by Kate's irony. His mother, too, had loved popular music. "Trash!" his father's voice had said, in the front seat when he was a child; inside him when Dr. Ignatz used to improvise with his college band; and now when he looked at jazzy Kate. Kate, too, had his mother's flickery, here-and-gone quality. *Pursue me!* And then he thought: Three hours a week I make her think she's the most important, the most interesting person in the world, that she is the world. And: I'm fully clothed, and I'm watching her fantasy of herself naked. She's teaching me how to unlock her. I could make love to her if I wanted. He saw his analyst's wise face, the long doglike ears of age, the stern yet sorrowful eyes that were so like his own father's. *Don't you want to be an analyst?* the Sup's gravel-and-ash voice would say. *This temporary infatuation could be the end of your career!* Dr. Ignatz willed the wilting of his cock. I'm not going to play the sap for her, he told himself. She's making a rapid transference. A good hysteric. But it was already becoming a mantra. Agoodhysteric. Agoosteric. A goose A trick. He wanted to make himself feel as if he were reading about Kate in a textbook. But the soft, sweet feeling, the desire to blend himself with her, wouldn't go away. She remained warm, round, compelling. How could he prefer the blueprint of a house to a room that he could enter? *She slept with the upper-class fellow,* he thought, *I wonder if she'll sleep with me?*

Kate picked up her hat from beside the Kleenex box on the small table by the couch, a round hat made from blue velvet, with a veil tucked around the rim, not in any decade's style, yet *her* style. She swirled her black-stockinged legs over the side of the sofa and sat up.

She touched the hat, straightening the veil forward. "Let's fuck," she said. "Hey!" she added, as if surprised by her own voice. "I can swear!"

"What?"

"I meant, *trust me.*" Kate smiled. She held her arms out to him, a little stiffly, unbent at the elbows, waiting.

He thought: I am not a good boy anymore, and felt his heart beat with hard wacka-wacka willfulness. He went to her, and she circled him with her arms. "My arms bend, too," she said, with what sounded like genuine surprise. Maybe she, too, was shocked that they were able to do this thing. Sup would be horrified. He wanted Dr. Ignatz to be moral, nourished by rectitude, unhappy like all the Jews since Abraham. Well, who was more important—this lovely woman or his fathers? Kate was, would be, had to be. Good, Dr. Ignatz thought, I'm bad! And, as if in response, Kate kissed him with theatrical fury, hurting his lips. He nuzzled a quarter-sized patch of discolored skin on her collarbone, and Kate made a pleasant growly sound from her throat. He slowly stroked the soft skin of her thighs, between the tops of her stockings and her lacy underwear, drinking her with his hand. "My fingers work," he said, playing with her. But his fingers *did* feel special, as if he had just recovered from a long, numbing illness, as if Kate and he had almost invented touch.

She smiled, her lips together, and purred lightly. "Oh play that junkyard music! Whip it, horns, whip it!"

The leather of his couch was vinyl and had stuck to their skin, making crackling sounds as they rolled about.

"Thank you," she said, when it was over.

It wasn't over. His career might be over. But not their lovemaking. That mustn't be over. Yet fucking had been a bittersweet disappointment, not what he had imagined. The breast that had returned to the crib wasn't precisely the one the child had had such delicious fantasies about while Mom was away.

It wasn't like what she had imagined, Krazy thought.

Ignatz Mouse stared into the distance. "It's different," he said, bemused. Yet there was something about the bitterness that could only be sweetened, satisfied, fulfilled, if they did it again.

"I want to try again," Krazy said. *By turning and turning to come round right!*

"Once more," Ignatz Mouse whispered.

* * *

"Thank *you*," Dr. Ignatz had said.

She had put her stockings back on, snapping them to her garters. Smiling at him distantly, she had smoothed her rumpled cotton skirt.

He watched her walk out, a blonde ignis fatuus, a faery light. And he knew that he would soon run after her, an Ignatz fatuous. Was that why he wanted her so, because even as she opened her arms to him, she seemed to be moving away, drawing him onward? Because she wasn't, like his wife, so always wanting, endlessly wanting, ready to chew him completely with her anger and anxiety? Perhaps chasing Kate would break the gauge symmetry, free him from his unhappy marriage-that-wasn't-a-marriage. And throw him out of the career that he loved!

He smelled her perfume on the fingers of his right hand mixed with the magical oil from her cunt—a new fragrance called DISASTER. Well, she had made him happy, and one shouldn't be happier than one's father, or than the dour substitutes he had found for his old man, like the melancholy Sup. One shouldn't move in more dimensions than one's ancestors. One *should* be punished; hurled from the Institute; trampled on by the new candidates on their way up the Commonwealth Avenue steps to Dream Seminar.

His next patient—a black philosophy student at Harvard—was due in five minutes. What if he finds me perched naked on my desk? "What a fine mess I've gotten me into!" he said to the empty air. Dr. Ignatz laughed, and a sour heaviness formed around his eyes. Then he wept, his face scrunched up like a baby's.

■ ■ ■

"Stroke your cock," she ordered.

"Thank you," he said meekly, kneeling in front of her on his office floor. Kate knew that he liked to stroke himself, or to hold his cock with his hand gently underneath, like a jeweler—or a butcher—showing off a choice piece of goods, and he performed with a pleasing small boy's innocence, not adolescent cock-proud, but as if he were delighted and surprised that he had one. Not that his cock was *that* important to Kate; she loved Ignatz one and indivisible. But *he* sometimes acted as if Mr. Cock might have its own favorite flavor of ice cream (strawberry?), presidential preference, plans for secession. In truth, though, maybe she was especially fond of his cock, so much longer and larger than one would have expected. (Expected why? Because of his height, or his job? You would think this was her first man, that she had no experience in country matters. But love was a sappy song and Korny Kansas was how she felt.) Perhaps she would even have him measure his cock for her, as she watched. He would like that. He would be proud and humiliated at once!

"Thank you," he said again.

"What?" Kate turned down the corners of her mouth with mock anger. Her haughty irritation was like wrestling or gossip—more fun to believe in than not.

"Thank you, *mistress,*" he said, looking down at the floor. "Please let me give myself to you."

That was the signal to continue a "scenario," just as the nonsense word "Pup" would mean that one of them was scared, that they should wrap for the day. How had this begun? Their scenarios—and why had they each thought to call them that?—had certainly started with some pretty straight stuff. And even now—she knew from service magazines and ladies' room gossip—they were still conventional in their plots, a graduate student and a psychiatrist, bourgey s/m, a little spice, a little dose of strichnice . . . strikenine . . . poison mixed with amyl nitrate; the galvanic kick confused with a dance step. So far there had been no cause to say "Pup." They would never draw blood, never mark the body. Would they? There was a tingle in wondering how much farther they *might* go. The second time they had fucked, he had held her hands to the couch, and murmured that she *had to take it.* What a funny phrase! Where had Dr. Ignatz learned such language? Whose script was this? A funny phrase. She had smiled, but it had made her face flush with pleasure, her coming stronger. Her attentive lover had noticed. And the next time *he* had said to *her,* "Please, make me take it." What could that mean? Each time she wondered if she would be able to continue, to improvise, new . . . humiliations! . . . for him. And then the biting and the crawling—like a baby, like a slave—had followed (but from *where?*) . . . and making him lie on the floor, sucking the high heel of her shoe as she took disdainful sips of sweet liqueurs . . . and the whipping, and . . . then? It was only a game. And what was really at stake? (*A life together,* her mother's voice said, *a marriage; the intimacies of the childbed, the sickbed, the deathbed.*)

How had this begun, Dr. Ignatz wondered—teasing himself for a moment, before giving himself up to the pleasures of the scenario—how could the Sup have let this happen? When Dr. Ignatz had announced the affair, Sup had said, "You must not see her anymore in therapy. Not even once. I'll find a referral for her." The severity had all been in those last few words: *not even once.* Each session that Dr. Ignatz spoke of Kate—and what else did he speak of anymore?—he waited to hear another lash of anger in Sup's voice. (Sup's voice was weaker these last weeks, his breath wheezy.) Was Dr. Ignatz disappointed that the anger had never come? If anything, he felt that Sup *wanted* to hear more, wanted the scenarios to go on. (But that was impossible!) And the scenarios? Had Sup been producer, there, too? Had they begun when Dr. Ignatz had held Kate's arms, pinned against the couch? That morning, during analysis, Sup had said something to him about Kate wanting to be restricted as her mother had restricted her. Had he said restricted or tied up? Anyway, Dr. Ignatz had gotten the notion that he should hold Kate down, perhaps tie her hands. He had remembered a fantasy that she had told him when she had still been his patient. (Had she ever really been his patient?) Stealing a fantasy she had entrusted him with during therapy, using the words to excite her was a crime, like . . . like plagiarism. "You're asleep in a field," he whispered. He felt like one of those phone services— your Visa card number the golden key—where a seductive voice recited your choice of fantasy from the limited menu that was the human. But he knew that if he told her what she dreamed of, he would have a powerful aura in her eyes. "Asleep on a mountainside, in a red top, naked below the waist. You can feel the grass on the backs of your legs, and it enters your dreams. A beautiful Oriental carpet. A man, a hiker, comes upon you, and your beauty is so great that he grows stiff. He has to enter you, and as he enters you, he enters your dream. If you were to wake up he would cover your mouth with his." He pressed her harder into the couch, moved inside her, releasing her arms. Her hands moved on his chest with a grasping, stroking motion, like an animal taking suck. She came.

Afterwards, Dr. Ignatz, poor prig, told her that it was a fantasy of being released from responsibility for her sexuality.

"It's a fantasy," Kate had said, smiling with closed-lip innocence, "about being held down in a field, while I sleep." And she was right—what difference did the abstractions make? They were on the same level as the fantasy—part of that other fantasy of Ignatz as a knowing doctor. He wanted to murmur in her ear again, watch the scene form in front of them, have her come.

And soon after that he had begun to tie her up, put her against the wall, pretending to whip her with his black leather belt.

All duly reported to the Sup—who said nothing, just coughed. (What did those coughs mean? Dr. Ignatz wondered. Were they perhaps Sup's way of signaling his disapproval? Or did they mean that Sup was aroused, eager for more? *Or were they a cancer in Sup's throat and lungs?* Dr. Ignatz knew that his own hopelessness often skewed his diagnosis, dumping him head first into the most melancholy possibilities.) Sup analyzed the scenarios, but—impeccable therapist—he did it without condemnation. Well, except for the slight disapproval that adhered to all psychoanalytic terms: phallic mothers and fathers with breasts, false self and narcissism. As if to have *those* desires, play with those figures, made you a fool! (Were there other kinds of desire, or was it desire itself that made you a sap?) Oh, Sup analyzed his fantasies; and for a moment Dr. Ignatz felt free—his confession in therapy redeemed the humiliation he had begged for on the floor of his office. Dr. Ignatz—through the magic of Unconscious Productions—had identified with his own fleeing fleeting mother, became her so that he would never lose her. S/he would serve Kate, would be her wife, would be punished by Kate for ever having left little bitty doctor-to-be Ignatz. And Kate was the nurturing, loving, angry father, the father with breasts, the woman with a penis. Dr. Ignatz listened to the wrap-up, Dr. Ignatz understood, but then he returned to his office, to hotel rooms, to his apartment, to wherever Kate would meet him, whenever she, in her complicated internal negotiations—as labyrinthine as any involving agents, stars, studios, rights—found herself free to want him, to do it all again. Oh, she had turned out to be a Katch-Kate-As-You-Kan, a will-of-the-wisp Higgs

Bosun! They would be embracing each other on the couch when the radiator's knocking would make Kate shiver uncontrollably, like footsteps walking over her marriage bed. It was her husband! "Crawling through the pipes?" Dr. Ignatz said, hoping to josh her out of her fear, hoping he would get to enter her. "You don't understand! You don't understand!" she would sob, meaning this time: *you don't understand.* He would spend the little time they had stolen holding her, stroking her high forehead, gentling the thoroughbred. "It's your mother you're really scared of," he analyzed. But she continued to shiver and to cry, until her stomach began to hurt, and she was unable to make love that day. Even when he was inside her cunt, he felt he didn't have her, she remained withdrawn within herself, a cat he might pet who was never *his* pet—even when he led her around the room by her hair. And, of course, this uncrossable inner distance made him want her more.

Sup analyzed. Dr. Ignatz analyzed. Kate, he supposed, with whatever new therapist she was seeing, analyzed. Oh, analysis took them backstage, so they saw all the unconscious ratchets and levers by which they were manipulated. But watching their gadgets was just part of the hypnotic show, they knew the why of things so they could let it all go on, as if they were in control. They didn't "renounce," they didn't "modulate according to the demands of reality." Instead they "acted out" the new variations he or Kate had improvised, so that the scenarios might continue, changing yet not changing, over a set of fixed chords, moving forward then backward with the endlessly repetitive rhythm, the same same of a soap opera.

"Beg," she said now, as a director might say "action," for she was an inspired . . . entertainer, an artist, really. "Beg, my dear little pet, my dreamy little boy." She wore a black felt hat shaped like a flattened paper boat. The comedy of the hat, tilted on her head like a wink, made the scene possible for him, not too serious, yet serious enough, a shared joke, so he was backstage and onstage at the same time. On his knees, he downcast his eyes before her cunt. "May I lick you, mistress? I long to serve you, to lick you, to suck your clit, to suck you off."

Krazy didn't dare look over at Ignatz Mouse. What if *he* had become, once again, that plastic nut case who had, the afternoon of her tiger-tea debacle, begged her to be hurt, just like this Dr. Ignatz begged with his "I long to serve you!" Oh God, Krazy thought, what if it's all starting again, and she was wearing the necklace of skulls, was once again the goddess filled with mother power! "Whip me with your tail! Make me your slave!" Yuch! Yuch! Yuch!
   But why was it so thrilling?

Kate stroked her own cunt. "Do you love my cunt, little one?"
   "I adore it," Dr. Ignatz said, staring at the wooden floor. "Please may I look at it?"
   She pulled him by the hair, and brought his lips to her cunt, then—O luxury!—she drank from a balloon of cognac while he licked her. Then, dribbling the last of the brandy on his black springy hair, she lay back on the couch, where he had once given a shape to her by telling her what her fantasies meant. Now, for as long as she held his head between her legs, she knew what he wanted, her studio owned the rights to him.
   He licked, lightly, quickly. "Oh that's nice," she hummed. "Now, strut it out!"
   He licked harder, and she came skimmingly, as if she were the boat, yet she was the wind, and she was the ocean the boat moved across.
   She took his head from her legs, pulled him up, and lay

him down on the couch. Straddling him, she sucked and bit his nipples, pulled lightly, then harder on their curlicues of brown hair.

"Please, mistress," he implored in a sleepy yet insistent voice, "harder."

"Are you begging to be hurt?"

"Yes, please, harder." *You're being the good mother,* he remembered the Sup saying to him, *the one you wanted, the one who could stand anger, the one who wouldn't turn away. And you're seeing that your mother is punished for the times that she did turn away.* Her teeth dug into him like claws, and the formulations scattered from his mind.

Kate hummed another Cole Porter tune, a favorite of his mother's (he had doodled it on the piano endless nervous college afternoons, as he said an anxious good-bye to jazz and hello to pre-med adulthood), *oh why can't you behave, so your baby can be your slave?* He *would* behave, he said, he *was* her slave. And he knew it pleased her when he begged for pain—he could feel the wetness of her cunt against his leg. It excited her to hurt him, to be his mistress, his goddess. And it exalted him! She could destroy him if she wished— hey, not really, right?—but she chose not to. He was chosen by his goddess to serve, and to survive.

He let himself sink into the pain; the dark pool was a place where she was there *with* him, for certain; sharply joined; inseparable; fused together.

What had he just said? *Please let me suck you off. Please make me take it!* Turnabout was fair play, but what could that mean? Take it? What *it?* Kate felt she needed a new line, and the words might lead her to it. Oh, what was *always* the It? He wanted her to have a cock! Then she would really be the It girl! Well, she couldn't grow one. But she would do the best she could—not, of course, that *she* had ever wanted to be other than she was, but she *did* want to be what he wanted.

So, an advocate of fair play, she turned him about, making him lie on his stomach. She told him she was taking a white vibrator from underneath the Kleenex in the box beside the couch. In the future, she said, he would keep one there for her. (She smiled. What if one of his patients found it—like that handsome black philosophy student with the lovely scarf that she sometimes saw in his waiting room. He reaches out one day—wailing as all patients did about what Mama had or hadn't done to and for him—and, whoops!, he finds the doctor's dildo, the Cracker Jack prize in the therapy box.) She made Dr. Ignatz imagine crawling to the desk drawer where in the future, she commanded, he would keep a jar of cold cream for her. He would lie down across the couch, and she would oil the vibrator for him.

"Beg," she said, but sweetly, softly.

He begged: "Please, mistress. Please open me. Please fill me."

"Go on." She smiled, remembering when Dr. Ignatz the therapist would encourage *her* free associations. "Go on."

"Please give it to me. Please make me take it."

The pain of her opening him, he imagined, would fill him with a warmth that would spread through his legs and arms, pushing his legs apart. *There,* he was open, flat, all his embarrassing secrets for anyone to read—giving a kind of innocence to this silly, splayed-leg, humiliating display. Am I a man or a woman? He was pinned to the hysteric's question as he was pinned beneath an imaginary cock that was an imaginary vibrator in his girlfriend's once real—for fantasy seemed to make even solid objects spectral—hand.

* * *

Kate said she would move the white vibrator in and out in long, slow strokes. He must move to meet her strokes, and then she would push him down into the couch, where she had once lain, opening *her* dreams and fantasies to be judged by him. Now she dominated, now—for him, to please him— she played the part of the false male. (After all, *she* had no anger against her lover.) She stroked her clit with her free hand, then she lay on the couch and had Dr. Ignatz enter her, move inside her to the imagined rhythm of the vibrator she told him she was moving in and out of his ass. She felt herself close.

"Come, slave," she said. "Show you belong to me. Give yourself."

He came into her; spent; suddenly embarrassed. Without desire these scenarios were ridiculous, stale, no thicker than words on a page, than light cast on a quarter-inch screen. It was like going to the movies in the afternoon; blinking and blank, you returned to the sunlight empty-spirited, vacant, your time wasted like a crumpled sperm-soaked tissue you had jerked off into.

She came. Lovingly, Kate stroked Dr. Ignatz's curly hair. "Good boy. You came well for me."

"Thank you, mistress," Dr. Ignatz said, his voice still a bit sleepy-slavish, caught in the spiderweb ties of a dream.

Ignatz Mouse stared at the space in front of the table where the images formed. Maybe, he thought musingly, the whole world *is* flat, and only our desire makes it even seem occasionally round, makes the costumes luminous, turns the actors into stars. He would have to think about that. But right now he didn't want to think. He wanted to rest. It had been *so good.* Kate had given Dr. Ignatz what

Krazy had never given *him*. Always he had bricked her, pursued her. Now Kate had given him—well, sort of him— the brick back to the . . . *the certainty that they were connected.* He spoke to the air near the kitchen where the scene was being played. "Oh thank you, goddess, for finally having revealed yourself!"

"Oh, thank you," Kate said to Dr. Ignatz, remembering the strength of her coming, stroking his beautifully formed back, his thick hair, his face, as he put on his pants. His skin was so smooth, his face so young looking! Magisterially, the mistress still, she told him he must promise not to sleep with his wife again.

But that was real life. "I don't know," he said, cringing inwardly before Kate's off-screen spontaneous anger.

She was furious. "You were my therapist, *Doctor* Ignatz. You seduced me. You told me to trust you, and then you took advantage of your position."

I seduced *her?* Ignatz shuddered, trying to zip himself. But she was right, he shouldn't have, well, didn't she? hadn't she wanted him?—his thoughts tumbled like laundry caught in the guilt cycle—why had she taught him to open, raised her legs on the, fuck me, who? "You asked me to fuck you!"

"I did not! I asked you to trust me!" She began to cry. "Oh God, Ignatz, I trusted *you,* and you really brainpanned me! I mean brainwashed me! I love you! Why can't you behave!"

He reached to hold her, but she pulled away and stood with her back to him, showing her lovely ass, full, rounded like firm melons. She dressed slowly, pulling on her stockings, her black lace underwear, knowing he was watching, and that it aroused him.

* * *

"Where are you going?"

"I have to pick up Joe at his office. It's nearly dinner-time."

But how could she be so unreasonable? Why didn't she understand *his* difficulty, she who had to spend every evening with Joe!

But *she* was the only one allowed to be the victim! "Good-bye," she said, and, sarcastically, "Thank you for a wonderful afternoon."

"I'm sorry I made you so angry," he said. He felt a fake prep clown, his blue oxford shirttails still hanging out of his pants.

"I'm not angry. I'm just disappointed."

"Thank you," he said, pointlessly. *Of course* she was unhappy with him. He was too thin. His ears were too big. He was vapid, flat, talentless. Only Kate had ever made his body seem all right! He wondered when he would see her again?

■ ■ ■

Later that same week, Kate sat behind the couch in Ignatz's tall red metal chair, smiling at his office furniture's pleasing higgledy-piggledy eclecticism (though his therapy techniques had been Institute-pure until her beauty had—unintentionally!—made him play the sap for her). Probably the decor was mix and match because he couldn't stand thinking about furniture; his mother had spent too much time antiquing, and he still saw furniture as a competitor. (*That,* she thought, was a good analysis! She must tell him.) There was a large old desk that Emily had bought. (Kate and Dr. Ignatz had each exorcised the desk by using it as prop. S/he had leaned against it, begging to be whipped, to take it in the ass.) Behind the desk there were bookshelves full of decades of *The International Journal of Psychoanalysis.* A white upright piano stood facing the couch, and red plastic milk crates filled with sheet music and old issues of *Downbeat,* the pages all sticky with Dr. Ignatz's love. Desk vs. Piano; a diorama of adult renunciation vs. childhood fantasies. Some afternoons, when they couldn't make love, she had him accompany her on the piano. He was very good—or he would be if only he could allow himself to be a little more feelingful. When the tune got hot, he skittered away into more intellectual, hard bop territories. He sounded then like a clever teenager who had memorized solos off of records and learned to recombine the notes in calculus class. Often she felt closer with him when they played music together than when they made love—though she still had to keep her face turned away when they performed together, or she felt *too* close, *too* exposed.

She felt at one with him, too, when she sat back here, on his seat, high above the couch, and imagined what it would be like to be him, listening to the bourgeois blues that must play endlessly from below. Dr. Ignatz worked now behind his desk, trying to produce the draft of a new paper. To become more than an instructor at the Harvard Medical School one had to produce sixteen—or was it sixty?—or six hundred?—or six quadrillion?—published papers. Otherwise one remained enfant (terrible or traditional) forever. Dr. Ignatz's papers were different, not make-work, but truly brilliant. And that wasn't just transference talking. The other analysts—even a lay analyst like Joe—were such smug bureaucrats of the unconscious, without any sense of adventure. Dr. Ignatz wouldn't tell her what the paper was about, but she was sure it must have to do with their lovemaking. He would risk anything for his art-science—even describing really embarrassing things *he* had done! He probably ran back to his desk the days she left him here, his shirt untucked, and took notes, just as he would with a patient. But he—as well as she, of course—was the patient. After each scenario, he and the Sup—and she and the Sup—analyzed. Sometimes, she thought, they only made love so that they would have something to take back to the Sup to analyze— like misguided house pets dragging the master a gourmet pigeon, oh, juice! Dr. Ignatz was the woman, his own mother, the one he had lost, and she, fucking him, was the father with breasts, which equaled the mother with a penis—so she was both a powerful mother *and* an Ignatz-as-mother-fucker!—which made the Combined Object (which sounded to layperson Kate like a gadget from Hammercher-Schlamecher!), which meant the One Who Will Never Leave You—so there is no separation, no death . . . Yikes! Would they ever get the right body parts matched up again? The Sup, she thought, didn't often talk like that to her. Didn't Sup take her seriously enough to unfurl the real goods? Was it because she was a woman? (*Was* she a woman? In her fantasies—the ones that made reality?) Soon, she thought guiltily, she must tell Dr. Ignatz that she, too, was seeing Sup. Or should she leave that tasty revelation to the Sup himself? Dear Sup looked so thin lately. The doctors hadn't yet found an antibiotic that worked on his bronchitis, so they had checked him into Mt. Auburn Hospital for further tests. Of course, they *would* find a cure. After all, Sup was a doctor, too. Sup would be fine. Until then, he saw his patients in his hospital room. What splendid dedication! Sup had been Dr. Ignatz's teacher, and now they were both, in a way, teaching her.

Kate rarely thought about her own work anymore, for Sup's and Dr. Ignatz's was so much more interesting, more involving, more important than what she now thought of as the Job, or Yet Another Dissertation About Jasper Johns. Therapy was like a detective story, where she was the detective, and she was the murderer, and she was the corpse, and it all never happened (yet somehow it did). So now she was perched on the stool as the doctor himself so often was, poring over Abraham, stodgy, reliable orthodox Abraham, in a moldy-oldy blue-bound volume from the Institute's own library.

"The displacement of libido from in front to behind and to the mouth indicates a desire to be a man. It shows her treating her own genital as nonexistent, and so softening her displeasure originating in the castration complex by thus turning away from her genital region. And the mouth allows for active castration, by biting." Yum, she thought, chomping, a wienie sandwich! So, if a man wants to be fucked in the ass it indicates he wants to be a woman. If a woman does, it means she wants to be a man. And a guy sucking cock is really mouthing a breast, and a breast is an ass is a cunt is a mouth unless you think your breasts are penises and dreaming makes it so. "Will you look at the pair of cocks on that girl," she said out loud, and laughed.

She heard Dr. Ignatz's sharp chicken-scratch pen stop, so she brought him a cup of java (with skim milk) from the Braun coffeemaker she had bought for the office, their secret place. She wanted to help him in his work, to be part of it. (And she *was*—his crucial co-star in the scenarios he was analyzing.) Serving him his coffee, she bent down low so he could see the new half-bra she was wearing, and the tops of her breasts. Today she wore a maid's apron to show she was his slave. *But he would have to have her;* and the more humiliated she was, the more he wanted her, for that was part of the no that was yes. She handed him the cracked cup. "Thank you," he said, and smiled at her.

"To bow and to bend is our delight," she said, shocking herself with her own sacrilege. She put her hand underneath the band of her skirt, reached between her legs, and painted her mouth with the wetness from her cunt. How could he want the flat diagram of a house more than a room that he could enter?

He pushed his papers aside and took her long hair into his hand. She fell to her knees, and he led her to the couch, she crawling next to him, like a pet, her cunt growing wetter as they covered the few feet across the rug. For so long she had resisted this desire to belong to someone, to be cared for, attended to. Soon he would touch her all over with his beautiful long fingers—more than his cock, more even than his imagination, it was his lovely hands that she desired, stroking her, petting her, smoothing her out, admiring her, warming her, training her. He lay above her, and she turned her face from him. "No," she said, to excite him, "no." He took her hands and tied them behind her back with his belt. She didn't resist. (And just as well, she thought, smiling with closed lips. Her resistance would have bloopered the scene— she was taller than he, stronger than he, her legs in better shape from her morning roller skates by the Charles!) Straddling her from above, he held her mouth to his cock, making the snake. She sucked him. It was her mother's breast, sure, it was her father's cock. OK. Fine. Good. And it was fun.

In her room, Krazy hid her eyes behind her paws. Her mollyclues felt so jazzed that they were about to bunny hop away in excitement. There was hatred in his love; love in her anger. She was biting her own tail. She couldn't watch them trying to get inside each other. It reminded her of her analysis with Ignatz. That delicious surrender of herself to a commanding voice! Had she really *ever* been innocent, even before the atoms had fallen apart? What had she and Ignatz been doing! What was Kate doing? She peeked out.

And Ignatz Mouse spread his arms wide, turning his head in excited confusion. Dr. Ignatz was Kate's master. He was her god. He was really Big. He could hurt her. *Could he?* Whose fantasy was this anyway? If it was hers, then it was just like the damn bricks, he *thought* it was his plan, when really she *wanted* them! But if it wasn't her fantasy, then he wasn't wanted, and the joy went out of it for him. God and worshiper, the yes that's no, the no that's yes. Once again a confusion whose only cure was to continue, to fuck again and again. Good. Fine. OK.

"Again," Dr. Ignatz said, as sternly as he could manage. "Suck me more."

Next scene he had Kate kneel with her breasts pushed into the couch. "Harder," he said, "push them more deeply into the couch. Raise them higher." He paced behind her, whispering harshly, his voice in the scenarios hardly feeling like his own. Whose fantasy was this? he wondered. His? Hers? Some patient's? Some pornographic film producer pinned to the traumas of his childhood, making his dreams unreel over and over on Dr. Ignatz's VCR till they had colonized his mind? He felt as if *he* were being made up by talking animals who borrowed his body so they could walk about in the human world. Who was he? Animal, human, man, woman? How could he become his own person? Yet it was as if the only cure for this confusion was to fuck Kate again and again.

He undid the belt from her hands and gave her the tip of it to kiss. In this scenario it was meant to be a cock. Why were men excited, Kate wondered, by a fantasy whose real enactment would drive them crazy with jealousy? Yet she enjoyed imagining that he ordered her to service another man, make him come in the air in front of her mouth. She did it for Dr. Ignatz. She couldn't betray him; her mouth, her ass, her cunt, her coming all belonged to him. He would order her to serve another, to prostrate herself before the whip, and then he would be enraged that she had opened herself to someone else and would punish her severely.

"You think you're inferior, Kate," Sup had wheezed. "A second-class citizen."

"Because I'm black."

He shrugged his shoulder, the mildest slow raising of his bones, bones nearly showing through the hospital gown. He sat facing her in a chair, with his bed between. "Because you don't have the rights to yourself. You still belong to your mother. Her restrictions were all mixed with love. You know: all those elocution classes, acting classes, being-her-daughter classes. So now you feel restrictions as love, and love as a restriction. You *want* to belong to someone again. You want someone to bind you, to own you, to hurt you."

Elocution classes? What was Sup talking about? Maybe the drugs they were giving him for his broncohightis made him forget things? Kate hadn't had many prodigy-child classes. When she had wanted to take more singing lessons, her mom had convinced her that it wasn't a worthy thing to do, and besides, despite her teacher's lavish praise, Kate didn't have enough talent. Even being an art historian—let alone an artist!—was more Kate Kareer than Mom could bear! Sup must be confusing Kate with one of his other cases—some stage mom who had wanted a star daughter. But Sup's mix-up made it easier to bear his analysis—like consulting a psychiatrist about, you know, this friend of yours who has a problem. And, oddly, what Sup said was true, in a way—Kate's mother had cried from the first day when kitten Kate had gone off to kindergarten, Mom had always wanted Kate to stay home with her, bake bread, play house. Oh, well, wrong patient, but right analysis. Restriction = love. Maybe it was like sex—there weren't that many positions and there weren't that many stories. One size fits all. Because everybody has a mother!

"You want Dr. Ignatz to hurt you. You think of being hurt as love. Brick after brick."

Bricks? *That* must be the imaginary whipping Dr. Ignatz gave her.

Krazy looked down into her cup and saw the tea-stained afternoon when the plastic Mouse had come alive. Krazy had worn a lovely skull necklace, and Ignatz had begged her to whip *him*. But really it hadn't been Ignatz—just a piece of plastic mixed with some tiger tea and *her* desire. The friend of Kate was Krazy! Krazy felt suddenly faint, from the confusion, from the remembered tea, from Ignatz's bizarre longing for pain. Her vertigo was her mind racing over a cliff, trying to escape the meaning of Trojan Ignatz's pleas for pain. But the knowledge waited at the bottom to catch her— her mother's soft fur become a bed of barbed-wire brambles. If you had mothers like hers and Kate's, moms who were so yummy and controlling at once, then you were bound to feel the pain they caused you as all mixed with the soft sticky stuff of love, you were bound to feel taking orders as sweet. Call that kindness? Well, what *else* was there to call kindness?

So had she been agreeing all these years, in every daily strip, every bonk on the bean, that the love women *get* should always be mixed with our hatred for Mom? Girls are like Mom—we deserve to be pelted! So bam comes the brick to milady's head! And, the only love anyone recognizes *from* others is one that feels like mother love, like restriction and pain? So love was like death? So throw the brick? So drop the bomb? So whip her? Whip her!

"I will whip you," Dr. Ignatz said. "And you will prove your devotion to me by coming when you are whipped." What could be more godlike! He could make her feel pain as pleasure, bricks as valentines!

Of course he wouldn't actually whip her. Standing behind Kate, he described what the pain would be like, the stinging against her beautiful ass, how she would long for the painful strokes, they would bring her ass alive. Stroke after stroke after stroke, his voice repeated, till she must have felt hypnotized by his dream whip. And then, as if his own voice had put him under, or the mad animals had changed the script, the belt was actually in his hands, and came down across her ass. A tentative stroking, like a long leather tongue. He was shocked. But Kate said, "Thank you," and he brought the tip down harder. Whose belt was it anyway? He remembered when he and Emily had bought the thing at Bloomingdale's, and he was suddenly angry at himself for his inability to leave Emily, at Kate for making him betray his wife, his career, his sense of himself as a decent, compassionate man. Kate was a witchy woman, a seductive cat. He must break her hold over him, maim the cat! But every blow just bound him more tightly to her, as "Thank you," she said, and he struck her harder, and—thank you!—and harder, until her ass grew red.

"Please," she heard herself say, and "thank you," and "harder," and she felt she was becoming an extension of his will only, a part of him, a great therapist, a brilliant star. Each stroke connected them irrevocably.

He ordered her to come, and she found herself coming, lightly, an hors d'oeuvre, a short overture. "Struttin' with some barbecue!" she shouted. She begged to be fucked in her ass, to be bad-bottomed. An ass, she thought, was a cunt was a mouth was a . . . feather-bed mountain; it was good to have a nice bushy tail, she thought nonsensically. He oiled his cock with the jar of cream that she had ordered him to keep in his desk, and entered her from behind, with a warm pain that made her feel completely opened beneath him, truly full and taken, forced towards her coming. He had one of his beautiful hands on her breasts, and one of his long lovely fingers stroked her clit, insisting that she come ("Oh mess around!") again ("Play that riff!") and again ("It's tight like that!"), until she screamed wordlessly and couldn't come anymore. She pressed her cheek up against his. "Thank you," she murmured. "That was . . . that was steam-heated!"

Steam-heated? Where was that phrase from? Dr. Ignatz wondered. Who was this woman in her innermost being, where he wished to reside? It was as if the scenarios they sketched as they made love, the fantasies, had taken the place of their actual bodies, and so they never really connected. The feelings they aroused were directed at fictions, at spectral masters and mistresses, at nonexistent cocks. The feelings were very strong—when he came he felt it throughout his body, fissioning pleasure atoms nearly took the top of his head off!—yet they went nowhere, didn't fuse *him* with *her*, left him alone and more isolated. Maybe if they did it again?

■ ■ ■

Then, suddenly, the season of thank-yous was over, and Kate's weather changed to wind and showers. Kneeling, crying, she asked him to promise that he would stop sleeping with his wife on Wednesdays.

"I can't." He saw poor Emily sending plates crashing into the wall. "I can't act like Emily and me all never happened." It's easy enough to be nuts about each other, Kate, he thought, but I don't know what that amounts to. I should trust you? You who double-crossed my predecessor, Joe, a man you had nothing against, just like swatting a fly? I should trust you? And if I did, *and you turned away from me,* I'd be sure I'd played the sap. Emily is needy—tearing at him as if he were food—but that made her reliable.

Kate, furioso, screamed, "I've let you whip me, I've let you take me in the ass!"

But she had wanted . . . Ignatz thought, as guilt nibbled away the end of the sentence. He put his hand to his face to block her anger.

"Oh God, Ignatz, I'm not angry with you," Kate said. "I love you! Why can't you behave!"

But, to her mind, he couldn't. For months, they made love rarely, and between takes there were eons of: I can't come to you today, I have to try to work on my dissertation, have lunch with advisers, see Joe before he leaves for a conference, I'm too nervous about not working, so depressed I can't do the paper for the seminar, so scared that Joe knows something. And in the meantime, in between times, ain't they got arguments!—as many as high school debaters. The championship topic: Why couldn't Dr. Ignatz leave his wife? (He learned: Argument was lovemaking carried on by other, more intimate means.)

"For God's sake, Ignatz, she's a professor at Harvard Law School! She can take care of herself!"

"You don't know her," he said, seeing Emily weeping in bed, her small vulnerable breasts half-covered by the duvet. In the back of The Daily Catch restaurant, a dark man, trapped between huge cutting boards and a stove covered with black pots, sliced live lobsters in half, their shells almost maroon in color, and tossed them into the boiling water. Do lobsters scream? Or only cowardly analysts? "Besides, that's just it, she's not a professor yet. She's up for tenure this year. I can't leave her till that's over." Poor Emily, she was to be the featured speaker at Northwestern's Critical Legal Studies Conference. She stared for an hour at the phone, unable to make a plane reservation.

"Why don't you just say you don't love me enough to leave her?" Kate said.

The Harvest waiter, his blue and white Marimekko tie tucked into his shirt like a St. Paul's student, brought them their martinis. He placed small cocktail napkins on their table, with a closed-lip smile, as if he knew a delicious secret. Behind him stood shelves of glass canisters filled with pickled onions, and pickled roots, and pickled tulip bulbs that looked like lab specimens. Fetuses. Not yet born. Like me, Ignatz thought. "It's not that I don't love you," Dr. Ignatz refrained. What was this blues called? he wondered. Name that tune! (Singing, ah, that was *both* argument and lovemaking carried on by other means. Made into a soufflé! He wished they were back in his office now, playing music together. Kate sang so beautifully, it was such a natural direct imprint of her being, that for the time of the song Dr. Ignatz felt liberated from his guilt, from his unpossessed self, from his weak, earthbound body.) "I just feel that I *owe* Emily, I feel guilty towards her." Besides, he knew that Kate didn't really want him to leave Emily, didn't really want possession of him, didn't want to wake up next to his sour-milk smell every morning. But her pride made her bat him back and forth between her paws.

"Ah, yes," Kate said, sipping the oily gin, sharpening her claws. "The Infinite Debt, right? You owe your father for your life, and he owes *his* mother, so you all have to pay the Old Fat Lady forever. Unto the fourth generation, right? One way or other, the Jewish boy pays the Implacable Woman." She sipped her drink and laughed with small sharp perfect teeth. "It's not over until the Fat Lady sings."

Had he told her all that? Dr. Ignatz wondered. It sounded like the kinds of things Sup said to him. He saw Emily, small, dark, well muscled, not fat at all, pounding the phone receiver she couldn't use against the table with mad frustration. He reached out to stop her hand, sending her into a raging whirl of tears. She screamed at him for his lack of commitment to her, for his coldness, for abandoning her when she needed him most. Her anger was like a viscous medium he couldn't extricate himself from, a tie stronger than love, as fierce as the grave.

Emily, herself no slouch at analysis when angry, offered an incisive view of his character: Dr. Ignatz was still the little boy tied to his father, making a pact that they should both be sad forever. How could she even have thought he could be committed to anyone else? Emily had justice—was Justice—dark-eyed Rachel weeping for her husband, for he was a jerk. (Oh God, what if she saw the deep red scratches Kate's long red nails had left all over his back!) And Dr. Ignatz knew that he was as she said, flat, insipid, incapable of commitment. Anyway, what was the point? People just couldn't get along; the world was a dung heap, and humanity was a suicidal thought in the mind of God. Heavy black ink filled his veins, drawing him downward. He could barely keep his eyes open. Emily's words, Kate's words, were like a hod load of bricks falling on his head, until he grew more and more depressed and had to sleep under the weight of the masonry.

Had they all spoken to his analyst? Or did he chatter with his fingertips, he, the flat character surrounded by three-dimensional women, open to their inspection, anger, judgment? He couldn't stand up to the women. He didn't want to. Dr. Ignatz-become-his-own-mother found "fathers" to punish him everywhere, in Kate, in his wife, in whoever might most lovingly torment him.

"Oh, let's dip the bill," Kate said, favoring him with a closed-lip smile. She used more and more slang now, like her hats, unplaceable, pieces of street talk, tough-guy wisecracks from detective stories, jazzbo slang. Loving Kate meant reliving the history of jazz for Dr. Ignatz, white piano player—warm and welcoming at first, full of sly

winks even for an offay, and pig-latin codes that wanted to
be broken. Then hard bop rhythms, and angry rap, whose
staccato shots said *not you, not you.* He was on a slide, he
felt, from doll boy to candy man to Mr. Can't-Dance, the
honky bastard.

"You'll never leave her," Kate said sourly. She looked
lovely in a man's blue suit with widely spaced chalk stripes.
She had streaked her blonde hair black in some new style,
or some new Kate fashion that he couldn't get down with.
"You think you're a real tough gee. But you've got a cream
center." A Chinese boy of about twelve sat behind the I
Shing's cash register doing his homework. His grandmother
stood by the door, beady-eyeing the till and saying good-bye
to customers. Kate didn't want the Peking duck tonight, she
didn't want to paint pancakes with plum sauce for Dr. Ignatz, she didn't want to watch him fumble with chopsticks.
She desired something spicy, faddish Cajun cooking maybe,
a little pain in the mouth to remind her jaded appetite that
she was eating, that she was alive. Creole gumbo for the
creole.

"What about you, doll face?" Dr. Ignatz had said. "The
only reason we can have dinner tonight is because your
husband's away at a conference."

"You and I have the same conversation all the time."
Through an opening to the kitchen, Kate saw the huge tar-
nished hood of the oven where The Cajun Yankee cook
blackened the redfish, flown up each day from New Orleans.
She swigged her Rolling Rock from the bottle, and drops of
water beaded on her black leather pants. "Only the backgrounds change."

"See," Ignatz Mouse said to no one in particular, "in America
the people don't change. Just the commodities."

"Not just their modesty," Krazy muttered, "the things

change, too." After all, what had smarty-mouse added with his political homily? "Just like Kate already said."

Ignatz didn't even look over to her. "They need avant-garde popular artists to show them the way, to show them how to have new facets."

Krazy looked for her teacup so as not to sneer at Mr. Know-It-All Avant-garde, Mr. All But Dissertation, who squid inked Terrorist New Art and New Sciences but couldn't change himself, couldn't leave his wife. But it was getting dark, and the cup had disappeared into the shadows. Had she *had* a Zuni teacup? A flowered cake plate? It was like the month the strip had stopped, and her overstuffed furniture had simply disappeared! She wanted to glance away from the screen, to see if her rug was still here. But she couldn't. She had to know how the fight came out—not, of course, that it ever "came out," brick after brick after brick.

Dr. Ignatz caught the swishy waiter looking too slyly at him. (He had an earring in his left ear. Did that mean he was gay? The world seemed suddenly filled with signs that Dr. Ignatz, a refugee in his own country, couldn't read. Or did "left ear" mean that the man liked it in a certain way? And how did Dr. Ignatz like it? And what did that mean? Dr. Ignatz suddenly felt like a refugee in his own body—animated now by desires he didn't understand.) Why the sly smile? Dr. Ignatz touched his left nipple. "It tastes different," Kate had said that afternoon—one of their now-rare lovemakings—"as if it's bruised." Throughout the day, doing therapy, he had felt the pain there as a distinction—a part of his livery. But tonight he worried (a medical impossibility!) that his nipple had grown larger (wasn't it?).

"How goes the dissertation?" he said. He sipped his martini at Kelley's Atrium Room—another of the Scottish developer's high-style metamorphoses, rehabed red-brick market buildings become restaurants. Her dissertation, Dr. Ignatz thought, was something else she wouldn't share with him. She had never told him word one about Jasper Johns.

Kate understood: Dr. Ignatz thought he was her-own-gooding, but really he was just being spiteful, for he knew that questions about the Job would make her uneasy. Maybe fake concern, she thought, was spitefulness carried on by other means? She heard her mother asking her if she had liked kindergarten. Yes, she had loved it. But was she *sure,* Mom asked with that special sweetness that made sour anxiety form in Kate's stomach, that she wasn't afraid of the bigger boys? Invisible ropes snaked out around Kate's little ankles, tethering her home.

"Oh, Ignatz, who wants to talk about that!" He handed her her Valentine's Day present, a small flat box with a red ribbon on it, the squall of her anger—no, *not* anger, *disappointment*—suddenly past. She avidly tore open her box, from Victoria's Secret, and held up the gift for the waiter to see—a pair of white stockings with a light diamond pattern, and a lacy white garter belt. ("Hello," his tag said. "My name is Fred.") Dr. Ignatz blushed. Who was she humiliating now, herself or him or Fred?

"And I have something for you," she said.

It was an even smaller white box. His arms, chest, and face flushed with sweet expectation, remembering last year's present—a cologne that he also thought of as part of his livery. Inside the box, this year, was an earring, a small blue stone, in a setting of four tiny claws. Frightened, he looked away; fascinated, he looked back, like an animal being toyed with. He raised his head from the earring in the palm of his lined hand, to the beautiful woman smiling at him.

She adjusted her round purple hat. "You will wear it for me."

The waiter put down two small napkins and two martinis. This place served them in jelly glasses. In old-fashioned glasses. In martini glasses. Shaken but not stirred. Stirred but not shaken. He waited for the waiter to leave. "I'll wear it for you when we make love."

"No," Kate said. "You'll wear it always." She sipped her fresh fruit strawberry daiquiri. "Have your ear pierced. Your left ear."

"Why my left ear?" Why was he even asking? He couldn't do this thing! What would they say at the Institute?

"Your left ear because you belong to me and *I* say it will be your left ear."

Dr. Ignatz's cream center melted with warm, masochistic desire. He *wanted* to be hers, to belong to his goddess, irrevocably, *beyond her leaving.* "Yes," he said, in a sleepy voice. "Thank you."

Kate laughed, contentedly, to herself. "What will they say at the Institute?"

Kate was less afraid of him now that he was her slave, so she risked taking a big book from her green nylon knapsack. She laid it on the table. Maybe she *should* try telling him about her dissertation. Sup had been very hard on her lately, saying she didn't take her own work seriously enough.

"You think you aren't good enough to do anything yourself. Just to serve coffee to men."

"Castration?" Kate said sweetly, as if it were a furry animal. Doctor and patient had changed positions. She sat in a chair, and he lay in the hospital bed, the blanket tucked tightly around him, staring up at the ceiling.

He coughed and it sounded as if a feral animal were running its claws over his throat. "Which came first," he whispered, "the penis or the egg? Stop trying to become like *me,* Kate. Stop acting like a movie producer, saying what you think *I* want to hear. Fantasies don't change *you* unless they're *your* desires."

She looked down at the gray lino of the hospital room, chastised, confused. Why was he being so harsh with her?

"Because I'm dying, Kate." He still wouldn't look at her.

Dying! No! That was unimaginable! "Sup, the drugs . . ."

"The drugs just make me sick." He waved her from the room.

The next day he had said, "You think *you* shouldn't be ambitious, Kate. So you identify with men who write earth-shattering articles on hysteria, or make earth-destroying bombs, like Oppie."

Oppie? The demigod her father had talked about? Kate couldn't have picked him out of a police lineup, let alone identify *with* him.

But Sup had made her think that maybe she should get back to *her* own work. Which was not psychotherapy, not jazz singing in a therapist's office, but art—art history, any-way. And maybe telling Dr. Ignatz about it could be a first step—declaring to the world, the mom, and the devil that *her* work was serious, too. So she opened the book to a picture of an American flag. "People use modernism in the most terrorist ways. As if the audience were a bunch of kidnap hostages! But really this art is about innocence. See," she said, "Johns won't paint anything except what is already flat, like a flag. So there're no illusions, no lies."

"So high art wants to be flat?" Why did he suddenly feel so bewildered? Tears were starting behind his eyes. Why should he care so much about an American flag?

Kate saw his sadness. But why? She was just doodling, not angry, mixing up bergy bits (Green——, Stein——, Rosen——), with sprinkles of vernacular spice—because she had let him whip her and fuck her in the ass, but she wasn't sure she could trust him with her work, her thoughts. And so what that she was making Mr. Man cry? *That* was spicy, too. She wasn't angry, no meanness intended. Kate laughed, thinking this conversation itself was a conceptual art piece, called "Why should I care about your tears if you won't leave your bourgeois wife and your annuities?" because art isn't a commodity—no, it's a middle-class dinner-table argument. "The flag is what it is. So it has real presence. Fantasy = Reality. Art = Life. Just like in popular art where Hammett = Spade = Bogart. The hero walks like a hero. He's an icon, like comic strip characters. Mickey Mouse, say, or Krazy Kat. Mickey isn't a drawing *of* Mickey. The drawing *is* Mickey."

"I don't understand. I mean . . ."

She turned to a Rauschenberg of stop signs, dead birds, smudged astronauts. "And the high arts want to be open to improvisation, like the popular ones. See, this picture is like a city dump, no above or below, no better or worse, no richer or poorer, no marriage or giving in marriage, just promiscuous fifty-two mix-up. There's no unknown outside, no nature, no background. You know, like we get explanations from the . . . from our analysts, but really they're on the same *plane* as our symptoms, not behind them. We're one-dimensional people mucking around with our cultural detritus!"

Detritus? Kate thought, flinching from her own somewhat shrill, too insistent voice. Gracie Allen wasn't an America-is-the-stomach-of-the-world-goat-garbage-disposal! Nowadays something crucial *was* missing from the high arts, Kate thought, as she watched Ignatz cry and didn't feel a thing—*real* pain was missing, *real* compassion, and *real* pleasure were all AWOL. All the good things she felt when Ignatz played and she sang some standard. (So there *were* standards.) The high arts were no crying Stan and fat Ollie. I'm the same as you, the high artists said, over and over, breaking their sword across their bare knee. But first you had to see the sword, first you had to accept that they were princes, so they could tell you they were naked and get a kick out of your shock. The popular workers provided pleasure scenarios, liberated zones; the high arts stylized them and gave them back, as if they were a scandal. Trademark soup cans, flatness, same-same repetitions. But who were they shocking? Their own tuxedo dignity! Shock was spicy strychnine on the palette. (Hey, she could say it now!) The popular workers hadn't meant to shock, just to master a sorrow, improvise a pleasure.

She shut up; drank; then said, "I am black but comely."

Dr. Ignatz began to weep. Kate was moving away from him, into a world he didn't understand. What did "real presence" mean anyway? Medical school, he thought, feeling hopelessly inadequate, had been just a trade school! Kate lectured him on how these artists wanted to have fewer dimensions—yet she had more sides than he did. It was silly, but he couldn't stop himself from crying. "Pup," he said, as she turned the page to a colored map of the United States and a goat with a tire round his neck. "Pup. Pup."

Mickey Mouse? Eye con? What the hell was that? How come *she* knew words he couldn't even pronounce? In Krazy's living room, Ignatz Mouse looked at the Fantasy art book. Could these be the same pictures he had thought-reformed kidnapped Krazy with? His plans for high culture—for roundness!—were being betrayed by his supposed COMI-SALAD allies, the high-culture artists! He stared. Was it a flag? Should he salute it? No, look at Johns's lovely brush-strokes, calling attention to themselves. A painter's work, a work of art. No, it was just some bars and lines on a piece of paper, like a flag. Not *like* a flag. It *was* a flag. No, it was a piece of art. Whatever he did was wrong! He just wasn't smart enough for this world. Not hip enough for this world. Not black enough. He was too flat; he wasn't flat enough. He turned and turned, but he couldn't make it come round right.

Kate, blurred by his tears, looked furious.
"You hate my dissertation," she said bitterly. "You're just like Joe. You don't want me to go beyond you. No wonder I can't work when I'm around you people." She picked up her knapsack and swirled her green felt cape around her back. "Thank you for making me talk about it," she said savagely. "Thank you for making me think my work is shit!" High-heeled, a New Jersey red-hot in tight jeans, with a pink handkerchief in her back pocket, she marched out of the restaurant with a crick-crack, break your lover's back, over his grave, out of his life.

■ ■ ■

Except for her spectral appearances on his apartment's answering machine—which she called only when she must know he would be at the office seeing patients: "I'm at Stapleton Airport," she said at the beep. "They're de-icing the plane. I'm on my way to Los Angeles to see Stan." Ignatz blew on his hands, the long fingers that she had once been so fond of. His hands had been the best part of him, for his body was too thin, his chest hairless, pink, ugly. Now his hands, too, looked ungainly. He felt the tops of her stockings, the smoothness of her thighs, and the memory only re-iced his fingertips . . . Beep . . . "I'm at a pay phone, near The Harvest, I can't talk long. Miss Le Blanc has a date to meet Fred." Dr. Ignatz turned towards his microwave. *You* couldn't stick your head in *that,* he thought, weeping. Your stupid nose would stick out. Was she lying to him? He ran down the steps of his two-family, and on to The Harvest. But she wasn't there. Had they already gone back to her Somerville apartment, a place where he was never allowed? He walked back home, the sniffles inside his too long nose telling

him that he had forgotten to wear a jacket. Every reminder
of his body was like receiving a Hallmark card that said, *Hi,
Pal! You're inadequate!*

That night, he masturbated to Kate's tune. He held a
piece of paper the precision length of his cock (a metal or
wood ruler wouldn't follow the curve and might miss a nano-
inch of valuable meat) to see if misery had shaved a quarter
inch of adequacy off his poor little doodle-doo. He stood in
a crowd of men, all in leather collars and business suits, their
cocks poking stiffly out of the open flys. Kate, on a platform,
surveyed them. "Choose me," Ignatz shouted. "Choose my
cock!" . . . Beep . . . "I'm in Paris, and I miss you terribly,
darling, I wish *you* were here with me. Why couldn't you
have turned a new leaf over, so your baby could be your
slave. Oh, Ignatz," she snuffled, "why couldn't you behave?"
Was she really in Paris? He played her back to check for
French-sounding static on the line. "Cary is showing Miss
Wonderly the Louvre. I wish I were showing it to you. 'Bye,
darling." Was she lying to him? Had she once mentioned a
Cary? Was he the upper-class fellow, the art historian, the
American-born Oxford don? Like the fantasies making her
hand spectral, these messages were making the world disappear. Had she ever really been his patient, his lover? Was
there really a Kate, he wondered, a Louvre, a Paris? (Well,
he *had* seen Paris in movies, so maybe *it* existed.) "I love
Paris," Dr. Ignatz sang in his sad, high, nasal voice, for since
Kate had left he found that he had become her, humming
Cole Porter songs, unable to concentrate on the articles he
was meant to write, surprised, like her, when he heard himself swearing. "Why, oh why do I love Paris? Because my
love is there." If she ever had been his love. If there was a
there, there.

These noms des affaires—aliases, ha-ha-ha, from *The Maltese
Falcon*—made her amours unreal and somehow bearable—a

new art form, the phone-machine serial (called "Heartbreak Hotel"), where he was certain to get Kate back in the last episode of the season, 'cause it all never happened. Until, that is, the beep was followed by homeboy Jack, Smart Jack, the Harvard philosophy student, Black Jack, his patient, Lumber Jack, the big man who always had money because women *gave* him money, Beau Koo Jack. Beep . . . "God, he's beautiful, Ignatz! But I hate him! He's such a dear fool." She rapped in Jack's New York whine: " 'My name is Jack/ And I'm good lookin'/ I'm the chocolate Descartes and I'm . . . I need a rhyme that isn't cookin', that's too corny, well, took in maybe' . . . I mean that's him, Ignatz, he can't even finish his raps! He wants to be street smart, when really he's a classroom boy." . . . Beep . . . "He tells me how other women buy him clothes, as if he were an uptown pimp, you know, to get gifts out of me. I swore I wouldn't give him anything, but yesterday he admired a scarf at Louis—and check this out!—it was *one hundred and eighty dollars.* And I bought it for him! I *know* I'm playing the sap. But he's so sweet, too, and I can't work and I can't stand being alone anymore. Why aren't you with me?" Her tormenting voice was as sleepy sadly sweet as when she had been his patient, and from his red perch he had looked down on the perfect bones of her face, her almond eyes.

From where he now looked down at hateful Jack. Jack who was *done to* always, Jack who shouted at his department chairman for his racism, grabbed recalcitrant library assistants by the necktie ("Sir, you can only take out five boo— aaargghh!"), demolished opponents—verbally—at conferences, and then, having acted out, went his way untroubled by responsibility. Consciousness, Ignatz thought, comes when you dam emotion up instead of expressing it, turn it inward, develop nooks, crannies, coigns of vantage to peek out from. Fear makes the soul, fraidy mouse Ignatz thought. But this was just the Dr. Ignatz way—Dr. Ignatz

knew, hip to his own Semitic jive—of triumphing over supposedly flat Jack. (Dr. Ignatz accepted the B'nai B'rith Brotherhood award for declaring Jack to be as crooked, craven,
and fucked up as the rest of humanity. And the nothing-but-
the-truth was that Jack himself had been so troubled by his
temper that he had sought this therapy.) Really, it was easy
to look at Jack from Kate's p.o.v.: six-foot-six, well-muscled,
with quick brown eyes and a lovely gap-toothed grin that he
used with malicious skill. Jack smart-mouthed with whiplike
meanness, and then, if you jumped back from his Jack attack,
he flashed a rainbow grin that said you were stamped "OK
by J."—OK by the redblackgreen nation. Jack knew you
longed for his approval: the street's high-five, black-white
reconciliation. (Apparently being a black philosophy student
at Harvard was almost as good for working people's need-
for-approval levers as being a psychoanalyst!) He felt Jack's
weight over Kate, moving in Kate, and wondered did he find
it maybe *too* easy to imagine Jack's sticky honey for Kate?
Dr. Ignatz wondered: Am I a man or a woman? His body
shivered on the stool.

Jack, meanwhile, ran down the week in review—the
mother who smothered like a one-woman Department of
Human Services, the Ayatollah dissertation adviser who
treated Jack like a freak. *No wonder,* Ignatz thought, saying
analytically neutral nothing. Summer, and Jack's hat was a
shower cap. Fall, and Jack wore unlaced high-top sneakers.
(You'll trip, motherly Dr. Ignatz had wanted to warn him.)
And this March the fashion trend was suspenders worn *down*
the front of his pants legs, inexplicably holding up air. Dr.
Ignatz thought Jack must be getting style tips from his inter-
galactic masters. (Oh God, what if Kate actually preferred
someone who *didn't* wear a Brooks Brothers shirt!)

In his litany of complaints, Jack never said word one
about a Kate Higgs Bosun. Probably, Ignatz doodled on his

pad, the affair was a LIE that clever Kate had made up to torment him. *"You are a liar." "I am." "Is there any truth to that story about you and Jack?" "Some, not much . . ."* She *put her arms around him. "I'm so tired of lying and think-ing up lies and not knowing what's a lie and what's the truth."*

But the next snowstorm, Jack arrived wrapped in the most beautiful scarf Dr. Ignatz had ever seen, a rich plaid that looked like delicate varicolored plants had been woven into soft wool and lined with dark blue silk. Probably Jack had always had such a scarf. Kate had seen it in the waiting room. Kate had stuck it in her phone collage for Ignatz-insanity-inducing verisimilitude. Could he go on seeing Jack as a patient, he wondered, being as he wanted to crush his skull under his loafer? Hadn't Freud written somewhere that it was wrong to want to murder a patient?

Dr. Ignatz's affair with Kate was destroying his career—but not by public censure. He hardly listened to his other patients anymore—what could they tell him about Kate? And during the Jack hour, he only had ears for the magic word —Kate's name—so the duck could drop and Dr. Ignatz could give his Institute-trained, anxiety-inducing, we-have-ways-of-making-you-talk "Yes?"

But Jack never said *Kate,* just endless boo-hoo-hoo about Mama. Ergo Kate *must* be lying. Or maybe Kate was low tomato on Beau Koo Jack's long vine. The bastard!

"Lovely scarf," Dr. Ignatz said, knowing that he shouldn't have.

Jack stopped bawling and grinned—remembering his power had drawn him up, for a moment, from the salty, pounding ocean of his mother. "Yup. Lovely women just love to buy me lovely things."

What lovely woman? He looked down, and saw a small jewel in the large lobe of Jack's left ear. "A lovely earring,"

Dr. Ignatz said, dropping another line. How fatuous he must sound!

"A lovely, lovely woman bought that for me, too, Doc," Jack said.

What lovely woman, you narcissistic bastard! Dr. Ignatz's inquiring mind screamed. But terror of the answer—disguised as analytic neutrality—meant that he couldn't bring himself to ask.

Jack wouldn't have heard. Bawling about Big Mama Too Much, he had reached over for a Kleenex, and came up with a white cock-shaped vibrator. It loomed large in Jack's small hands. (Jack had big feet and small hands. What did that mean? Left ear. What did that mean? What did Jack like? Where did Jack like to put it? To take It?) "Whoo-eee, Doc, what have we here?" happy Jack nearly screamed. "Special treatments for high-strung hysterics?" He pointed to the plastic cock with his other hand—a new-wave TV pitchman who worked in rapper's rhythm. *"What do women want? Dr. Ignatz knows! It's the buzz on the buzzer that gives them the glow!* Tell me, Doc, what kind of bird is this? Is this handy-dandy device the solution to Dr. Freud's patented penis envy? If we can put a man on the moon, why not a penis on a woman, huh, Doc?" He held it to his crotch, a white plastic missile, and waggled it.

Alas, Jack's hour was over. But as they stood and shook hands, Dr. Ignatz smelled a cologne on Jack that stung his eyes into tears.

That night's episode on Radio Hell: Beep . . . "Hi, baby doll, it's your little Brigid O'Shaughnessy, high on snick-snack, crack your comrade's back! Boy, stop the presses! This stuff is tea for tigers! It's bye-bye blues! Guess what Sup says about all this? Whoops! Guess I let the Kate out of the bag, there, huh? I've been seeing Sup, too, darling. Hope you don't mind? He said, wait, I wrote it down for you: Sup says

BKJ's being so pretty is just the key that unlocked my *real* desire—which is for *power*. BKJ, wait a minute, is . . . is the dangerous, *phallic* part of my personality. Jack doesn't consider any desires but his own. Whooeee! Jumpin' Jack! I fuse with men, then I feel like I've lost the rights to myself. So I want to hurt them, to get myself back. Like this message! Hey, I think the drugs they've been giving Sup . . ." Beep . . . "This stupid gadget is just like you! It cut me off . . . Anyway, I think that the drugs they've been giving Sup for the bronchitis make him talk a little out of his head. I don't want to hurt you. I mean I'm just kidding around now. I love you! Hey, baby, BKJ finally finished a rap!" An interval of rhythmical noises followed, like a trumpet farting. Then Kate giggled and a false male profundo chanted: "Look now, lady, my cock has got *size*. It'll go in your cunt and out the other side . . . No, stop, let me rap it once more, talking 'bout my cock is one heavy chore. Fucking Jack is never a bore, I fuck so hard you're bound to get sore! Look now, baby, my cock's not like another, it will go in one side and right out the other." Then more giggles and a bright, "Bye now."

On the dirty yellow lino of his kitchen floor, Ignatz stared up unseeingly at his kitchen light bulb. Mother of God, he thought nonsensically, is this the end of Ignatz? He had overdosed on the great American delirium, the tiger tea of sex and race (with a Supçon of psychoanalysis). Where, he wondered, oh where can I score some crack? But he no longer knew where you went to cop, he didn't know if it was even called copping. It was all a three-part series in *The New York Times* to him. His kitchen light fixture was speckled with dead moths. "Pup," he shouted at the light. "Pup! *Pup!*" Really, he didn't want to get high, he just wanted to go where Kate had been, Kate disappearing down the rabbit hole into the wonderland city of her sexuality ("My, but he's pretty"), the urban center of her blackness ("Oh, Ignatz, get up offa that thang!"). His fingers jabbed the answering machine's buttons, erase, erase, erase, *it all never happened.* What about *my* hands, Dr. Ignatz thought, clutching at his long straw clutchers, remembering all the sweet things Kate had said about his touch on the keyboard of her body. The only keys he massaged anymore were on his answering machine. He couldn't even play the piano without Kate; when he tried to soothe himself with blues his chords were maudlin self-pity or jangled anger. He wiggled his fingers. My hands work! Aren't they special? Well, he thought, remembering BKJ's tiny mitts, *everybody has hands.*

The next morning Dr. Ignatz wrapped himself in his oldest comforter—a bathrobe woven of blue wool and sweet black lethargy—and sat at the Formica kitchen table, cherishing the heaviness that muffled the edges of all his harsh thoughts in whatdoesitmatter cotton. He thought of his betrayer, his savior, his Sup. When his mother had looked away, only his grave-eaten father, his dying analyst, could protect defective little Ignatz. Or was he maimed because he had made himself into his father's obedient son? How could he ever take possession of himself, say good-bye to the bastard Supervisor? What makes an animal into a mensch?

The unconscious, the Sup had said once, in his new gnomic extended fortune-cookie style, is like two people, no, two *animals* locked in a room, dealing out tarot cards for you to read. The Hanged Man. The Woman with a Penis. Who knows what makes one a man or a woman? *That* question could take one deeply into things. But Ignatz was *nailed* to the question. He had to speculate—make new connections between the cards.

Sup, shatteringly, had cleared his throat. Dr. Ignatz, still musing inwardly, had asked what Sup's cough meant, not realizing he spoke aloud.

"Meant? *Meant?* It *means,*" Sup had wheezed, "that I'm dying."

His best friend, Mr. Coffee, burbled consolingly, wondering if Dr. Ignatz mightn't like a cuppa? Ignatz cherished the bitterness that he drank alone from the cracked cup. To hell with the Sup, Dr. Ignatz thought, seeing Kate without telling him! *Undoubtedly* Sup was in love with Kate from the first—all those questions about what she wore! And Dr. Ignatz's own therapy hour must have been a fascinating, bitter, porno loop for Sup! He had been Sup's body, possessing Kate! Sup probably came in his pinstripes! The stupid old eunuch! The dirty dying old man! Dr. Ignatz recited his father's strangely comforting mantra: *Why bother? The world is a suicidal thought in the mind of God and we're all little animals crawling in a dung heap.*

As, for example, Kate, standing on his porch in a red sweatshirt and blue jeans, her yellow woolen legwarmers down around her ankles, her blonde-black hair stringy with sweat on an overcast March morning. "God, I'm sorry," she said. She was crying. "I know I look a mess. I know I have no right to come here. But I didn't know where else to go!" Jack had knocked her to the sidewalk outside the Harvest Restaurant.

"Why?"

"That's it!" she screamed. "Blame the victim! For no reason, Ignatz, that's why! Jack doesn't think. Jack doesn't criticize himself. Jack doesn't analyze himself. Angry at the bitch. Bam!"

"I know Jack acts out," Dr. Ignatz said. Rain (that would become sleet that would become snow) began to sprinkle down. Too fuddled to go upstairs, Dr. Ignatz brought Kate inside his bathrobe, and tied the robe shut around the two of them. How thin she felt! He decided to hell with doctor-patient confidentiality. He bet Sup didn't respect it! And he express-mailed his Brotherhood award back to B'nai B'rith. "Jack has no inner life." Meaning: *He's flat. Look: I'm round.* "Jack's a jerk."

"He's not a jerk, really." Kate was breathing more slowly, more calmly. "I wasn't being fair. I was just saying what I knew you wanted to hear. God, when will I stop doing that! Trying to please everyone! Why can't I be like Spade." She added, musingly, "Do you think I'm afraid of you?"

A spade? "Afraid of me?" Ignatz said. "I would never hit you."

"What? I keep missing words! Ignatz, I think you better take me to the hospital!" She started to cry again.

The intern at the Mt. Auburn emergency room said that Kate had a punctured eardrum. They wouldn't be able to measure the degree of her hearing loss till they saw how well the healing went.

Shivering in the lobby, Kate asked Ignatz to come home with her to Somerville, to stay with her that night.

"You know it's Wednesday, Kate. I have to celebrate Emily's tenure."

"What?" She turned her bad ear towards him. "I can't hear you anymore." She gave him a closed-lip smile and walked to the elevator. The heavy metal and rubber doors closed behind her, the goddess back into the machine.

■ ■ ■

Sup's face above the blankets was a slab of bone, with giant eyebrows painted on. The bronchitis had raked the fat from his pleasant Mr. Potato Head face, revealing this massive, solid, implacable structure that would last forever. Wattles of skin flapped from his neck. Kate was terrified. If Sup couldn't help her, no one could, and he suddenly looked beyond helping himself. She turned the chair to the side of the bed, so she could keep her good ear to him, and she put her hand over her wound—to keep the shameful sight from the Sup. Jack had violated the most intimate part of her. *Sup had to help her to get her hearing back!* She knew that was crazy. He was an analyst, not a faith healer. But she *had* to be able to hear again! Hear perfectly. Hear everything. So she could sing! That was all she had ever really wanted to do with her life, not stupid scribble scribble scribble about Jasper Johns, but to show her true soul before an audience, to sing, to give pleasure. Not art history, but art! She *did* have a soul! Her singing *was* art. And her mother was wrong: Kate was good enough to do it! If only she could hear again! A soul is a funny thing, she thought. You find it at the very point you seem to be losing it. She confessed to the Sup about her damaged eardrum.

"You identify with men for power," he said in an off-hand way. Underneath the blankets, his hands moved up and down his thighs, scratching, scratching. "But having power makes you feel guilty. So you let the men punish you. Brick after brick."

Bricks again? More madness. She wept. For Sup. For herself. What if there was no help here? Then there was no help anywhere. But it *was* true, in a way, during the stupid hungover-from-crack-and-brandy fight about the car keys she had seen BKJ as one of the bat-winged monkey slaves of the wicked witch. Equals Mom. Punishing her for stepping out.

"Your mother taught: nothing too ambitious for Kate. No showing off. Dinner with Joe, then home to bed. But what if we make our lives so poor we don't care if we die? Then some irritable, almost indifferent hand will reach out . . ." He stopped, pulled his arms from under the covers, and stared at his blotched hands, his bony fingers, as if he didn't know whom they belonged to. He extended a skeletal finger, ". . . and push the button."

What button? She kissed him on the forehead. She wanted to soothe the madness away.

"Well, who can blame you, Kate? It's *death* I'm talking about, not table manners. God, that stupid Ignatz gets everything wrong!" He stopped; gasped at air. "The opposite of sex isn't table manners, it's anger and ambition—death, Kate, death. No wonder you're afraid of your ambition. The bomb made you think that anger leads to the end of the world. You just want to hold still, to hug yourself to keep your mothercules from leaving."

The bomb? The bomb her father had made? Kate didn't think about the atomic bomb from one end of the day to the other! Did Sup think she felt unconsciously responsible for what her father had done? She remembered when she was very little, her father saying that the bombs had left poison in the grass that the cows ate; Kate wasn't to drink moo milk, but to take special chalky calcium pills instead. Was that like the bomb being her ambition—and that anger made her mother's milk go away?

She stroked his forehead, then pulled her hand away— the bone *wanted* to come through! *To show off.* (Body becomes corpse becomes bone, becomes . . . becomes. becomes.becomes. Her mind shuddered; stopped.) The bomb, she thought, *was* an awful thing. Who wouldn't be terrified of it—if they ever thought about it? It was our anger grown too large—a cup filled with blackness, with pure death. Everything would be swallowed up indifferently. No more milk. No more mother. Maybe it *would* be better if no one was ambitious, no one got angry.

Sup tried to lift himself out of bed. She looked away, so she wouldn't shame him by seeing his withered genitals through the flap of his cotton johnny, or his sagging belly, a comical paunch above his skinny legs. He leaned on her, as light as bird bones wrapped in parchment, and she slowly led him to the bathroom, shutting the door behind him, so he could have some privacy.

He spoke to her over the stop-and-go tinkle of his pee. "Your mother wouldn't allow anger. No animal in Kate. Only a false, flat, innocent self. So you won't even see it. That's why you won't see that I'm dying, Kate." He kicked open the door and held his cock out. "Look at that!" He shook it up and down. "It doesn't work anymore!"

Kate kicked the door closed.

"You cats are such clean animals. So full of not-my-fault innocence. No dirt, no shit, no aging, no death!" There was a nnnh, nnnh sound; he might have been straining to urinate; or to laugh; or to breathe.

She helped him back to bed. I'm not an animal, she thought. I mean, I am, but I'm not. I mean, I talk, she concluded nonsensically.

"Here, tuck me in."

She straightened the blanket, crimping it tightly under his shoulders, the way he liked it, as if the thin pink blanket were his new shirt, vest, suit, and bow tie combined. Cats? God, this was terrible! His brain circuits were firing at random. She couldn't take much more of this. "You'll be better soon."

"Kate. Listen to me. You *want* this, too." Sup took a tissue from the bedside table and coughed. She could see his body shake like the overlapping frames of a film that had come off the sprockets. "Here," he said, "a gift. Token of my affection."

The tissue held a clump of sputum and blood. She gagged and hurled it across the room.

"I'm dying, Kate. Dying. Dead. The thing you can't even imagine. Accept that you want it. You love me *and* you want me to die, Kate. You can't take much more of this. Listen to me now, Kate. *I* want you to be angry. Why shouldn't you finally *pounce?* Write songs for me. Write a song to say good-bye to Jack. And to Joe. And to me."

"But I don't want to say good-bye to you."

He turned his face away from her. "Kate, I *want* to die. I want you to help me. Sing to me. Here." He patted the side of the bed. "Sit here."

Kate sat.

"Now sing. Sing something that will help me die."

Kate sang. One of her ears caught only pieces of the tune, so she had to hear the whole inside her. The song had no words. She hummed and the humming formed into notes, and the notes came from a dark empty cold place deep in her, the place where the black snakes intertwined. Was this her heart—the *not* of its *not yet, not yet* beat? Without that she couldn't have a heart. There was something inside her that she had kept holding back from herself and from the world, so that time never passed and yesterday was like today and no one aged—and she was sad all the time. Sup *wanted* her to release that *not,* no matter what the cost to him, *because* of the cost to him . . . and the notes came and came . . . and made a song filled with the care one gives a dying friend as you help him towards death, a song filled with the bedpan, the urine and shit on the sheets as he loses control of his bladder and bowels, the morphine suppositories you put in his ass, the ravings endured. Her mother's death, her poor dear loving mother who had died with so many unlived lives inside her. Stars do age, Mama, must age. And die.

As she sang the Sup lightly scratched the patch of discolored skin on her shoulder with his sharp nails, as if he was trying to scrabble the stain out. Like a foretaste of the grave, no one had bothered to cut his nails.

"You're great, Kate," he said weakly. "You really slay me!"

After he fell asleep, his fingers continued to scratch for a moment. When they stopped, she put his arm back down next to his body.

■ ■ ■

The rest of the dark March afternoon she spent in T.T. the Bear's Place, a comfortable Central Square bar, old wood and better times, a refugee from the sixties, flotsam cast on the shore of working-class Cambridge. A small cave, the bar suited her mood and the light snowfall outside. "Quarter to three," she hummed, "and only one other woman in the place," a gal a few drinks past forty, who held her cigarette with three fingers and gulped the smoke back, as if she were sentenced to the cigarette, as if she had to suffer the smoke, suffer the songs on the jukebox that made her brown eyes blue. She had a five-inch stack of quarters next to her drink, which she used to bribe the jukebox into taking her hostage over and over. Kate, too, had gotten some quarters, thinking she might cut in, but her new bar pal was too intent—under a curse, paying off a debt—and Kate didn't dare break the force field of her sorrow.

On the top of a paper napkin, Kate wrote *Good-bye Songs.* She began a rap for BKJ. Writing had the bitter tang of freedom where she was the boat, and the ocean, and the wind—though the ink ran, widening her words to near illegibility. The barrel of her maroon Waterman pen had a nice heft to it, though, like wielding a gun. Well, not a real gun, of course, a gun that turned into a Zippo lighter. And songs were bombs. Well, not real bombs, but play bombs, like water balloons. Not real death, but symbolic death. Because we want *that.* To slough off the old self. Or Kate did. *She didn't have another ear to spare.*

Kate felt under a strange house arrest—the only way she could affect the world outside was through her art. Only that would tell the truth, not leaving out her sweetness, or her anger. But was writing songs what she—Kate, by herself, Kate *alone*—wanted to do? Or was she just trying to be the Sup, wearing a cock suit again? Well, she could *learn* from a man, couldn't she—even if Sup, like a modern artist, was just showing how powerful he was by giving up his power. Not that she could actually have killed him today! (It was a let's-pretend water bomb, more fun to believe in than not.) She loved Sup. (She thought of him waving his shriveled dick about in the bathroom. Waving his dick? She hadn't seen it! Snip . . . Wait! She *had* seen it. He had *wanted* her to see it.) And she loved Fred, and Stan, and Cary, and Dr. Ignatz, and Jack. She hadn't *just* desired their power! After all, she had power of her own—real sap-making capabilities. She looked at her lovely long legs in the white stockings Ignatz had bought for her, felt the satisfying tightness of the garter belt around her belly.

She waved to the bartender for another beer.

No. That wouldn't do. Why just be Brigid, the enchantress, the woman with a cat inside her, the morals of a cat? Why be what *they* thought her? Why not have the Bogart part? *A Star Is Born*—but this time Judy cops to her own ambition!

She looked over at her companion—ma semblable, ma looney tune. One more little piece of my heart, one more trip to Phoenix, one more public display of how men have danced the mashed potato on your soul, and Kate would be crazy, too. She went and took the cigarette out of her friend's hand. The woman tossed her beer on the front of Kate's jeans. Kate took the pink handkerchief from her pocket and patted herself dry. The woman pointed at Kate's pee-pee fly, and began the chorus to "MacArthur Park."

Kate returned to her table. Well, *she* would live by her own code; *she* would be Sam Spade, would be Sup, would be, even, the good parts of Dr. Ignatz. Gods were OK if they were like cakes and you *ate* them. Her pen and her voice would be her gat. No. Even in this world where no code held, she could do better than *that*. To make the new round Kate, she would add the great mothers to her cake, add the deep implication of *feeling with,* add Baby Snooks and Ginger and Sippie Wallace and Moms Mabley's motherwit and Gracie. They knew how to maintain the love and connection, and still have their anger and their dignity. George, so patriarchal with his cigar, till Gracie's jiu-jitsu made him into the straight man. All that wonderful stuff was always there for us, a second childhood to help us grow up, a grab bag of new inthrowjacks to collage a new self out of. That's how refugees like Kate (a cat in a woman's body, a woman in cat disguise) got reborn as Americans!

The jukebox was free now, but Kate decided to use her coins in the phone booth near the bathroom. Better to sing the songs, she thought, than to suffer them. Though she knew that she would never sing effortlessly again. Her voice, now, came after experience—and that should show; whatever beauty she could make would be *made.* She put "Thanks for the Memories" on her husband's answering machine. And for BK a bluesy version of "Hit the Road, Jack." Then she added the rap she had scribbled on the napkin. "You said you were a fellow who really had size,/ Reach in your shorts and find the big Cracker Jack prize./ You said you'd fuck me till I said when,/ but what you put in me was just a carrot julienne!" How he would sputter! But her song was too wacka-wacka angry, too silly. Why be what they saw you as—furry-fury, temptress-cat? What do they know about cats? *Cats belong to themselves!* " 'Bye, Jack. Good luck with your dissertation!" Then she rapped once more. "OK. Tiny Jack, I wish you well,/ But if you go upside women, we'll see you in hell."

Then she dialed Ignatz. But when he answered—live— she didn't have a number for him. She wanted to see him. You can have my husband, she thought, but don't you go messing with my man. She could *do* things with Ignatz. At least some times, she thought, smiling at their love games, he *wants* me to have power. He's *teachable*. So she invited Dr. Ignatz for a drink.

"We could be partners," she said, "like Nick and Nora. Or Stan and Ollie. You'd play the piano, I'd sing."

He laughed. "Sure, Judy. I've got a barn. Let's put on a show!"

She wanted to smack him. He would have to accept her anger, so she wouldn't be ashamed of herself, and feel guilty for her ambition. Was that too much to ask of that curly head, that less than Greek figure? And he would *have* to leave his wife.

"Kate, this is silly." Outside the snow must have started; droplets fell from Ignatz's curly hair. "If you want to stay here, we can see if we can work things out together. I don't trust you, Miss Wonderly. I can't just throw everything over and dance off to New York with you. If there even really *is* a New York."

George and Gracie would have done the six-minute egg. Fred and Ginger would have flung each other across the parquet. Calm, smiling, Ollie Higgs Bosun would have reached across the glass table and poured a whole pitcher full of beer inside Dr. Ignatz's pleated pants, then waited patiently for him to pour water down *her* pants. They'd be even then, the world would be in balance, and they could make love.

But Dr. Ignatz Laurel would have missed his cue. "Why did you do that?" Ignatz would whimper. "Do you hate me so much? Oh God, I *deserve* to be hated." Like her drinking companion, he made a show of his pain to shame the world.

Boy—they hit you, or they bricked themselves, just as long as there was hitting. Guys—how 'bout a little *style*, please? "I don't hate you *anymore*," Kate would have instructed. "I *was* angry."

"Good-bye, Ignatz." She looked at his lovely creased face—how had she missed those lines around his eyes, those cracks that make us more ourselves, that remind us that our existence is a mirrorkell, that show the black background we shine against, the almost of loss? Oh, she loved him still, the little coward! She got up to leave. "See you in the funny papers."

Ignatz Mouse gasped. Do something, you idiot! She really means it! The light was waning from Krazy's living room. He turned to ask the Kat for more tea, and some reassurance that everything would come out all right, she wouldn't leave him. But she wasn't at the table, and her Zuni tea service was doing a Cheshire cup disappearing act. He looked over to the rug, the kitchen. No Kat! He was alone in the room! Outside the window a cactus was turning into a church spire. Ignatz wanted to tell Krazy how the Sup's dying brain changed like the Coconino backgrounds. Or like the Producer endlessly changing plots till the continuity was lost. But Krazy wasn't here! There was no one to tell his clever insight to. For the first time since he had left his father for work in the comic pages, Ignatz Mouse, brave Ignatz Mouse the rebel artist, wept. But, teary or not, he knew that he *must* keep his eyes on the imaginary screen, he must keep the story going somehow by himself, but in a way that was true to Krazy, too—*he*, alone, would have to *imagine* the kinds of things that meshugina Kat would say!—for otherwise, he knew, the screen that was their co-creation would disappear and he would be trapped here, alone, forever!

■ ■ ■

The next day when Dr. Ignatz went to visit, the nurses had sat Sup up in a green padded chair by the bed, fastened him to the chair back by the long cotton straps of a special light-blue johnny. From his time as a resident, Dr. Ignatz knew that this funny suit was more humane than other kinds of restraint, a great help to the staff in controlling patients too weak to break the lightest bonds, yet strong enough to wander about. But it made the dying Sup look pathetic. *Which he deserved!* Dr. Ignatz was furious at Sup for having seen Kate all these months without telling him. Furious that Sup loved Kate! Well, who could blame him? She *was* magnificent, so brave in that bar with her cockamamie plan to become a singer. (Didn't she know that the fire of one's talent didn't guarantee anyone's attention?) Besides, he loved the old man, too, the dying old man. And he needed his help.

"This is degrading," Sup said, his raspy voice a wisp now. "Undo these ties and I'll undo yours."

Well, that was sense, Dr. Ignatz thought, the Sup's business was undoing ties. He released him. Sup walked off to the nurse's station—all the more implacable in his mission for his weakness—will alone propelling him forward down the bright, fluorescently lit corridor. (Ignatz didn't stop him. He felt as if there was an unbridgeable holy aura around the Sup, the prestige of dying. Ignatz was held in the fist of his youth, and Sup lived in a different county, one where people aged; died.)

At the nurse's station, Sup took off his johnny and flapped his penis up and down at the girls. Dr. Ignatz led him back to bed, and—still in the analysand's thrall—wondered if this striptease was meant therapeutically for him? Something about display? cocks? overvaluation of same?

"Want to get in bed with me, little Mouse?"

"What?"

"Oh Ignatz, it was always the contact with me you wanted. So you threw bricks at Krazy and then came to me to be arrested."

Bricks? Crazy? Sup was raving again, and Ignatz felt his own identity flickering. The Sup had been his mentor, his mirror, the daily strip starring Dr. Ignatz. Now his past was disappearing. "What? Arrested?"

"You know, you'd rush to analysis to tell me about it." He laughed. Sputtered. Coughed. "To be penetrated," he said in his wisp of a voice. "Intellectually." He gasped, reaching for the oxygen. The plastic mask with its long clear tubing tail looked like a small animal clinging to his face, taking breath away instead of giving it.

"Mouse," he said, after a few breaths, "stop being mom and looking for fathers to fuck you. You have to give birth to your mother inside you. The one who looked away. Use your anger against her to push her out of yourself."

Again he motioned for the clear plastic oxygen mask— like a dog's muzzle, say—and, for a few moments, he breathed clarity and light.

"You should write songs for Kate, songs from her point of you." He gasped. "Of view."

But my father, Ignatz thought, didn't want a musician. He would rather have seen me dead. Ignatz saw a lifetime of bitter opposition.

"Make your songs restitution for leaving him."

"He wouldn't listen."

Sup turned his withered hands palms up, and slowly, with evident pain, shrugged his bony shoulders. "Who listens?" It was the tag, Ignatz realized, to the oldest psychoanalytic joke. "Who ever listens?"

▪ ▪ ▪

Dr. Ignatz canceled his afternoon appointments. Sup had been no use. Songwriting as therapy! What nonsense! Kate and Sup were in league to drive him mad. He played the blues on his upright. But his chords veered between beery self-loathing and wild-swinging rage.

BKJ—not picking up his messages anymore since Kate

had made his phone-mate a jukebox of nasty surprises—
came in for his three o'clock psyche-massage. When he saw
his doctor at the piano, Jack said nothing, just stood and
listened. Analytic neutrality, Ignatz supposed. Or maybe he
thought the concert was part of the therapy, done for his
benefit, like Sup's cock waving.

"Kate's gone," Dr. Ignatz said. Dignity no longer
seemed necessary. Or *possible*. BKJ must have seen reels of
his affair with Kate, Ignatz's dereliction as therapist, his odd
proclivities.

"I heard. Strange girl. My America, my newfound land.
I'll miss her."

"America? I guess. Black and white in one?"

"No, I mean she's like America. Seems to give herself
completely, guilelessly, to each passing fancy. But in the
morning, she's gone. On to the next song. Our love wasn't
here to stay."

"I think she's changed," Ignatz said. Kate had meant
what she had said at T.T.'s. Now she really wanted him to
leave Emily. He couldn't. So he played his blues, thinking of
poor sad him, and his dying, much-loved rival, the Sup. The
opposite of sex isn't table manners, he thought—adding
more blue notes to the vamp, it's death, the loss at every
moment; Kate turning away from him as he played. So he
pressed her into him. But then he was furious at her for
turning away from him, so he tormented her inside himself,
tormented himself. The world is a dung heap, he thought.
But that was self-laceration, not the blues. So he tried to
make Kate come out in the notes. ("Trash," his father said,
but Ignatz ignored him. "Listen to my song, Dad," he said.)

"I'm listening," BKJ replied.

Kate was the theme—pop standards, blues-inflected,
blues with high heels on—going off into different variations,
then coming back to him. He tried to accept her, not punish-

ing her as his father had punished his mother, but cherishing her. He banged down hard, using his anger to give birth to her. She *would* go away. But if he helped her to go, maybe she would come back to him. Theme and variation, call and response.

"That's nice," Jack said, shuffling from foot to foot in a little improvised dance step, this foot that foot, lifting and swaying. "I like it. Not like that ugly rap shit."

"You don't like rap?" Ignatz said, surprised.

"Nah," Jack said, and he sang. "Can't rap, don't make me/ Can't rap merci beaucoup/ My blues won't let my mouth/ Do things it shouldn't do./ Can't rap, don't make me/ Can't rap, merci beaucoup/ I lost my girl, and I can only sing the blues/ I need a new therapist and so I sing the blues/ Accompanied by this smart, though somewhat lustful, Jew."

All in all, that was sweet of Jack. They laughed together, and, self-consciously, embraced before they parted.

■ ■ ■

Three months later Kate and Dr. Ignatz met again at a service for Sup at Harvard's Memorial Church. The whole Boston analytic community was there, even the anti-Institute renegades. Sup was worth honoring. Sup was worth crying for, if the analysts hadn't thought that an excessive acting out.

Ignatz was in a special analytic limbo. His own analyst dead before termination, he nursed his patients without relish. Why should they be fed when he wasn't? And he stayed away from the Institute. Overcome by orphan's paranoia, he was sure his colleagues looked at him oddly, as if he had killed the Sup.

Kate sat in the same pew, not touching, her lovely legs in long black stockings. Who knew mourning could be so sexy? He told Kate of a dream of Sup he'd had. (It had been months since he'd told anyone a dream. Dreams now felt more intimate, more magical, as if one should tell them not to analysts, but to Gypsy lovers. Well, Kate would do for that.) In his dream, Sup was still alive, his arms withered, his hands like claws. Dr. Ignatz had felt guilty that in his dream he hadn't wanted Sup back, alive again.

He thought that Kate, beneath her long black veil, smiled. "He *wanted* us to help him die, Ignatz. It's better this way. For him. For us." She took his hand, pressing it lightly, so that they needn't be embarrassed. His fingers flared with life.

The president of the Institute droned on. Dr. Ignatz couldn't take his eyes from Kate. She was beautiful in the nearly flat black hat from the scenarios, and the widely meshed veil added mystery to her already fascinating face. He remembered the pain of imagining himself-as-Kate under Jack. He remembered being angry at his patient on Kate's behalf when Jack never mentioned Kate's numinous name. He remembered his own refrains as they argued about Emily at The Harvest. What was the name of that tune?

Suddenly he ripped a page from the prayer book and wrote down some words. What would his father think of such desecration of a holy—albeit Protestant—book? (Jesus Christ, his goddamn life was *The Jazz Singer*! Fine! *Well,* he had his mother's voice say, *Ignatz, you belong to the world now.*) The name of that tune was "Dollar Brand"!

He handed it to her. She looked down, hummed to herself. "You've got a Zippo lighter, got the dollar brand/ But you can't light my cigarettes if you won't be my man." She read on. It was a silly little song for Kate to sing, saying good-bye to him, from her point of view—so she wouldn't have to leave him, or that, leaving him, she might return.

She squeezed his hand. "Ignatz, dahling, have you got six minutes to spare after this? So I can make you some breakfast?"

"Six minutes?" he said, though he felt he knew what was coming. "Why six minutes?"

"Why, dolling, so I can make you two three-minute eggs."

■ ■ ■

One year later. Kate sat in a French Provincial–style chair at the Plaza Hotel, her legs, in red stockings, stretched out on an ottoman. A stack of magazines and newspapers lay by the slightly bowed gilt chair legs. Ignatz, in jeans, sat across from her on the big double bed. As if defiantly holding himself apart from his surroundings, he hadn't taken off his loafers. Kate picked up *The New York Times,* and read out loud to Ignatz: "'In this world, where, at first it seems that no code holds, we all play the sap for each other. But then, as Kat'"—for that was Kate's stage name—"'and her accompanist, Ignatz, show us, this new sort of relationship forms rules of its own: You lead I'll follow. Or I lead, you follow. Improvisation—the making of music as an open-ended conversation.'"

Kate let the pages flutter to the floor. "It's too bad . . ."

An old refrain. Ignatz knew the song. "Yes."

"He would have liked listening to us."

Ignatz remembered Sup in the hospital bed, his face muscles drawn inward in pain, listening. To him. To *her.* Promiscuous listening, the bastard. His dying joke. "Who listens?" Ignatz said, shrugging his shoulders like an old Irish Jew. "Who ever listens?"

When she was upset her ears went back, and she narrowed her eyes. "They *listen,* Ignatz. Don't they?"

He tried to soothe her. "Yes. Of course, they listen. To

you. You have," he said sincerely, "star quality. And that's something you can't buy or learn in school."

She picked up another magazine, with a slick cover. " 'Kat and Ignatz show us that you can participate in your lover's success—and the electricity between these two is palpable; we can be certain that these two *are* lovers. She moves away from him, accompanied by the blues notes on the piano, as he mourns for her loss. But, won by his feeling-ful playing, his empathy for her—the way he embodies her in the song—she turns towards him with the melody. A game of hide and seek. In art—sharing the creation of a fantasy—they achieve their fusion with each other, drinking each other from the same cup, a cup they have created while we watched.' "

"This guy," Ignatz said, "is like all the high-brow critics you love so much. He's showing how smart *he* is by writing about us. See, he says, *I* can make something out of junk." Ignatz didn't like these new magazines, their six-dollar-and-ninety-five-cent price, their mocking covers (this one was an obscene panel of Nancy and Sluggo), their academic discourse peppered with jive talk, their "aren't we cool, we like to mix with garbage" attitudes, their wise-guy titles—like this one, *Bum Rap*. This was *not* avant-garde popular art, but avant people being ironic about a little uptown thrill. If everyone thought Kate's art was simply good, there wouldn't be any spice to their taking it seriously. If Kate and he didn't stay uptown, then where was the insult to Mom and Pop at the bourgeois dinner table? (Or downtown? Ignatz was still geographically out of it. He left Kate to cover the art water-front.)

"No. Wait. I think he *really* likes us: 'Listening to Kat and Ignatz one begins to feel that sex may be a lesser form of connection than playing music together. And Kat's rendering of Cole Porter's somewhat masochistic love songs—"so your baby can be your slave"—reminds one that these longings, too, can have their place in love-become-art, that they can be raised and transformed, so that love need not be same-same obsession but, instead, a field of playfulness.' "

"Jesus," Ignatz said, "we're just saloon musicians!"

"Just?" She knew that Ignatz was afraid that the don's sense of their importance would be gum in the works. She teased him. "If anything, I think we should make the act more complicated."

"It's a gift to be simple," the Mouse said.

"It's a gift to make it look simple," Kate replied.

"You sound like me!"

"A mirror looking at a mirror," Kat said. "No. Wait. I *mean* it's a complicated business nowadays to produce *real* simplicity." She picked up a weekly newspaper. " 'White people write songs. But their songs are just hungry ghosts till black people give them a soul . . .' " She tossed it across the room. "Want to hear *Variety*?"

"Sure."

" 'It looks like the man whom the Hearst Corporation calls simply the Producer has the making of another of his multimedia hits in Kat Higgs Bosun and her piano player, Ignatz. Their combination of torch numbers, original specialty items, and between-times blue George-and-Gracie-like chatter, are already wow on the club, concert hall, and college circuit. "There's no question about them as a live draw," the Producer said, "we've been SRO in all the Hearst clubs and casinos. Will it transfer to Hearst vinyl? Look at me," he said to this reporter. "Would you want to hear them on record? See the aura? See how round I am? Of course you would want to hear them! I'm readying their first TV special for Eastertime. And then my Assistant and I are thinking Christmas movie. An old-style musical. But I can say no more. Maybe it will be a Western? Do you like Westerns? Black hats vs. white hats? Kat is a gunslinger, and Ignatz is a whore, no, I said plays piano in a whorehouse, and . . ." ' "

"Genug," Ignatz said, as if the Producer brought up distasteful memories. "Better the art-rap nonsense than that."

"We're a comodesty, dear. Art history waits for art, and the market waits to snatch up our song. They still *do* own the rights to us." But, as if she, too, were eager to forget those unpleasant silken ties, she picked up the don's article again: " 'Kat is the incarnation of the mystery of sex for our decade. Androgynous, open, seemingly guileless in her sexuality, nothing overwhelmingly predatory about it, except as that, too, might be the occasion for playfulness.' "

Ignatz laughed. "Sure! Come here, little Mouse. Let me *dance* with you."

" 'Kat and Ignatz live, as we all do, in the acceptance *and* the fear of death, the joy *and* anxiety of their sexuality, in the knowledge of change, *and* in the flat, unchanging, relaxing dream of innocence. It is a painting *and* a flag.' " She licked a finger, and turned a page. " 'As with so much modernist art, Kat's questions seem to be on the surface. Kat, her blonde hair streaked black, her black hair markered with blonde, can be a vamp. And then, like a restless American switching the station, she simply changes. She does what she wants, not minding if others look on, simply turning a deaf ear to hecklers. A whore? A madonna? A . . .' "

"A cat," Ignatz said, curling his long lovely fingers into claws.

"A woman." Kat smiled.

"Was this the guy who was your lover?"

"The don? That coyote! I always had the feeling he was gay. I don't think he was really interested in sleeping with me. He wanted to *be* me." Kate lifted up the glossy pages. " 'Kat often sings songs Ignatz wrote for her. The oddly affecting "Abraham's Song"—sung from the point of view of a cat—or "Dollar Brand"—the story of an affair with a married man (Ignatz himself) unable to leave his wife. Thanks to their assiduous interrogation on the "Duck Tells" TV show—which Kat and Ignatz use almost as an extension of their stage act, to add a confessional aspect to the very surface of their work—everyone really knows their offstage story. (Yet we *demand* that there be still more, something unknown. And out of our desire for romance, we, the audience, *imagine* that intriguing, shadowy "something more" behind what we see—hidden motives, sexy quirks, secrets within Kat's silent prowls around the piano. Kat and Ignatz—by their rigorous gossiping about themselves, which puts *everything* on the flat surface of the stage—let us feel how we *make* one area the unconscious, the background; *we* create perspectives, create roundness—that beautiful fiction—collaborate in creating people with shadows on the stage.) Ignatz, we know, wrote "Dollar Brand" as a way of showing that he understood Kat's pain. Singing it, she accepts his gift, alters it, and shows him what he had missed in his guilty view of the situation—he had overlooked her power, her pleasure, that she had always been so much more than his victim. Kat is aptly named. For she is making katzenmusik, a song out of her pain, like the cats whose fur men ripped off during Germany's Lenten festivals. But like all the great blues singers, she offers us, from her pain, a deeper implication in life, all of it, its angers and its love, its *passion*. Even the breaks between registers in Kat's voice are undisguised, and work to add sincerity. The cracks make her more herself. Her beloved, played by Ignatz, her piano player . . .' "

"Played by?" He held a finger-barrel gun to his own head. "Your art or your life!"

Kate laughed.

"I think I'm going to call room service. Order a nice mouse for you." Ignatz still got a kick out of using room service at the Plaza for a hamburger. Was that like academically trained critics ordering Kat and Ignatz on their tony critical instruments?

" '. . . her piano player, accompanist, songwriter, straight man, is weak-looking, thin, with big ears and Harpo curly hair—' "

"Yuch!"

" '—yet clearly beloved nonetheless.' " She turned the page. " 'So when Kat sings "My Funny Valentine," one is reminded that this was a song that Larry Hart wrote for the woman he loved, the love that he hoped would "help" him to become heterosexual. (A symbolic problem, Kat and Ignatz show us in their highly sexual onstage banter. Who is a man and who a woman—and when each of us takes up or turns those roles—is not, finally, a matter of organs!) His beloved was to sing it to him, from the Broadway stage. Yet to hear these two play this song, to hear Kat make it her own, is to go far beyond such ventriloquism. Here the mirror-looking-at-a-mirror ("I look into your eyes where I see me looking at you looking at me—isn't art empty, aren't we both grand!") nature of so much modern performance has been transformed into something feelingful, freeing. As she sings, "Is his figure less than Greek, is his mouth a little weak?" (And as it's Ignatz she's talking about, that is certainly the case! When he opens it to speak, does he squeak!) she sounds as if this is precisely the sort of creature she wants. Just a thin man. Nothing special. Except to her. Almost as if she had made him up! And the cruelty of that—for after all *he* might have preferred to be seen as taller, to be lied to, to be said to be stronger of chin and chest—that cruelty is openly shown, yet redeemed and transfigured by the loving gaze of the artist who has—with all her capabilities, her cruelty and her desire—entered, as if his creator, into the mildly grotesque form of the beloved. Together, Ignatz and Kat give us a figure of reconciliation.' "

Kate closed the pages, humming to herself, looking at Ignatz, eyes closed on the bed, a small blue stone glittering in his left ear. " 'When he opens it to speak, is he smart?/ Don't change a hair for me/ Not if you care for me/ Stay funny valentine, stay/ Each day is Valentine's Day . . .' "

■ ■ ■

On a deserted mesa wind blew into a house that now had only three walls left, no, two, no, one. Tumbleweed blew past a table, shaking a cup that seemed to have been half dissolved by the wind, a partial cup that, as the table disappeared, stood in midair. Outside—if one can speak of an outside when there is only one wall—was a small empty stone building, unchanging, eternally itself, with a faded wooden sign over the door: JAIL. Behind it, a cactus turned into tall church spires, and a mesa in the background became maroon bells for the spires. It must have been the light playing tricks.

Appendix

DOLLAR BRAND

We were sitting at a cafe,
Warmed by money and sun.
I said: This isn't fun
Anymore. I can't do what's wrong.
I've got to learn my craft
I've got to write this song.

Now you: you got a Zippo lighter, you got the dollar brand
But you can't light my cigarettes if you won't be my man.

I know I wore a black hat,
I know you wore a grin,
The whole stupid cafe scene
Seemed to fit right in.

I said:

I don't want you in the afternoon, want you all night long,
This sneaking up the backstairs, can't you see it's wrong?
I can fly on airplanes, I can talk on the phone
But I can't stand weak drinks, and sleeping all alone
You've been watering the whiskey, and throwing meatless bones.

So I'm putting my black hat on my head now,
And my cape round my back
I'm leaving for New York, and I'm not coming back.

Now you: you got a Zippo lighter, you got the dollar brand
But you can't light my cigarettes if you won't be my man.

I called you up to say my momma died
Won't you come on your scooter, bring flowers for her grave?
You said, I know you're sad, know how you've cried,
But I know how you've lied, too, and I won't be your slave.

Well, I'm putting my black hat on my head,
Wrapping my cape round my back,
I'm leaving for New York,
And I'm not coming back.

Now you: you got a Zippo lighter, you got the dollar brand
But you can't light my cigarettes if you won't be my man.

I have the voice and I have the wings,
And you can't hold *me* here with a silly silver ring
You have three meals, and a nice warm bed
And I'll bet you have the feeling you'd be better off dead.
You have a Zippo lighter, the dollar brand,
But you can't light my cigarettes, if you won't be my man.

You sat at the cafe, the sun was slicing down,
The sunlight cut your throat, left you bleeding on the ground,
You bled a while on the terrace,
Then you went inside.
You made a nice display
And something in me died.

Now you: you got a Zippo lighter, you got the dollar brand
But you can't light my cigarettes if you won't be my man.

ABRAHAM'S SONG

Sung by Kat as a Kat:

We curled up near her warm furry belly, and my mother sang:

> The secret hidden since the world began
> Is the tormenting of cats since stones became Man!

And then Mom would say:

> As the patriarch Abraham grew old, sullen, and stiff, his son Isaac grew strong, buoyant, quick. His mother's favorite: She called him, "My little kitty-kat."

And then mother sang:

> Abraham loved Isaac, and hated him, too.
> This pain became God, and spoke to the Jew:

(Then all we kittens joined in, pretending to have deep voices):

> *END THIS DIVISION! GO SLIT HIS THROAT!*

Then Mom moaned these blues:

> Abraham found a rock to pillow his son's head
> Thought: This life is a dung heap. The boy's better off dead!

And we kitties said, with a mixture of relief and contempt:

> *But then he couldn't do it!*

Mom nodded:

> He hated his son
> For signing his death.

He loved his boy!
He'd given him breath!

The kitten khorus sang:

He hated his boy, and loved him, too
For being *his* death, *and* the hope of the Jews!

And:

Over Abraham's head a light bulb flashed on!

Mom:

Based on a pun!
A kid for a kid,
And Thy Will Be Done!

Us (and we loved saying this!):

So he *slit* the kid's throat and *saved* his own child!

Mom sang:

His heart gamboled, yet his heart was still sad!
He'd saved his own son—so he *still* was a dad!

Well, what worked for him once, might work once again,
Like pills for our pains, and forgiveness of sin
—The torment of animals since stones became Men!

PERMISSIONS ACKNOWLEDGMENTS